Deadly Triad

Book Three

Deadly Encounter

Deadly Triad

Book Three

Deadly Encounter

By

Nancy Kay

Deadly Triad

Deadly Reflection
Deadly Revenge
Deadly Encounter

Desert Breeze Publishing, Inc.
27305 W. Live Oak Rd #424
Castaic, CA 91384

http://www.DesertBreezePublishing.com

Copyright © 2012 by Nancy Kay
ISBN 10: 1-61252-916-X
ISBN 13: 978-1-61252-916-5

Published in the United States of America
eBook Publish Date: September 2012
Print Publish Date: May 2012

Editor-In-Chief: Gail R. Delaney
Editor: Marcy Dyer
Marketing Director: Jenifer Ranieri
Cover Artist: Jenifer Ranieri
Photography Credit: Nancy Schneider
Model: Joe Schneider

Cover Art Copyright by Desert Breeze Publishing, Inc © 2012

Dedication

To my friends and family, for their encouragement and support throughout the years. For pep talks when I faltered and wine toasts for success. To Karen, for believing in me; to my fellow writers who have kept me focused; to four special friends, for their unwavering faith; to my boss and co-workers, for their tolerance; and to Joe, the love of my life and my lifeline.

Chapter One

Howling wind and driving snow created perfect cover. Taking full advantage, Jack LeFavor squeezed the trigger and drilled a neat hole in the center of Frankie John's forehead. In a split second, he had erased the look of shocked surprise from Frankie's face. He lowered the gun and backed out the passenger side door. Inside the car, Frankie sat behind the wheel with his head tilted back and angled to one side. At first glance, he appeared to be resting, just another tired motorist napping at a Pennsylvania roadside rest stop.

The nickel-sized hole in Frankie's forehead said otherwise.

"Holy shit, Mr. LeFavor! Why'd you do that?" Skinny Lastowski's eyes bugged out like a barn owl. He backed up several feet, pulled his knit cap low, and staggered against the force of the wind.

Jack straightened and glanced around. Now he'd have to deal with Skinny. Too bad. He liked the wiry little guy. Skinny must be in his mid forties, but he wasn't much bigger than a twelve-year-old. Jack carefully shut the door. Skinny hunched deep into his worn jacket. His gaze kept flitting back to his dead friend still behind the wheel inside the car.

"He screwed up, Skinny," Jack said, forcing calmness into his voice he sure as hell didn't feel. Skinny edged closer, and Jack turned to face him. He squinted against the sting of icy, driven snow. "You know the rules where I'm concerned. No personal contact. *Never* involve me." Keeping the gun low, Jack tightened his grip and rested one finger on the trigger. Might as well get this over with.

Arms wrapped around his shivering body, Skinny frowned and shook his head. "Frankie said there was no choice. He had to call you. That guy, you know, the one from Ohio? He met us, just like we planned. Then *shit.* Outta nowhere, Frankie insists on payment *before* he turns over the shipment. At first, I thought the guy'd refuse. He eyed us both up. Damn, Jack. I was shittin' bricks, but Frankie... he stared him down. I could tell the guy didn't want to give it up, but finally, he gets a bag from his car and tosses it to Frankie. The rest is a freakin' blur. Frankie kneels down, snaps open the bag, and looks inside. Then all of a sudden he jumps up, tosses the damn thing into our car, and shoves me in after it."

Skinny pulled his collar up, grimacing when snow slipped down inside, and rubbed the side of his head. "Smacked my head on the door. I saw stars, damn it. Then Frankie jumps behind the wheel and slams the door. The guy freaks out, grabs the door handle. We take off and leave him standin' there, waving his arms like a maniac."

"Frankie never handed over the shipment?" Jack knew the answer, and knowing burned a hole in his gut.

Emphatically, Skinny shook his head. "No, sir. We're haulin' ass outta there, and I'm screamin' at Frankie, 'What the hell's goin' on?' All while we're flying down the road like a bat outta hell. Cool as a damn ice cube, he fuckin' tells me he doesn't trust the guy."

Jack paced in a tight circle. He couldn't believe his ears.

Skinny shifted from one foot to the other, tucked his hands beneath his crossed arms. "Frankie drove like hell until we got to Bayside. He stashed the money *and* the stuff in some deserted garage, all the while goin' on about how the guy's a liar.

Jack rolled his eyes. What an unholy mess. He'd just killed a man, and a shipment of drugs and enough cash to choke a damn horse was missing.

"But Frankie had a plan."

"What?" Jack stopped pacing and narrowed his eyes on Skinny. "A plan?"

"Yeah. He knew you'd be pissed if he brought anything with him when he met you. That's why he stashed everything. He insisted when he told you what he'd found out about the runner, you'd be okay with it."

"Could you find the garage, Skinny?"

Looking miserable, Skinny shrugged and screwed up his face. "Maybe."

Bayside, Ohio, half the damn town was made up of rundown houses. Jack bet his ass ninety percent of them came with dilapidated garages. Christ, even the lone service station in town was boarded up.

What the sleepy lakeside community did have, though, was a backwoods, small town police department. A department so shorthanded they shut down at night. If something happened, a rare occurrence, they called in the chief to take care of things. Nobody got rich being a cop in Bayside, and that worked to Jack's advantage. He knew exactly which man in blue could help him locate a dilapidated, deserted garage in the sleepy little town.

Jack scanned the deserted lot. Parking at the rest stop was two tiered. A lower level for trucks and the upper one near the building for cars. He'd left his big SUV in the lower lot and traipsed through knee-high drifts to where Frankie had parked.

Lights from the building housing the restrooms were indistinct blurs amidst swirling clouds of snow. In the distance, cars on I-79 crept along like silent ghosts in the deepening twilight. The snow-covered ramp from the interstate was almost invisible, except where he'd plowed through with his Escalade. He could barely see the tire tracks he'd left behind. If his luck held, nobody would stop until after he took care of business and got the hell out of there. Jack had never thought he'd be thankful for a damn blizzard, yet tonight it had played in his favor.

He shifted, shuffling his booted feet in the snow. If what Skinny had said were true, Frankie had stumbled onto something. Could be he'd discovered the runner worked for a rival drug supplier or was some sly undercover cop. Or maybe even someone from Ohio's Investigative Unit had managed to get to the guy. Those sons of bitches had been on Jack's ass for awhile.

Maybe the exchange *had* been a setup. He shivered despite his bulky, down-filled jacket. Right now, he didn't have time to sort out everything. *Could bes* and Skinny's *maybes* weren't good enough. Either way, Frankie had screwed up, and now Jack had to cut the loose strings and tidy up the mess.

The last loose string stood right in front of him, hunched against the cold.

Chapter Two

"Almost home," Lanie muttered, heaving a sigh of relief. Or what she now considered home, since she'd moved from near Pittsburgh to Erie, Pennsylvania. The move had been scary at first -- a new city, a new job, a new place to live. She'd found a log cabin in the country and notched up the scary factor by moving away from the city. Apartment living had been okay in bustling Fox Chapel, but furnishing the sturdy, basic little rental cabin and turning it into a home had presented a challenge.

Elaine Daphanie Delacor loved a challenge.

Moving hadn't been on her radar two years ago. She'd managed a private fitness club, a job right up her alley, and she had loved her work. Then an arsonist had turned Fox Chapel Fitness into a pile of ashes. So Lanie had spread her wings, and after landing a similar position in Erie, she had moved north.

Lanie tended to leap into things with both feet, always had. She tackled the job and the rustic cabin in the country with determination. Her landlord had given her full reign, so after hours of scraping, painting, and hauling junk away, she'd carved out enough space to meet her needs. This final trip had netted the last of her meager belongings and effectively cut the cord.

Her former boss at Fox Chapel Fitness, Cassi McGraw, who also happened to be Lanie's dearest friend, had relocated to a small town near Erie after the fire. Aside from Cassi, the only thing Lanie had ever really cared about in Fox Chapel was her job that no longer existed, and dear Uncle Charley, whom she hoped looked down on her from Heaven and approved of her decision.

She'd been a teenager when her mom had died. One screwed up teenager. If not for her mom's brother, Charley, and his relentless quest over the years to save her young ass, who knows where she'd be today. He had made sure she went to college, and he'd lived long enough to see her succeed. Besides Charley, no one else in her fragmented, dysfunctional family gave a rat's ass about her.

A few snowflakes smacked her windshield. She peered at the road ahead. Maybe she *should* have checked the forecast before heading out. As the sun set, Lanie barreled north on I-79, leaving the past behind and looking forward to her future. Then just south of Edinboro, a wall of white engulfed her. The road disappeared, as if she'd entered another dimension.

"Damn." She squinted through the windshield and slowed to a crawl. Even with the heat blasting, bone-deep cold accompanied the blinding snow. She gripped the Miata's wheel so tightly her hands cramped. The thick, butt-ugly gloves she'd passed up for the ones made of eye-catching red leather flashed in her mind's eye. Stylish leather gloves might be great for driving, but what if she ended up out *there*?

How many times since she'd moved north had Cassi warned her, "Lanie, get sensible winter clothes; Lanie, pay attention to weather reports; or Lanie, get a friggin' four-wheel drive!" She loved Cassandra McGraw. They'd been best friends since college, but sometimes Cassi's cool, practical voice just plain ticked Lanie off. Two days ago, when she'd left for Pittsburgh, Cassi had warned her to check the road conditions before returning. But Lanie had never given weather a second thought, until five minutes ago when she'd driven into this white twilight zone.

Ah, there. Blinded by the driven snow, she'd almost missed the sign. Pulling into a deserted roadside rest stop probably wasn't smart, but she had to get off the road and take a break. Tightening her death grip on the steering wheel, she eased off the interstate and crept forward. Faint tire tracks ran the length of the exit ramp, but she saw no sign that a snowplow had ventured off the thruway. She followed the tracks until they turned into the lower lot for trucks. Holding her breath, Lanie kept right and headed toward the restrooms. She rolled to a stop in front of a brick building that sported a peaked roof and protective high walls leading up to the door. Tall pole lights speared skyward, silent sentinels lining the parking lot. High atop them, light from silver capped globes were faint halos, at times swallowed by horizontal sheets of snow. They provided little, if any, illumination to the deserted roadside rest. Unable to see more than a few feet in front of her, she blew out a long, shaky breath.

The wipers struggled with the heavy snow. She shut them down. At first, cocooned in her car and bathed in the greenish glow from her dash lights, the steady hum of the heater pouring warmth to her freezing limbs soothed Lanie. But before long, an overwhelming sense of being totally alone washed over her.

She flipped on the radio. No luck there. Reception for Erie stations was spotty at best, and to her dismay, Sirius XM Satellite Radio only provided weather conditions in major cities. She smacked the dash with her palm. Who in the heck had determined Cleveland and Buffalo were worthy of weather reports, but that Erie, a city smack dab in the middle of a freakin' snow belt, wasn't?

She'd never even heard the terms *snow belt* or *lake effect* or *white out* before moving here. Erie County had its own unique way of labeling every damn snow event to come along throughout their endless winters.

Deciding to take a break and regroup, she chose XM's all-50's channel, tilted her seat back, and just rested. Outside, the storm raged. Despite violent wind bursts that made the car rock, inside the car's dim interior Sinatra's crooning voice soothed Lanie. Before long, her eyes grew heavy and drifted shut.

She awoke with a start, disoriented and groggy. A lull in the wind caught her attention, and nearby, outlined in sharp contrast to the snow at the far end of the lot, sat a dark, late model sedan. Lanie snapped her seat upright. She wiped the frosted window for a better view and peered out. Had a car been there earlier?

Mini snow tornados danced between her car and the sedan. The other car would disappear, engulfed by the swirling gusts, only to reappear again as if by magic. The interior of the vehicle was dark, but Lanie had the distinct impression of two passengers within. She studied them. They didn't move, making her wonder if they were napping or... maybe watching *her*. A chill whispered over her skin, so she notched up the fan. How long had she slept?

Her car's defroster wasn't coping, and snow coated both the front and rear windows. If she were going to continue on, she'd have to get out and clean them off.

She dragged her tall leather boots from behind her seat. They were her only concession to the winter weather. Having heels, they wouldn't work for walking very far in the thigh-high snow, but for the short term, they'd keep her feet and legs dry while she cleaned off the car.

Contorting in the confined space, she donned the boots, secured her scarf, and tipped up the hood of her jacket. She paused, her hand on the car's latch, to see if the two strangers had made a move. Nose pressed to the glass, her breath fogged the spot she'd just cleared, adding more frustration. Maybe she should just march over and say, "Hi, guess we're both stranded." They could be just average people stuck in the snow like her.

Or not.

A couple of rather scary scenarios played through her head. None of them made her want to open the door and plow through the growing mounds of snow to their car. No, best to just scrape off her windows and be on her way.

She lifted the latch. *Nothing.* The door was frozen shut.

"Damn it, damn it, damn it." She pounded on the door, her red-gloved hands clenched in tight fists. After several thumps and a couple of hard bumps with her shoulder, the stubborn door flew open. A backlash of snow whirled inside. Sputtering, she wiped a fine layer of white from her face, then fished a long-handled snow brush from beneath the passenger seat. She eyed the tool for a moment, measuring, considering how effective the thick plastic scraper would be as a weapon.

She pushed the door open fully, stood clutching the brush, and faced the icy wind. Wind-driven snow bit into her exposed skin, and strong gusts created slithering white waves that glided eerily over the frozen ground.

Lanie went to work, brushing loose snow from the windows, hoping the defroster would take care of the thin layer of ice left behind. Feet braced, she leaned into the gusty blasts. She darted fast looks at the dark sedan, prepared to leap back into her car at the first sign of movement.

She cleared the front window and managed a tiny hole in the rear. That would have to do. Then just as she pried open the door to reenter her car, Lanie noticed a heavy duty SUV parked in the lower lot. Had it been there all along, too? A steady stream of warm exhaust lifted like the hot breath of a silent dragon and whirled away through the steady gale, drowning out any sound from the big vehicle's engine.

Creeped out, Lanie shot into her car and snapped the lock. She switched on the wipers and flipped the control to full defrost mode. Some of the ice coating the windshield melted, forming droplets, and the wipers cleared a growing path. In her rush, she upended her purse with the unwieldy snow brush and dumped its contents onto the floor.

Well, shit.

She tossed the brush into the back. When she bent down to recover her stuff, her eyes lit on her cell phone. "Oh, for Pete's sake. This storm's sucked the brains right out of my head."

She flipped open the phone, and her stomach dropped. *Oh, no. Only one stupid bar on the power grid.*

Okay, where was the auxiliary cord? She dug through the stuff she'd dumped, stuffing things back into her bag as she went. No cord. "Well, fuck."

As a rule, Lanie avoided such strong expletives. This unraveling predicament called for something strong, so *fuck* filled the bill. She glared down at the single bar. Should she risk a call? Her gaze lifted to the idling SUV, then slid on to the silent, snow covered car at the end of the lot. Was her imagination in overdrive, causing needless panic to override her common sense? Or should she get the hell out of there?

A call would use up precious battery life and then, if they followed or tried to stop her, she'd be shit out of luck.

Her hand hesitated over the contact key. Whom should she call? Cassi? Lanie grimaced. A call to her friend guaranteed a lecture on *what she should have done.* On the other hand, Cassi's brother-in-law was a state cop who patrolled in Erie County.

Maybe T.J. was on duty tonight. She grinned. T.J., with the prime butt.

He had a way of rattling her on so many levels whenever they ran into one another, but right now his tall, lanky body in that trademark gray uniform would be a welcome sight. She put aside her brief flight of fantasy and turned her attention to the idling SUV. Maybe her imagination *was* in overdrive, and her stranded companions were harmless, waiting out the storm like her. Lanie chewed her lower lip.

She just couldn't shake the creepy feeling of being watched.

Trying not to panic, she scrolled down and hit Cassi's cell number. Crossing her stiff, red gloved fingers, she sent a little prayer to the cell phone gods and waited. The line rattled and scratched. She gave the phone a vicious shake as a combination of fear and anger lifted goose bumps on her skin. She was about to press *End* when Cassi picked up.

"Cassi! Oh, Cass, thank God. I need--" A loud beep stopped Lanie mid-sentence.

She stared down at the black display. Tears burned her eyes as she tossed the useless phone aside and slumped into her seat. Her sullen gaze drifted out the window as the door of the SUV opened and a man in heavy winter gear got out and waded through the snow toward her stranded Miata.

Lanie bolted upright.

*****

"Nick. Nick, I've lost her call!"

Nick McGraw strolled into the room, rubbing his shower-damp hair with a towel. Cassie's frantic fingers flew over the cell phone keys. *Must be Elaine.*

He heaved a sigh, comparing his wife's best friend to a large pebble tossed into a deep, still pond. When she hit, ripples spread, gathering speed until they crashed into the shore.

He moved closer. "Hey, what's up?"

"I can't reach Lanie." Cassi held up her cell. "My phone rang and I heard her voice, then the call dropped. I can't get her back."

"Hon, you know Lanie." Nick draped the towel around his neck. "She probably forgot to charge her phone again." Cassi didn't usually come unglued over a dropped call. Maybe he'd missed something.

He smoothed a wild strand of her hair. "Wasn't she going to Fox Chapel this weekend? It's possible she heard about the weather and wanted to let you know she was staying over until the storm passed."

Cassi's eyes broadcast emotions like front page news. Nick recognized the fear, verging on panic, swimming in their dark depths. Relenting, he pulled her against him. "Tell me her exact words."

"I could hardly make out her words." Cassi looked into Nick's eyes. "That's not what scares me. It was her voice."

Nick raised a single brow.

"I know, I know, Lanie overreacts. But Nick, she sounded... panicked. I heard raw panic in her voice."

"You can't recall exactly what she said?"

"Well..." Cassi broke away and paced back and forth. "She said my name, then something like 'thank God I need...' And after that, nothing. I think she needed something, but I only caught a few words before the call ended."

"Okay." Nick followed her around the room with his gaze. She really was bent out of shape, and that was uncharacteristic for his strong, level-headed wife. He grasped her arm as she passed, halting her nervous movements. "First, try calling her place. Maybe she's at home and was using her cell to save money."

Gripping the cordless, Cassi dialed and waited, her head bent, tapping an impatient foot. "I got her machine." Eyes brimming, she held out the phone.

Nick wrapped an arm around her tense shoulders. "Come over here and sit down."

He steered her to a sofa by the fire, sat, and pulled her down beside him. "You know Lanie tends to be an alarmist."

Cassi's brows snapped together. He sandwiched her hand between his. Hers was ice cold.

She linked her fingers with his. "Nick, I've known Lanie for years, and yes, she sometimes overreacts. I can't ignore this, though. She's always been there for me whenever I've needed her."

Nick agreed. Before he'd married Cassi, Lanie had helped his wife through the death of her parents, the loss of her business, and an attempt on her life. He'd been involved with the whole investigation when a twin sister Cassi didn't know existed tried to kill her. The deranged twin had also been responsible for burning Cassi's business in Fox Chapel to the ground.

Lanie Delacor had managed Cassi's business, Fox Chapel Fitness. After the fire, Lanie had decided to take a job offer in Erie, not far from Pine Bluffs where he and Cassi now lived. His wife had been thrilled. From the day he'd met Lanie, Nick couldn't ignore the bond she and Cassi shared. A sixth sense that at times was a little scary.

Cassi's gaze went to the wall of windows across the room. Outside, the storm raged. "Something's wrong, Lanie's in danger."

"How about I call T.J.?" Nick suggested. "If he's on duty and time allows, he can check on her." He flinched inwardly for making such a promise. He knew damn well that if T.J. was on duty, he'd be swamped due to the storm. Being a state policeman stationed in Erie County guaranteed pandemonium during any lake effect event.

"Oh, Nick, could you? Please? It's a horrible night out there, and I don't want to bother T.J., but I'd feel so relieved if I knew Lanie was safe."

Nick didn't doubt Cassi's feelings about her friend's safety were genuine, or she would never agree to his bothering his cousin on such a night. He dropped a quick kiss on her lips and went to retrieve his cell phone. On the way, he tossed another log on the fire and paused to peer out at the blinding snow. He considered himself lucky. Being chief of police in a small town had its advantages on a night like this. Erie was less than an hour away, but in Pine Bluffs everyone appeared to be staying home out of trouble.

Cassi switched on the TV. As he waited for T.J. to pick up, Nick caught a weather warning scrolling across the bottom of the screen. Significant snow in early November wasn't unusual for Western Pennsylvania, especially when the lake waters were still warm and a cold Arctic blast blew in across them. Tonight's conditions were perfect for just such an event. Nick's mood sank as Accuweather confirmed his greatest fear.

Accumulations would be high, and the weathercast said to expect wind gusts creating total white outs. Travelers were advised to either slow down and use extreme caution or stay home. His chances of reaching T.J. and enlisting him to check on Lanie dropped.

He wrapped one arm around Cassi and pulled her close. Together, they watched the ominous scroll across the screen.

*****

To Lanie's way of thinking, the strange man traipsing through a blizzard toward her left her no choice. She slipped her car into gear and inched forward, casting nervous glances at the approaching stranger. His big SUV still spewed exhaust in a steady stream. He wasn't stranded, but for some reason, he'd decided to leave the warmth and safety of his vehicle behind and stroll over to her car. The move didn't make sense, and when something didn't make sense to Lanie, she opted to get the hell out of Dodge.

Making it back onto the thruway wasn't as difficult as she'd imagined. The wind had created patches of bare pavement on the ramp, and whenever her tires gave an ominous spin, she'd hit one of those spots and jolt forward.

She chanced a look behind her. The man stood where she'd been parked, hands on his hips, staring after her. Swirling snow soon engulfed him, and as she escaped, his outline faded and became an indistinct dark shadow amidst a sea of white.

She kept moving and slid in behind a large truck, following its steady, blinking taillights. Maybe the big rig would clear a path for her. Despite her one concession to winter, four brand new snow tires, she feared the sheer depth of snow would bog down her Miata.

Her hands ached from gripping the wheel. She kept her eyes glued to the road as she crept forward. They tingled and burned from constantly straining to see. Her pulse quickened when the truck sped up and pulled away. She'd never be able to keep up.

A few long tense minutes passed until the truck's lights faded from view, then the Edinboro exit came in sight. She'd had enough white knuckled driving, so she peered through the blinding white onslaught hoping to see the off ramp. Light from the huge Wal-Mart complex just off the exit created an eerie glow through the falling snow. Her heater fan rattled. A stubborn chunk of ice beneath her wiper blade refused to dislodge. Visibility deteriorated rapidly.

When a car in front of the semi exited down the ramp, she pressed forward, easing off the thruway and following the other car's tracks. She could think of worse things than spending a night at Wal-Mart. The car she had attempted to follow disappeared down the ramp, so she focused on the faint tire tracks it left behind.

All of a sudden, lights flashed behind her. Someone was right on her bumper.

Lanie's heart leapt into her throat. Through the frozen sheen on her rear window, she made out a huge, snow encrusted grille with an emblem in the center. Snow swirled in front of the blinding headlights as they bore down on her. She froze and braced for impact, helpless in the path of impending disaster.

Seconds later, the monster from behind rammed into her and shoved her off the ramp.

Her Miata spun around and came to rest in a drift. Buried in snow as high as her window, she now faced the glaring headlights. She squeezed her eyes shut. Then her car settled, tilting as it slid sideways down the embankment. The car lurched to a stop.

Lanie panicked. She couldn't breathe. Her seatbelt cut across her chest, holding her in and letting her dangle like a broken tree limb. Every loose item in the car skittered past her and came to rest against the passenger door. She released the steering wheel, and her hands trembled. She fumbled, gasping and panting, until she could lift the clasp on the seatbelt.

She dropped like a stone. Lying helpless atop her purse, cell phone, and an assortment of takeout cups, she peered out the driver's side window above her.

A shadowy figure suddenly blocked Lanie's view.

She gasped, and a scream lodged in her throat. Legs braced wide, his thick body outlined by the twin beams piercing the night, the man stared down at her. Fear gripped Lanie, for somehow she knew he was the man from the rest stop. He'd not only pushed her off the road, but appeared ready to climb down the embankment after her.

"No. Leave me alone," she cried. She put all she had into her fierce demand, yet it sounded weak. *She* sounded weak. Weak and helpless. She clenched her teeth, determined as she struggled within the cramped interior. Unmindful of the pain, she bent her arms and legs and rapped against the seat, then beat on the door at her back.

No. I'm trapped!

Tears streamed down her cheeks. She didn't dare take time to look at the threat. To look at *him*. Helplessness swallowed her whole and threatened to cripple her.

Then out of the blue, above the howl of the storm, came a boom louder than thunder, followed by flashes of light. The ground shook and rumbled.

Lanie froze. She'd somehow managed to twist onto her knees, crouching awkwardly with the gearshift digging into her thigh. She gasped for breath. The sky through the window above her flashed with light, once more outlining the man. Then in an instant, he was gone. The headlights streaming into the night above her swung around and disappeared.

She stared at the nothingness of flat black window glass.

Relief washed over her. She laid her throbbing head on the tilted seat. Hushed stillness surrounded her. The Miata's engine was silent, yet the car's interior lights cast a ghostly glow within her lopsided prison.

Determined, Lanie grasped the edge of the seat next to the door and pulled, until inch by inch, she straightened and stood on the passenger door gazing through the driver's side window. Disoriented because of the angle of the car, she fumbled for the power window switch. Finally she made contact, and the window glided down.

Snow poured through the opening, making her cough and sputter. The icy shower worked its way beneath her coat and slid inside her sweater. She tugged her coat tighter, then grabbed hold of the open window frame and lurched up, pushing with her feet until she managed to clear the window and tumble out into the snow. A quick glance around assured her she was alone. She flipped onto her back and took a few seconds to catch her breath. As she lay beside her upturned car, shouting and voices calling to one another filtered through the falling snow.

Was she dreaming? Had she smacked her head when that bozo had pushed her off the road? The snow kept coming, a solid, white curtain pouring from the sky and covering her like sifted flour. Her hands were freezing, the leather gloves stiff and unyielding as she brushed snow from her face. Cold seeped through her clothes, and she shivered violently.

Suddenly sirens cut through the night, and vivid colors bounced off the falling snow. Weird sweeps of blue and red danced in the sky overhead. She eased onto her side. Unable to stand in the soft snow, she rolled onto her knees and crawled to the rim of the road. Pulling herself over the edge, she collapsed into the twin depressions left by huge tires. Using what little strength she had left, Lanie rose up and sat back on her legs, gaping in wonder at the chaos unraveling before her.

Interstate 79 looked like a cockeyed parking lot. Several large jackknifed semis blocked the road. Cars were strewn over both lanes and beyond, as if they'd been tossed there by giant hands. Indistinct figures moved amongst the wreckage, using high powered lights to check each vehicle. Parked along the interstate and lining the exit ramp, emergency vehicles clogged the way, their lights flashing madly.

Lanie plopped down in the snow and pulled her knees in close to fight the bone chilling cold and debilitating fatigue. Her ears buzzed. The shouts around her echoed hollowly. She gasped and jerked back when unexpected light flashed into her eyes.

"Hey, over here on the exit ramp!" a voice called out, "There's a woman on the ground."

Lanie squinted against the light and raised her hand.

"Are you all right?" A man dressed in heavy clothes knelt beside her. Bright reflective markings on his coat flashed when he moved.

"I will be when you quite blinding me with that light." She shoved at his hand. The sudden move made her dizzy, and she swayed in place.

Gently but firmly, he gripped her shoulders and lowered her onto her back. "I'm an EMT, let me check you over."

"Hey, this stuff's cold. Could you help me up instead of making me lay on ice?"

Another figure approached them. "Is she hurt?"

A pair of long legs in gray pants with dark stripes down the sides stepped into Lanie's line of sight. A surge of welcome relief shot through her muddled brain as her gaze traveled up to the man's black outer coat to a state police emblem on its sleeve.

"She must have crawled up the bank," the EMT told the trooper. "A red car's almost buried down there, but other than complaining, she seems to be okay. I don't know how long she's been here."

The trooper squatted down, and Lanie met TJ McGraw's gaze through the falling snow. She swallowed hard, forcing down the nausea that threatened to climb up her throat.

Then she asked, "Hey, Trooper McGraw. What took you so long?"

Chapter Three

T.J. stared down into Elaine Delacor's luminous green eyes. Her smart-assed remark didn't surprise him, but the lack of punch behind it did.

On his way to a reported multi-car pileup on I-79, T.J.'s stomach had plunged when he'd gotten a call from Nick. His cousin's wife had been unable to reach Lanie. Cassi McGraw was probably Lanie's best friend, and was as down to earth as they come. She didn't jump at shadows. So when Nick asked him to check on Lanie, T.J. figured he had good reason.

He'd traveled nearly impassable back roads, detouring through McKean to reach the Edinboro exit at Route 6N. The intersection where the interstate passed over that highway was notorious for accidents -- bad ones -- and from what Troop E Headquarters had relayed, this one qualified. The storm was one of the worst he'd seen since he'd been on the job, and he'd dreaded finding Nick and Cassi's friend amongst the crash victims.

He'd promised Nick he'd check on Lanie, but at that point he didn't mention the accident. Now relief spilled through him as he helped Elaine Delacor to her feet. She swayed, and he caught her before she sank back into the snow. He didn't like the pallor of her skin or the glazed look in her eyes.

"Lanie, are you all right?" he asked.

She opened her mouth, then closed it and just nodded, and that concerned him. The woman usually had plenty to say. Her dark hair stood up in spikes covered with a fine layer of snow. She began to shake violently and gripped T.J.'s arms with both hands. The EMT who'd found her had been called away, leaving T.J. no choice. He scooped her up and headed for his patrol car.

"Hang on Lanie," he said as she went limp, becoming dead weight. He shifted her compact body in his arms. "You need to get warm."

"I'm fine," she mumbled, slurring her words. Her teeth chattered as she burrowed against him. No sass now. He suspected hypothermia, and the sooner he got her out of this freezing cold, the better. Upon reaching his unit, he managed to open the rear door and slide her onto the seat. As he eased back, she grasped the front of his coat.

"T.J., I need to get my car. I need to get away!"

He halted her pitiful efforts to climb from the car.

"He's after me," she cried, sobs breaking through.

While he gently pried her hands loose, T.J. scanned the area. Every EMT attended other accident victims, and what little traffic there was had come to a standstill. *Damn it.* He needed to get back to the scene, but he couldn't leave Lanie. She remained conscious, a good sign, but her clumsiness and confusion set off alarm bells.

Who the hell does she think is after her?

Heat pouring from the state car's heater escaped through the open door, doing little good, so T.J. pushed Lanie over, slid inside with her, and closed the door. He checked in with other troopers at the scene, letting them know his position before turning his attention to Lanie.

He needed to keep her warm, yet protect her exposed skin. Direct heat could damage cold tissue, and her skin felt like ice. She blinked sleepily at him. Gradual warming should help. He pressed his fingers gently to the side of her neck, checked her pulse, and then slid his hand around and cupped her cold face. Her soft, feminine, vulnerability beneath his fingers gave his hormones a hard jolt.

He'd avoided Elaine Delacor since the day he'd met her. To him, she epitomized all complicated, irritating women. She was sexy and sensual... *oh, yes.* But nonetheless complicated and irritating. He'd intentionally avoided the compact, curvy woman with those bold green eyes. She baffled him, and T.J. didn't like being baffled.

Outside, nonstop snow surrounded them. Inside the cozy interior of the marked state police cruiser, T.J. McGraw was more than baffled by Elaine Delacor.

Touching her silky, sweet-smelling skin aroused him.

*****

Lanie's heart drummed a sporadic cadence. Her fingertips and toes tingled and burned as heat seeped through her system. The constant hum of an engine soothed her, along with a pleasant mixture of leather and a man's spicy aftershave that swamped her senses each time she took a breath.

Using every ounce of energy she could muster, Lanie dragged her eyes open.

"Lanie?" The man's voice was familiar. His hand caressed her cheek, and she burrowed closer to the warmth he provided. He drew her in and wrapped his arms around her. He not only made her feel warm; he made her feel *safe.*

"Lanie, look at me," he ordered when her eyes drifted shut.

"Give me a minute," she murmured. Her shivering had eased, but the slightest movement drained her. "Oh, ooh," she groaned. "My arms feel heavy, and I can't move my legs."

"It's the cold, Lanie. You'll feel better once you're warm, but you'll be weak for a while. Your system got a shock out there. You're lucky to be alive."

Alive?

Her mind reengaged, and her breath caught as a she recalled being pushed from the road. She pushed away from the man holding her.

15

"Let me go. Please, let me go." Her voice hitched, and her demand lacked punch. She sounded like an old lady pleading. Though her strength had faltered, her focus cleared, and her gaze came to rest on a familiar face. One that matched that familiar voice.

She narrowed her eyes. "T.J.?"

"Yeah, it's me." He switched on an overhead light, making her squint. He grinned at her. "Never thought you'd end up in the back seat of a parked car snuggled up with me, did you?"

His thick lashed gray eyes met hers. They were dark with concern, and the light caught a hint of blue within the smoky gray. "You've been out of it for a while," he told her. "We found you sitting in a drift on the exit ramp."

"My car," she rasped out. "Did you see my car? He pushed me off the road and came after me."

"I think you just slid off the road, Lanie." T.J. frowned. "You must have climbed up from where your car landed. Being exposed to the cold for even a short time can lead to hypothermia."

"No, T.J." She wriggled from beneath his arm and turned to face him, propping her arm on the front seat. When he reached out to steady her, she batted weakly at his hand. "Don't," she said, pausing to catch her breath. "Let me think."

She rubbed between her eyes, making her head pound. Outside, lights pulsed. Piercing white, dancing red and blue. An ambulance moved away, followed by a wrecker towing a van. Stranded cars sat everywhere, and a short distance up the thruway she made out the vague outline of a semi jackknifed across the road.

"I wasn't part of this," she declared, and turned to stare at T.J. "This hadn't happened when he pushed me off the road." Blatant disbelief on T.J.'s face made her jaw clench. She had to make him understand. "He *followed* me and rammed into my car."

"Lanie," he began patiently, "There are several semis and more than a dozen cars strewn all over the road out there. They rammed into one another, a chain reaction. My guess is you just got caught in the middle of it."

Lanie pushed at her disheveled hair and glared at T.J. Damn it, how could a state trooper be so clueless? Physically she may be weak as a kitten, but her mind still functioned.

Her hands shook as she buttoned up her top button and double wrapped her scarf around her neck. "Stubborn as ever," she muttered "Where's my stuff?"

"Uh, for Pete's sake. Calm down. If you mean your purse, it's probably still with your car in the ditch over there." He gestured with a jerk of his head. "As soon as I know you're okay, I'll go see if I can get it towed."

He grasped her arms and forced her to look at him. "Lanie, listen to me. The kind of exposure you experienced can be dangerous. You need to settle down, conserve your energy."

Much as she hated to admit it, his level-headed reasoning made sense. She'd been educated to respect one's body and knew he was absolutely right. Twisting her arms from his grasp, she relented. "All right. Get someone to tow my car. Can you arrange for someone to take me home?"

"I'll see what I can do," T.J. said, pulling on his gloves. "Stay here until I come back for you." He placed a hand under her chin and forced her to look at him. "Promise me you won't do anything stupid until I take care of things."

Their eyes were only inches apart.

Lanie's heart skipped a beat. She'd always considered T.J. handsome, but up close he was a woman's wet dream. A boyish cowlick sprang up from his close-cropped, thick red hair. It's subtle color fell somewhere between copper and strawberry blond. Her gaze dropped, and Lanie used every ounce of self-control not to lock her lips on the stubborn set of his mouth.

His brows snapped together. "Elaine, did you hear what I said?"

She pulled away. The cruiser had little room. A radio system and some kind of computer set up took space in the front seat. A briefcase and extra outer gear piled beside them in the rear left her nowhere to go. Unless she wanted to crawl into the man's lap. As tempting as that seemed, if she got any closer she feared her will power would shatter despite the borderline hyperthermia.

"I heard you," she snapped. "I'm getting kind of squished here. Could you move your butt and see about my car?"

T.J. gave her one long, narrow eyed look, crammed on his hat, and got out of the car. "Stay put," he warned.

"Wait," Lanie cried out. "T.J., please lock the door."

He paused, but nodded and closed the door.

She held her breath, waiting until the locks clicked shut. Fatigue dropped over Lanie like a heavy quilt, and she curled up and closed her eyes.

Chapter Four

Jack crushed the empty take-out cup and tossed it aside. If he sat here much longer drinking day old convenience store coffee, he'd have to hit their restroom again and take a piss. Customers were few and far between on a night like tonight, and he couldn't risk a bored, curious clerk remembering him. Best to keep a low profile, suck it up, and wait. His location enabled him to see everything exiting the thruway, and, sooner or later he'd get lucky. He switched on the wipers and cleared the fast accumulating snow. *Son of a bitch.*

The damn stuff just kept coming down.

Another wrecker headed down the ramp, towing yet another crumpled car. Each time one passed, he hoped to see the little red Miata in tow. So far, zilch. He shifted and struggled to keep alert. All he needed was a plate number in order to track down the woman from the rest stop. He'd counted close to half a dozen ambulances leaving the scene, but he had no way of knowing if she was in one of them.

Her fancy schmancy car was the key. If she'd survived -- and a sick feeling in the pit of his stomach told him she had -- he had one more damn mess to clean up. He'd taken care of Skinny and Frankie, a messy task, but he'd accomplished the mission. Home free, with no witnesses. Perfect. Then that little red car had rolled in off the interstate and changed the game.

One more problem in a series of pain in the ass mop ups.

A sweep of lights illuminated the sky and a lumbering Pennsylvania Department of Transportation plow appeared, clearing the ramp. Close behind it came a flatbed wrecker. *Bingo!* The wrecker had a red Miata on board.

"About time," Jack muttered, and he prepared to follow it.

He jammed on the brakes. The damn Pennsylvania State Police cruiser right on the truck's ass could wreck his plan. Jack heaved a huge sigh of relief when the wrecker turned left and the cruiser headed in the opposite direction, toward Edinboro. Once the marked car's taillights disappeared down the hill, Jack floored it and hurried to catch up with the wrecker bearing the crumpled red sports car.

A short distance down the road, the wrecker pulled into a large lot. Alongside an impressive double bay garage ablaze with lights sat a haphazard row of vehicles. Rag tag remnants from the pile up on the bridge. Jack waited at the edge of the lot as the flatbed maneuvered into place. Several figures hustled from inside the garage to loosen the Miata's restraints and guide it into a slot among the other causalities.

"That's right, fellas, just tuck that fucker in there so old Jack can get what he's after."

When the last man ducked back inside the garage, the wrecker shot by him, heading back toward the thruway. Jack waited until its lights disappeared around the bend, then pulled closer. All he had to do now was get the Miata's plate number and get the hell out of there.

Under normal conditions, the drive to Bayside, Ohio would take him about ninety minutes. His contact at Bayside PD would no doubt be dead asleep by the time he got to town, but the late hour and the foul weather could prove to be an advantage for him. He'd roust the sucker out of bed to help him locate the money and the lost shipment, then call in one more favor. A little pressure on his small town cop buddy should do the trick.

He needed the name and address of the Miata's owner. The mystery woman was the only living person who could place him at that lonely Pennsylvania rest stop. The snowstorm had not only covered his tracks, but had also botched his attempt to eradicate that one witness.

He frowned and sped up. Overhead, stars poked through the swiftly moving clouds. The road ahead gleamed wet and black as he drove out of the relentless snowfall. As if a switch had been thrown, he soon left the swirling white behind. Up ahead, lights along I-90 brightened as he approached. Bayside was north of the interstate, just west of the Pennsylvania line along the shore of Lake Erie.

If the Miata's driver had been injured, that would be another complication. No way could he walk into a hospital and take her out. Judging from the way she'd flopped around, trying to get the hell out of her car, however, he'd bet his ass she'd already been checked out and sent home. Once he knew where *home* was, cutting off that one last loose string should be a piece of cake.

A small ornate sign welcomed him to Bayside. He turned down a curving lane and stopped in front of an impressive two story brick house. The neighborhood was upper-class. Not exactly where one would expect a part time cop in a one horse town to live, but hell, he wasn't about to rock that boat. Cash slipped into the right hands was often overlooked.

He chuckled, eased his door shut, and stepped into the chilly night.

The snow on the ground wasn't fresh. The storm had apparently skipped right over the little town. If his luck held, Frankie and Skinny had left tracks when they'd ditched the goods earlier. All he had to do now was wake his *tour guide* and find the fuckin' garage.

Shit, he could be back in Pennsylvania by daylight if things went right. He hitched up his pants and settled the snub-nosed .38 on his hip. Then he pressed the doorbell and turned when the door behind him opened.

"Evenin', Terry," he said. "I need you to take a little drive around town with me."

Chapter Five

T.J. waylaid a paramedic and asked him to recheck Lanie. She'd insisted on watching them retrieve her car, and he'd practically had to hold her up as they'd yanked it out of a snow bank and pulled it up to the road. She had point blank refused to go to the ER for a more thorough checkup.

"Then go home, drink plenty of fluids, and rest," the tired looking EMT ordered. "Get someone to check on you over the next twenty-four hours. Best not to be alone for a while."

T.J. thanked the man and bundled Lanie back into his patrol car after the men had secured her car on the flatbed. She all but collapsed in the seat. Her eyes drifted shut, and he took it upon himself to reach across and fasten her seatbelt, pausing when her soft breath feathered across his face. He stifled the urge to touch her, to run the back of his hand over the soft curve of her cheek. With her relaxed and half asleep, the stubborn line of her jaw was nonexistent. She didn't have the flowery scent many women he knew preferred. What he breathed in that set his hormones throbbing was different... an alluring subtle scent mixed with the aroma of an exotic spice.

In haste, he backed out of the car, slammed the door, and almost lost his balance. He ducked his head against the storm, hurried around to the driver's side, and slid in behind the wheel. His gaze roamed over Lanie's face as she sighed softly and settled deeper into the seat. Directing his attention to the road ahead, he put the car in gear and eased onto the ramp. They'd called Cassi and assured her Lanie was all right. The storm had moved inland, and Pine Bluffs was now taking a pounding, so there was no way Cassi could get to Lanie's place. He had reminded Lanie of the EMT's warning and suggested she contact a friend to stay with her. She hadn't answered.

Still, he wasn't about to leave her alone. His shift ended shortly, so he'd offered to stay with her so she wouldn't have to ask anyone else to come out in this weather. She'd fought off drowsiness long enough to offer him a curt, "Get real." Then she'd borrowed his cell phone and called a friend named Jen who had agreed to meet them at Lanie's cabin.

That worked for T.J. So with her intriguing scent driving him to distraction, he headed north out of Edinboro, hoping the storm would diminish as they neared Lake Erie.

*****

Lanie drifted in and out of sleep throughout the drive to her place.

She struggled upright and rubbed her eyes as they crossed beneath I-90 into Harborcreek. The inside of the cruiser was toasty warm, and a black velvet sky dotted with occasional pinpoints of light was visible through the front windshield.

"The snow stopped."

"Not quite." T.J. glanced at her. "We just drove out of the worst of it. It's still snowing a few miles south of here, and the forecast is for it to continue in the snow belt throughout the night."

Squinting, she leaned forward. "I see stars."

"What?"

The concern on T.J.'s face when he slowed and stole fast glances at her made her chuckle.

"No." She shook her head, grinned, and pointed skyward. "I mean, I *really* see stars."

"Means it'll be cold tonight, with no clouds." T.J. relaxed and turned right onto a road running parallel to I-90. "The lakeshore took a fast hit, and then the storm moved inland. Conditions are perfect for a real snow dump just north of Edinboro all the way south to I-80."

He stopped at the intersection and turned to her. "I have an idea where you live, but I need specifics."

"Okay." Lanie took a sip from the bottled water he'd provided. "My address is one and a half Hilltop Road. It's off Sidehill Road, in Harborcreek. The Reeds own the property, and I rent a small cabin on the ridge overlooking their apple orchards."

She glanced around. The snow may have stopped, but several inches covered the ground. "The drive to my place isn't much more than a dirt road, but I'm sure Jen will have cleared it by the time we get there."

She'd hated to bother Jen, and yet with Cassi unable to get there, Jen Reed was the only other person she considered a friend since moving from Fox Chapel. Jen's parents, Josh and Irene Reed, were great folks. Lanie had stopped to purchase apples at their farm market and had ended up renting her cabin from them inadvertently through her conversation with the warm couple.

Shortly after moving in she had met Jen, who'd been away at college and had then traveled around the country working a variety of jobs for several years after graduation. At first Lanie had pegged Jen as standoffish; someone who minded her own business and expected others to do the same. Lanie didn't have a problem with that. She understood exactly how it felt to want to be left alone.

Shortly after she had moved into the cabin, however, Jen had turned up at Lanie's door with a scraggly black kitten. She'd dumped the little guy, apparently abandoned by someone, into Lanie's arms and declared they needed one another. The little lopsided black and white face peering up at Lanie had sealed the deal. Since then, a strong bond had grown between the two women.

"This the road?" T.J.'s voice cut into her thoughts.

21

Lanie nodded. "That's Hilltop. My place is near the top of the ridge."

They wound uphill through the orchard. She'd been right. A clear path through the trees led them to her cabin. One of the Reed's tractors, outfitted with a serious looking plow, was parked beside it. The porch light beckoned her through lacey snowflakes floating lazily down.

"Your friend has a key to your place?" T.J. asked as he pulled alongside the tractor.

"Yes. I rent from her parents, and she's been taking care of Sam for me."

"Sam?" T.J. shot her an inquisitive look.

Lanie pulled on her stiff leather gloves and buttoned her coat tighter. "Sam Cat. Someone tossed him out along the road in front of the Reed's. They have barn cats, but this little guy wouldn't have survived with them, so Jen dumped him on me."

A slow grin spread over T.J.'s handsome face. "So you've got a soft spot after all."

Lanie squirmed, and her face heated. She loosened the top button of her coat. The *almost* flirty remark from T.J. unnerved her. Flustered, she reached for the door handle, and suddenly the night came rushing back.

"Wait," she snapped as T.J. prepared to get out. "Did they find the guy who pushed me off the road?"

"Lanie..." T.J. frowned and heaved a patient sigh. "I think you got caught up in a chain reaction crash. You need to rest and recover from the shock. Then you'll be able to think clearly."

"Look, you're a policeman, and I'm telling you some guy followed me from the rest stop, rammed into me, and pushed me off the road." She narrowed her gaze and crossed her arms. "He was ready to climb down that bank and do God knows what when all hell broke loose and cars started piling up."

She stopped to catch her breath. T.J. McGraw may be sexy as hell, but the man had a blind stubborn streak, and if he used that patronizing tone on her again, she'd deck him.

They looked up when the door to her cabin opened and a tall, thin girl wearing jeans and a sweater stepped out onto the porch.

"My babysitter's here," Lanie opened her door, while T.J. climbed out and circled the patrol car. He held out his hand, and Lanie pushed it aside. She hauled herself up and braced her hand on the car door. Her world spun crazily. T.J. caught her as her knees buckled.

Without a word, he wrapped his arm around her and guided her toward the cabin.

Jen scrambled down the steps and met them halfway. She and T.J. guided Lanie up the steps and into the cabin.

"Is she all right?" Jen asked, sending T.J. a worried look. "Maybe we should take her to the ER and have her checked out."

"I'm fine." Finally feeling steadier, Lanie untangled herself, crossed the room, and dropped into a chair. "Just give me a minute."

Hands on her hips, Jen turned to T.J. "Well?"

"The EMTs at the scene said she'd be okay. She'll be shaky, tired, and thirsty for a while, but they saw no reason for alarm."

Lanie pulled off her gloves and tossed them onto the table. She yanked her coat from her shoulders, squirmed awkwardly on the chair to get out of it, and dropped the coat on the floor. Dismayed when the move sapped her strength, she drew in a deep breath.

"In case you two haven't noticed, I'm right here. I'm not in a hypothermic coma, and I can still speak for myself. I repeat: I'm fine, and I'm *not* going to the ER."

Jen and T.J. exchanged a brief look.

Guilt rolled over Lanie. She sounded like an ungrateful bitch. They meant well. T.J. had gone out of his way to get her home safely, and Jen had braved the frigid night to plow her driveway.

T.J. stepped over and picked up her coat. He crouched down to eye level. "Get some rest. Let your friend take care of you and pay attention to what the EMT told you. I'll keep you posted about your car."

Lanie nodded, folding her arms and tucking her hands beneath them. He'd removed his hat and that damn unruly cowlick caught her eye. She wanted to reach out and smooth it into place. She didn't dare. The move would either embarrass him or give him the wrong impression. His ego certainly didn't need encouragement, and Jen's curious expression hadn't escaped Lanie. If she laid a finger on the man, she'd sure as hell have some explaining to do.

He started to rise, and she put her hand on his arm. "Please. I *didn't* imagine what happened. All I ask is that you check it out."

Without a word he rose and stepped away. He studied her a moment, and then turned to Jen. "Are you able to stay the night?"

"Yes, I plan to be here as long as she needs me."

"Good." He glanced at his watch. "I'm heading off duty now, but I'm on first thing tomorrow. I need to follow up on some things, and then I'll check in here."

Jen followed him to the door. He put on his hat and turned in the open doorway to give Lanie one last long, considering look.

"Goodnight," he said, and closed the door behind him.

Chapter Six

Lanie burrowed beneath the blankets and hugged Sam Cat's warm body close. He'd been with her throughout the night, providing a much needed touch of reality when the nightmares had ripped her from sleep. Her accident and the close brush with hypothermia had left her sluggish and listless. The effort needed to pull up her thick down quilt made her feel as weak as... well, as a kitten. Although the *real* kitten, now awake and bright eyed, didn't seem weak as he tugged and chewed on the drawstring of her pajama bottoms.

"Hey, Sam. Knock it off, will ya?" she mumbled, giving the compact little ball of fur a halfhearted shove.

Unperturbed, Sam Cat dove right back and attacked the frayed tie with renewed vigor.

She closed her eyes and let him play his silly game. The heady aroma of coffee drifted into her room, and she detected the comforting murmur of voices emanating from the flat screen TV tucked beneath the counter in her kitchen. Jen was a coffee fiend, too. She'd spent the night, and though they'd only known one another a few months, Lanie considered her a rock solid friend.

Reopening her eyes, Lanie turned her attention to the high window across the room. The bluish gray sky provided a backdrop for thick snowflakes. Not the driven sheets of white from the night before, but a floating curtain of white drifting steadily down.

With some effort, she crawled from beneath the blankets. Sam padded onto her lap and stood, tail waving, alert and ready to roll. She scooped him up and brought him nose to nose with her. "You're going to have to be patient today, fella. I'm afraid my batteries need recharging."

He bumped her nose with his and emitted a rumbling purr. Lanie planted a kiss between his ears and lowered him to the floor. She rose and reached for her dark blue robe at the foot of the bed, pausing to catch her breath before she pulled it on. How could she still be so wasted?

Her fingers fumbled with the robe's belt, and she finally settled on tying only a half-assed knot at her waist. Sam crouched, his furry butt held high, then shot out of the room. Lanie cautiously made her way to the kitchen, drawn by Jen's soft laughter as she scolded Sam.

Her friend set aside her mug and rushed to Lanie's side when she entered the kitchen.

"Hey, sleepyhead," she greeted, sliding her arm around Lanie's waist.

Lanie tilted her head and looked into her friend's serious eyes. "A hug, I can handle. If you plant one on me, I'm going to deck you."

Jen laughed and gave her a quick squeeze. She released her hold, but

24

stood close by. "I take it you're feeling better this morning."

"I feel weak and a little shaky when I move too fast. I'm also starving. I take that as a good sign, and getting some food on my stomach should help the shakes. But God," she muttered, pushing at her disheveled hair. "I must look like hell."

Jen crossed to the coffee machine, pulling a chair out from beneath a sturdy oak table as she passed. "Have a seat."

She nodded at the chair as she reached for an empty mug. Steam rose as she filled the cup almost to the brim. Lanie plopped down on the chair, relieved to get off her feet. Her *My darned legs feel like Jell-O.*

Jen placed the cup on the table, then retrieved a carton of half and half from the fridge.

"I had toast earlier with T.J., then decided to whip up some apple pancakes. They're ready to go if you're ready to eat. I'll heat up the griddle and--"

"Whoa. Back up to the part about the toast. T.J. McGraw was *here* this morning?" Lanie took a sip of coffee. The hot liquid burned all the way down, but it tasted heavenly. Warmth settled deep inside her.

Jen put the half and half away and pulled out a deep bowl with a whisk sticking out of it. She beat the batter as she moved to the griddle resting on the front burner of Lanie's stove. "He stopped by just after seven a.m. Said he wanted to see how you were doing. He's a cutie."

She grinned at Lanie and paused to adjust the heat beneath the griddle. Then she resumed whisking.

"Did he say anything about my car? Or the guy who pushed me off the road?"

"Wait." Jen stopped mid-stir. "Someone pushed you off the road?"

"If he didn't mention it, I'm sure he still thinks I was out of it last night."

"Trust me, you were."

"After I bounced around inside my car, then had to climb out and crawl up a mountain of snow, who wouldn't be a bit punchy?" She frowned at Jen and cupped her hands around the warm mug. Her fingers still felt cold and stiff. The heat helped.

"T.J. said you were headed for hypothermia when they found you. It's understandable you'd be confused."

"Jen, *after* the accident I was confused. When some jackass rear-ended me on purpose and sent me off the road, down an embankment, and into six feet of snow, I was *not* confused. I was scared out of my friggin' mind." Her voice broke, and she gulped more coffee.

Jen put the pancake batter aside and turned down the heat. She refilled her mug and slid into a chair across from Lanie. "Tell me. I can see there's more to what happened last night than a pile up in a snowstorm."

Lanie met her friend's curious gaze, and something inside her eased and settled.

"There is," she murmured. "And I'm not sure it's over, Jen. I'm not sure someone isn't going to come looking for me."

She took a deep breath and aimed a weak smile at Jen's serious expression. "Right now I feel hollow inside. So why don't you make those pancakes before I end up on the floor? Then while we stuff out faces, I'll tell you what happened before I nosedived off I-79 last night."

*****

T.J. brushed snow off his coat and climbed back into his patrol car. The wrecker eased onto the thruway and headed west, towing a crumpled Ford Focus. He yanked off his gloves and held his frozen fingers in front of the blasting heat vents.

"Is this damn stuff ever going to stop?" he asked aloud, as wind driven snow swallowed up the flashing amber light atop the tow truck.

He glanced at his watch. His shift had started at seven a.m., and it was now a little after nine. This was the third vehicle that had been towed out of the median on I-90 this morning.

"Can't people look out their stupid windows and see this crap coming down?" He scowled. "It's no emergency to get to the damn mall."

He checked in with communications. Nothing pending. He advised the desk he'd be grabbing a late breakfast, checked both ways, and swung onto the road. Visions of apple pancakes made his mouth water.

Up ahead, the wrecker took the Route 531 off ramp. T.J. eased into the exit lane and followed it, making a note to contact the Pennsylvania Department of Transportation, better known as PENDOT, to remind them to check the ramps. He hated to be a pain, but sometimes a little nudge helped shift their focus.

If this kept up, the storm would set a record. The white stuff had been coming down nonstop for over twenty-four hours. They must have had storms that had lasted this long when he was growing up in Pine Bluffs, but back then he didn't have to work in them. More than likely, he and his cousin Nick had driven his mother crazy whenever bad weather closed the schools. She'd been a good sport, though, most of the time, and had put up with their antics. He cautiously turned and headed east on Sidehill Road.

In his opinion, as far as mothers went, his qualified for sainthood. Right now, for example, if not for her offer to keep Hershey, he'd be in deep shit. She'd saved his butt, offering to keep the chocolate lab pup he'd acquired a few weeks ago, dubbing it *doggy daycare*.

He owed her big time now. Despite the turmoil and destruction he had experienced the first time he'd left Hershey alone in his place, the wet-nosed bundle of energy had stolen his heart. Returning her to the kennel wasn't an option, so he'd resigned himself to putting his furniture, at least the chewable stuff, in one room and living with a few old pieces until he could build an enclosure. The damned dog wasn't picky; she'd gnaw on anything. Still, the situation wasn't her fault.

Not long after, TJ had constructed a sweeping enclosure, complete with a private dog entrance into a secure part of his lower level. Now his pal could move about freely. He still didn't feel comfortable leaving her alone when he was at work, though, so for the time being he'd accepted his mom's offer to help out.

He slowed as row upon row of apple trees appeared on his left. Sturdy, low slung trees as far as the eye could see, with layers of snow decorating their bare limbs like white frosting. Hilltop Road cut through the orchard and wound up the hill. From the looks of it, Jen had made another run with the tractor and cleared Lanie's driveway again. As he climbed the hill, he eyed her log cabin on the crest. Here the snow fell thick and steady, instead of being wind driven like that on the open thruway and points south.

His stomach gave an ugly growl. He sure hoped Jen and Lanie hadn't scarfed down all the pancakes Jen had promised him earlier.

*****

"I can't believe I'm so tired already. I've only been up a couple of hours." Lanie bundled herself beneath a quilt and tucked her legs in close. Pleasantly full of Jen's pancakes, she scrunched into an overstuffed chair by the fireplace, let her head fall back against the soft cushion, and closed her eyes.

"You should have skipped the shower," Jen admonished. "You need to rest for at least a couple of days."

Lanie's eyes opened part way when Sam climbed onto her lap. Determined to rearrange the quilt to his liking, he dug in with sharp little claws to lift and push. His engine-like purr rumbled louder when Lanie stroked him. "Get settled, Sam. Maybe we'll both catch a nap."

"Ah -oh."

"What?" Lanie shifted, settled Sam closer to her, and frowned at Jen. "What?" she repeated. A chill shot through her despite the crackling fire and her being wrapped up from head to toe.

"He wasn't kidding when he said he'd be back."

"McGraw? T.J.'s here?" Lanie glanced down, thankful she'd taken the time to shower. She finger combed her still damp hair. Wasn't much she could do about the old sweats she'd pulled on, but at least she didn't smell like a gym rat. "Is he in a patrol car?"

"Yep," said Jen as she crossed and opened the door. "Hey, trooper," she greeted as T.J. filled the doorway, big and tall in his winter gear. He stepped inside and removed his hat, careful to keep on the mat by the door.

"Can you stay for pancakes?" Jen asked.

"I was hoping there'd be a few left." He grinned at Jen, then lifted his gaze and scanned the room. He zeroed in on Lanie. "I see you're up and about," he said. Slipping out of his coat, he handed it to Jen with a nod.

"Thanks."

Lanie breathed in chilled fresh air and leather. A strange combination, but somehow fitting. T.J. removed his boots and crossed to stand beside her chair. The leather holster resting on his hip squeaked when he crouched down and studied her with serious eyes. "You look better. How do you feel?"

Preparing to respond, she inhaled, and the smell of his aftershave swamped her brain. She blinked, then nodded like a stupid puppet. Until finally, irritated by the affect his nearness always had on her, she cleared her throat and responded, "Fine. I'm fine."

Sam's nose quivered. He untangled himself from the covers, placed his front paws on the arm of the chair, and rose up until he was eye to eye with T.J.

"Well, hello there. You must be Sam." T.J. chuckled and scratched the kitten gently behind one velvety black ear. "You've got a lopsided look going there, buddy."

Still testing the air, Sam tilted his head. His lopsided look came from a patch of white on the left side of his mouth. Unmatched on the right, the uneven color gave him a permanent smirk.

"You like cats?" Glad for the distraction, Lanie lifted Sam and repositioned him on her lap. T.J. stood and ran a hand over his hair. "Never knew any. I've got a dog... or rather, a pup. Maybe a cat would suit my lifestyle better."

"Lifestyle?"

"Yeah, shifts wreak havoc on routine. I'm finding out that routine is the key to training a bullheaded pup."

The mention of T.J.'s lifestyle brought current events front and center. Lanie sat up straighter. "Any news on my car?"

"Nothing yet." He tilted his head toward the window. "The snow's much heavier inland. Add thirty mile an hour wind gusts, and plowing is almost a waste of time. They didn't get the accident from last night cleared until about three a.m. this morning."

"First one up," Jen called out.

Lanie joined T.J. and Jen at the table, sipping bottled water as T.J. dove into a stack of pancakes dripping with sweet-smelling maple syrup. He thanked Jen when she placed a steaming cup of coffee beside his plate and added a touch of half and half along with a dash of sugar.

After polishing off the entire stack, he pushed his empty plate aside, leaned back, and sipped his coffee.

"Do you remember much about last night?" he asked Lanie.

"After I nearly froze my butt off climbing out of my car and up a mountain of snow, things got a little... blurry," she concluded. "Before I got *pushed* off the road, everything's as clear as glass."

"All right." T.J. frowned into his coffee and took another sip. "I'd like you to give me a blow by blow description starting at..." He paused, apparently unsure where he wanted her to start. "the rest stop, I guess."

28

Lanie gulped down more water and then set the bottle aside. She wasn't sure exactly when to start, either. While showering earlier, she'd reconstructed the events leading up to the accident and tried to pin down when things had gotten creepy. In retrospect, she'd decided that the moment she'd noticed the car, followed by the powerful SUV idling silently amidst the swirling snow was what she needed to focus on.

T.J. pulled out a notepad and pen. "Whenever you're ready."

Jen rose and took away T.J.'s empty plate, providing room for him to take notes, then looked at Lanie. "Can I get you anything else?"

"No. I'm fine, thanks," she said. Then she reconsidered. "Wait. Could you bring the quilt over here? I still can't seem to stay warm."

Once she'd draped the heavy cover over her lap and tucked it tightly around her legs and feet, she scooped up Sam and relayed all that had occurred after she entered the rest stop.

T.J. scribbled notes, nodded, and asked an occasional question. His expression told her nothing. He must be in trooper interview mode, she concluded. After she told him the part about the SUV pushing her off the road, he stopped writing and looked over his notes.

"Do you know what kind of SUV it was?"

"A black one, with a big emblem right in the center of the grille."

"How could you see the grille when it was parked facing north, just as you were?"

"I saw it when he crawled up my... my *butt*, right before he rammed into me. The grille looked huge, like a monster with a mile wide grin." Her hands shook as she took another swig of water. She smacked the bottle down onto the table. "You still don't believe me, do you?"

Ignoring her, he jotted a few more words and then laid his pen aside. "Until I get a chance to examine your car, I don't know one way or another. What I do know is that the list of vehicles involved in the pile up last night did *not* include a big black SUV." He held up his hand when her mouth dropped open. "Doesn't mean it wasn't there. Something that size could have just driven away."

"I know he drove away," Lanie insisted. "I was trapped in my car, and headlights outlined him as he stared down at me. Then I heard the crash, and he disappeared. Within seconds, the headlights swung away and vanished." She shook her head and stroked Sam's soft coat. Warm silky strands beneath her chilled fingers.

"I'd heard the crash," she continued. "Yet I didn't realize what had happened until I climbed out of my car and up to the road. I don't know how long I sat there. I was freezing and just felt numb and confused. Then you showed up." She shrugged. "You know the rest."

"Let's back up a minute." T.J. flipped through his notes again. "You said there was another car at the rest stop."

Lanie nodded. "Yes, a dark sedan. And no, I don't know what make or model."

"Okay." A smile tugged at T.J.'s mouth. "Tell me what you do know."

"There were two people inside it, and they never moved. Looking back, it was kind of wierd because they must have been there when I pulled in, and I drove past them when I left. At the time, I remember thinking they must be napping."

One of T.J.'s eyebrows rose sharply.

"It's possible," she responded. "I actually dozed off a few moments myself before I noticed the big black shape in the lower lot and got the creeps."

"The SUV?" T.J. asked.

"Yes. I felt as though someone inside it was watching me. That's why I got the heck out of there when he got out and came toward me. I mean, think about it. Why would anybody crawl out of a warm car in the middle of a blizzard?"

"Wasn't there a rest room just past your car?"

She hadn't thought of that, and T.J.'s tone sounded a bit too smug. She glowered at him and thought about it. No, her instincts were *not* wrong.

"No," she said aloud. "I trusted my gut feeling and would do the same thing all over again. That guy was *not* heading to the bathroom."

Sam sat up abruptly, his quizzical face alert as the cell phone in T.J.'s pocket buzzed.

"Excuse me. It's the barracks." He got up, stepped away, and took the call.

Seconds later, his eyes widened, and he swiveled around to meet her curious gaze.

"You're sure," he questioned, disbelief evident in his voice. He listened intently, giving one word responses. Then his expression turned cold; his gray eyes, stormy. Not a hint of humor in his tight lipped expression.

He disconnected and turned to Jen. "Thanks for the pancakes. I've got to run."

Without another word, he crossed to where his coat hung near the door and slipped it on. He yanked on his boots, giving Lanie the distinct impression that something was terribly wrong.

Carrying Sam, she approached him and put a hand on his arm. "T.J., what's happened?"

"They just cleared the ramps to the rest stop." He stared into her eyes. "You were right about the dark sedan. Two people were inside."

"Have they talked to them? Maybe they saw the SUV follow me."

"No. They didn't see anything." T.J. covered her hand with his. "They were both dead."

"Oh, no." Lanie's heart pounded in her ears. "They... they froze to death?"

"No, Lanie. They were murdered."

Chapter Seven

T.J. drove straight to headquarters, parked out front, and dashed upstairs into the lobby. The desk sergeant buzzed him through and met him in the hall. Mark Evans kept his six foot frame in good shape. He sported a crew cut sprinkled liberally with gray, and T.J. had never seen the man anything but clean shaven and clear eyed. As they walked to the conference room at the end of the long hallway, he briefed T.J. on the grisly discovery.

"They were shot," T.J. repeated, hustling along beside Sergeant Evans. "Do we know how long they'd been there?"

Evans shook his head. "We'll know more once they autopsy the victims. From what I've been told, one of the entry wounds was right between the eyes, and the other took off a good chunk of skull. More than likely they both died on the spot. Both were male. That's all I know."

They'd reached the long conference room at the end of the hall. T.J. put his hand on the sergeant's arm. Evans stopped.

"I want you to know I drove Elaine Delacor home after the accident," T.J. said.

Evans waited patiently.

"It was the end of my shift," T.J. went on. "She'd been checked out by an EMT, and the tow operator had already taken possession of her car. So I offered to drive her home -- plus, I wanted to make sure the friend she'd contacted was at her place."

"Okay." Sergeant Evans blew out a long breath. "Thanks for letting me know. See me after the meeting."

T.J. nodded, and they joined the group assembled inside. Glancing around, T.J. spotted several guys from the crime unit and a trooper talking quietly with Corporal O'Brian. The trooper gripped a steaming cup of coffee and stared into it, unblinking, as he responded to the corporal. Must be the poor sucker who'd found the bodies. Tough break, no matter how vigorous their training. The first time a guy comes face to face with a corpse, it always rips a hole right through his gut.

"Gentlemen, let's all take a seat." Evans stalked to the front of the room and slapped a folder onto the table. He waited while the men settled around him.

"T.J.--" The sergeant raised his voice above the scrape of chairs. "I want you up here." He pointed to the folder in front of him. "In going over your report, it came to my attention there may be something that connects last night's incident to ahh..." He flipped open the file. "Operator number one. Elaine Delacor."

T.J.'s heart sank. On one hand, he was thankful he'd mentioned

Lanie's suspicions. Yet on the other, he hoped like hell there wasn't a connection. Because if there was and someone *had* rammed her car off the road, the odds were she had unknowingly witnessed a murder -- and that big black SUV was still out there.

"Trooper Nicholas." Evans gestured for the trooper sitting with the corporal to come forward. "Please join McGraw up front. For those of you who are unfamiliar with him, this is Trooper Gary Nicholas from the Meadville Barracks."

The young man came forward, the cup of coffee still clutched in his hand, and slid into a chair two seats down from T.J. He nodded, swallowed, and resumed staring into his cup. T.J. wanted to say something, but knew any words at this point would be ineffective and might even be unwelcome. At some point, the trooper would need to talk, to help deal with the emotion boiling in his gut. Right now, though, was probably too soon.

"Okay," Evans said. "I'm going to lay out the details we have so far." He shuffled the papers in front of him, rearranging the folder's contents, then took a deep slug from the bottle of water he'd pulled from beneath the podium. "What looked like a typical multi-car pileup in a blizzard took a sharp turn with this morning's discovery. Here's what we've got so far."

He set the water aside and glanced down briefly. Those who knew the sergeant recognized his slight frown, an indication that he was organizing his thoughts.

He cleared his throat. "Sometime between five and six p.m. yesterday, a typical lake effect storm hit southern Erie County and most of Crawford. Shortly after dark, a truck heading north on I-79 jackknifed just south of the bridge over Route 6N and started a chain reaction pileup on the interstate. The location overlaps both Troop E Headquarters and Meadville Barracks. Units from both locations responded."

T.J. glanced around when Evans paused. Coffee still brimmed the cup of the trooper seated near him. The crap had to be stone cold by now, and the trooper's face was pale, his features set in hard lines. Off to the left and slightly behind him, Corporal O'Brian threaded a pencil through his fingers. Back and forth, back and forth, over and over.

"I'm going to skip the details about the actual accident." T.J.'s head snapped forward when Evans continued, "With one exception. Trooper McGraw, please come up and fill us in on what you encountered and relay the statement from that one particular accident victim."

T.J. laid out the details. He then explained his interaction with Lanie and her claim that she'd been deliberately forced from the road.

"In retrospect," T.J. concluded, "Elaine Delacor probably didn't imagine she had been targeted after leaving the rest stop. The discovery of the two bodies this morning, presumed to have been murdered, gives validity to her statement. She did in fact observe a single dark sedan occupied by two individuals parked at the rest stop. She also noted no sign of movement from either of the occupants."

The corporal stopped his pencil in mid-twirl, and Trooper Nicholas stared at T.J. instead of the cold coffee in front of him.

T.J. went on, "Elaine also stated that a large, dark colored SUV was also present at the rest stop. Being alone, she chose to leave the area after dislodging snow from her windshield instead of trying to wait out the storm. She entered I-79 northbound and made it as far as the Edinboro Exit, when she noticed an SUV closing in fast behind her. The vehicle connected with her Mazda Miata and drove her off the exit ramp."

The room remained quiet as a tomb as he relayed what Lanie had told him occurred after her car slid down the embankment.

"I spoke with Elaine again earlier today. She's recovering from hypothermia, but was still adamant about what I've just relayed to you." He turned to the sergeant. "Do you want me to continue, sir?"

"No. Thank you, T.J. I'll take it from here."

T.J. returned to his seat, and Evans succinctly laid out a course for the impending investigation.

*****

T.J.'s shift ended at three pm. Tired and mentally drained, he headed for Pine Bluffs. The minute he rolled to a stop at his parent's low slung house, Hershey bulleted out the door and leapt toward him through the chest high drifts. Laughing, T.J. stepped out of his compact SUV and absorbed the writhing happiness with outstretched arms. He ducked and twisted, trying to avoid the dog's avid tongue, and almost landed on his ass.

"Hey there, girl. Did ya miss me?" He gave Hershey a brisk rub. "Huh? Did ya?"

He stood and waved to his mom. Outlined in the open doorway as twilight fell, Mary McGraw waited for him, the warm glow beckoning him from within. His parents' house sat atop a ridge overlooking Pine Shadow Lake. Snow blanketed the landscape surrounding the house, solid white all the way to the ice covered lake. T.J. paused just to drink it all in. He'd been on his own for years. After college, he'd worked for Pine Bluffs PD, and then he'd gone to the State Police Academy in Hershey, Pennsylvania. He now owned a duplex on the edge of town and lived in half of it, renting the other half to a young, newly married couple. Recently, he'd acquired another piece of prime real estate, long time friend Rich McConnell's converted carriage house. Yet this place was still home.

Hershey raced in frantic circles around T.J. as he made his way to the house. She'd dash onto the porch, then reverse and fly at him, swerving just in time to avoid crashing into him. A light burned in the garage off to his right, and he bet his dad was checking out his ice fishing gear. This early winter would be well received by the former police chief, who was now retired and thoroughly enjoyed his freedom.

T.J. paused to scoop up some snow, make a compact ball, and toss it high and wide. Hershey took off after it.

"I'm going in," his mother called out with a laugh. "Take some time and wear her out. She's spring-loaded from being cooped up during the storm."

She ducked back inside and closed the door. He smiled after her.

Why not? A couple minutes of tossing snowballs for the dog to chase might help to unwind the knot in his belly. After this morning's meeting about the grisly find in Crawford County, he'd mentally sorted through a shitload of stuff.

He'd also met with the sergeant and explained in detail the how and why of his decisions involving Lanie the night before. A trooper driving a motorist home following an incident wasn't unheard of, but it also wasn't normal protocol. Evans was a good sergeant, and aside from raising his eyebrows when T.J. had slipped and called Elaine *Lanie,* he hadn't had a problem with the situation. Though he did give T.J. a long, hard look when he'd told Evans she was no more than a friend.

They'd discussed possibilities involving the case and finally concluded that they couldn't ignore the obvious. Chances were Lanie had seen something at that rest stop. Yet whether she could testify to what she'd witnessed or even realized its significance was another matter. One of the crime scene guys would contact her soon. Until then, Evans had agreed to have patrols check on her as time allowed.

T.J. had stopped by Lanie's on his way to Pine Bluffs. Her friend Jen had met him at the door and told him Lanie was dead asleep, and had been for most of the day. Jen asked him to wait there while she drove the tractor down to her parents' farm and returned with her Jeep.

Both agreed Lanie shouldn't be left alone.

While waiting, he had played with the curious, feisty bundle of energy Lanie called Sam Cat. Cute little guy. Fast as a whip and sneaky. Lanie hadn't stirred from her room while he was there, and he'd left as soon as Jen returned.

On the way to his parent's house, Lanie had stuck in his mind, and that annoyed him. Not the case -- he often mulled over cases after his shift -- but this sudden desire to *be there*. To just be there for her. Up until last night, he'd made it a point to steer clear of the curvy, green-eyed... ah, woman? Lady? Person? Victim? What the hell was she, anyhow? He'd best remember she was part of an accident investigation I anie Delacur just happened to be involved and--

Hershey hit him from behind. His knees buckled, and he smacked face first into a huge drift. From somewhere close by, his dad roared with laughter.

"Get off me, you idiot!" T.J. yelped, fending off the dog's wild leaps of joy while floundering in the snow.

"Hershey, get up to the house," his dad ordered. Then he extended a helping hand to T.J.

"Hey, Dad. Thanks." T.J. shot upright with the assist and paused to brush off his clothes.

Hershey dashed off toward the house.

"Quite an introduction to winter," Tom McGraw remarked as they ambled toward the house.

"A real bitch. I guess you heard about the pile up on I-79?"

"Front and center in the news. How's Lanie?"

"Didn't know that hit the news so fast."

"Nick stopped by earlier and filled me in. Cassi's been in touch with Lanie off and on all day. Or at least with Lanie's friend Jen. The cold took her down a peg, huh?"

"More than just a peg." T.J. shook his head. "The cold and shock knocked her flat. I don't think I've ever seen her so subdued. I stopped by after work, and she was still sleeping it off."

They'd reached the porch. Hershey danced in place, staring a hole in the door. She held up one paw and chewed it briefly to dislodge balls of snow from between his soft pads. T.J. followed his dad and the dog into the warmth of his mother's heavenly smelling kitchen.

She approached them and lifted her cheek for T.J.'s kiss.

He shrugged out of his coat, hung it by the door, and helped himself to a cold brew. Time to relax. To let himself be pampered, and to put thoughts about the woman with tempting curves and vivid green eyes on the back burner.

*****

"Look, Jen." Lanie leaned against the kitchen sink, peering out the window. "Our tree face has snow on his mustache. Kind of spooky lookin'."

Jen leaned in, sipping her hot chocolate and squinting into the gathering dusk at the spooky face, a pair of eyes, a prominent nose, and a sweeping mustache tacked to a tulip tree.

Lanie bumped Jen with her elbow. "Remember how gorgeous those leaves were just a few weeks ago?"

"Umm. I love tulip trees in autumn. All that golden yellow, and they're one of the last to drop their leaves."

They'd found the tree face at the garden center when buying mums. Laughing like a couple of loons, they'd chosen the tall, elegant tulip on the crest of the hill above the orchard and attached the cement cast eyes, nose, and mouth to the wide trunk. Now his somber expression greeted Lanie every morning.

Though the tree's branches reached stark and bare toward the sky, the face stood out against the rough bark. Wind driven snow gave him the look of an ancient mariner.

"Is there more?" Lanie held out her empty mug. She'd gulped down the first cup way too fast and wanted to indulge in another, only slower.

"Do you want more soup, too?" Jen asked, dipping a ladle into the simmering cocoa. She turned to fill Lanie's cup. Jen's mom had come by late in the day and dropped off a full kettle of chicken soup.

"I think I'll wait a while. All I've been doing today is eating and sleeping." She patted her stomach. "Not good for the waistline."

She moved from the window and settled at the sturdy oak table nearby. Choosing a napkin from the stack on the table, she blotted marshmallow cream from her upper lip. "You're sure T.J. didn't say anything more about the bodies?"

"I'm sure. He was only here long enough for me to take the tractor down the hill and get my Jeep." Jen sighed and sat across from Lanie. "He seems very concerned about you."

"T.J. McGraw doesn't particularly *like* me. I gave him a hard time when he worked for Pine Bluffs PD. Ever since the time he investigated Cassi, T.J.'s steered clear of me." Lanie shredded the napkin into neat little squares. She shrugged and let a tiny grin form. "I kinda got in the habit of yanking his chain whenever I could."

"I understand why you'd stand up for Cassi. But she *was* found standing over a dead man with a knife in her hand. Just sayin'," Jen remarked, lifting a hand to fend off Lanie's hard look. "He was a Pine Bluffs police officer then, and he's a trooper now. It's his job to look at everyone."

"You're right. In the end, he saved her life. Actually, he was quite the hero."

"A handsome hero."

"Yes." Lanie considered her friend's words for a moment. "He's a strange combination of buff and boyish, with a pinchable ass to boot. Regardless, we're like oil and water. Not a good match. Not to mention he's all about family, hearth, and home. I'm cut from a different cloth."

"Why would you say--"

"End of conversation, Jen. Even if I were interested in T.J., it wouldn't work. If he offered a quickie, maybe a hot and heavy affair," she shrugged, "maybe I'd take him up on it. But don't hold your breath. Usually he avoids me like the plague. Last night, he had no choice."

Lanie shoved out of her chair and went to rinse her cup. The room spun a bit, and she gripped the edge of the sink.

"Hey, don't overdo." Jen came to stand beside her. She draped her arm around Lanie's shoulder and gave her a quick squeeze. "I'll clean up here. You go sit by the fire with Sam Cat."

Lanie turned and wrapped her arms around her friend. "I hate being so dependent and such an intrusion in your life."

"You're not an intrusion." Jen leaned back and got eye to eye with Lanie. "If this situation were reversed, you'd do the same. I'm staying over again tonight. By tomorrow, you should be almost back to normal physically. Oh, and your boss called today. After I told her the situation, she insisted you take the week off, no argument."

Lanie wanted to protest. She wanted to object to her friend being a nursemaid and her boss thinking she needed recovery time. She was a *fitness trainer*, for Pete's sake. But relief flooded her and tears stung her eyes. Aside from Cassi, her dearest friend since college, nobody had ever taken time to care for her. Now for just a little while, she wouldn't have to fend for herself and put up the brave, feisty front she'd used most of her life.

Sam Cat trilled a soft greeting when she scooped him up and snuggled with him beneath a heavy throw. She sank into the sofa in front of the fireplace, comforted by the sound of Jen putting away the leftover soup and scrubbing the pan they'd used for hot cocoa.

Tomorrow would bring the trooper from the Pennsylvania State Police crime unit. She'd spoken briefly with him late this afternoon and arranged for him to stop by in the morning.

As far as T.J. was concerned, well... he'd done his duty. Jen had said he'd headed to his parent's place when he'd stopped by earlier, and she wouldn't be surprised if he had a date later. Why not? The man was hot, no argument there. Any girl would be lucky to have stalwart Trooper McGraw. Lanie just wouldn't be that girl.

Chapter Eight

Jack rolled over and checked the time. His raspy cough echoed in the quiet motel room. *Fuck*. He'd wanted to be on the road by now. The wild goose chase for Elaine Delacor had eaten up an entire day. Two nights ago, after dragging his cop buddy in Bayside out of bed, the two of them had spent half the night driving around, hunting for an old garage.

Damn town had way too many rundown garages. When they'd finally located the place, he'd been ready to explode. His frayed nerves had finally settled when they'd spotted tracks in the snow that had lead them right to the door, and his anxiety had decreased even more when they'd found the money and stash inside, exactly where Skinny had said they'd be. Jack had made a few calls, then they'd hidden the goods under a pile of boards and settled in to wait.

Just before sunup, a scrawny long-haired guy had showed up, retrieved the shipment, and slunk away. Jack had kept the payoff as originally planned, all bundled in packs of twenties.

In a way, he regretted having taken out Frankie and Skinny, but in his world he couldn't tolerate shit-for-brains idiots. If that cash had disappeared, he'd have been severely pissed -- and *his* life would have been worthless.

He rubbed his eyes, pushed the blankets aside, and swung his legs out of bed. He glanced across the room, assured by the sight of the beat up black gym bag exactly where he'd put it two nights ago. There were ways to make sure the cash wouldn't be traced, and he knew them all. He'd take his cut and then quietly pass on the rest. Jumping through all those hoops, though, was a royal pain in the ass.

Crossing to the window, he pushed aside the heavy drapes. The street glistened dark and wet as the residents of Fox Chapel made their way to work, and dirty piles of snow ringed the parking lot. A steady drizzle hazed the air, blurring the neon signs winking in the gray dawn.

Two days ago, he'd driven south on I-79 in similar gray dawn light. He'd left the snow behind, only to encounter freezing sleet, then rain. When he'd finally located the address in Fox Chapel Terry had tracked down from Elaine Delacor's license plate number, melting snow and steady rain had turned the landscape into a slushy hell. As luck would have it, the apartment had been empty, so he'd given up until later that day.

"Almost makes me want more of the damn snow," Jack murmured to himself, yanking the curtain closed. He stumbled into the bathroom and showered, letting hot water pound his beat up body, cursing the number of hours he'd spent closing in on his prey only to discover that Elaine

Delacor didn't live in Fox Chapel anymore.

Part of him wanted to drive right back to Bayside and put a round between good old Terry-the-cop's eyes. Common sense told him Terry couldn't have known the license plate hadn't been updated since the woman had moved, but shooting him would sure as hell relieve some of the tension coiled up in Jack's gut like a damn snake.

He hated wasting time, and for two solid days, that's all he'd done. Last night when he'd returned to the apartment, the door across the hall had popped open just as he was about to force his way into the place. Smooth talking a former neighbor into telling him where Elaine Delacor had moved had eaten up even more time, not to mention the effort it had taken for him not to force the issue.

He'd tried charm, asking if Miss Delacor was away, and the neighbor had acted as if Jack were a stalker. What he'd really wanted to do was smack the old biddy upside the head and tell her to spit it out. But he'd played the game. He'd smiled till his teeth ached, giving her some cock and bull story about being an old friend of the family. And apparently, his gambit had struck a chord, because she'd smiled, at last, and asked if he knew Elaine's Uncle Charley. He'd jumped on that odd stroke of luck, lied through his teeth, and she'd spilled her guts.

Whoever this Charley was, he must have meant a lot to *Lanie* Delacor, because old granny next door didn't hesitate to give him all the information he'd asked for, and then some. As luck would have it, she didn't have an exact address, though. Just that Lanie lived *somewhere* near Erie, and what a shame it was that she'd lost her job when Fox Chapel Fitness burned down.

Dead tired after his encounter with the old lady, he'd stopped at a local store and picked up a clean shirt and a change of underwear, then checked into a motel. According to the news, the snow had let up, but the roads were still a mess. So he wasn't about to turn around and drive north again. This morning, he was glad he'd stayed. A good night's sleep had cleared his head and helped him to focus his thoughts. He cut off the water and toweled himself dry.

He put on his new shirt and the slacks he'd worn yesterday, found the TV remote tangled in the sheets, and clicked on the morning news. The anchor mentioned nothing about police finding two bodies near Edinboro, so the story hadn't made the Pittsburgh news. No surprise there, but surely by now they'd found Frankie and Skinny.

A shiver snaked up Jack's spine.

He hoped so. They might have been a couple of screw-ups, but hey... he wasn't a heartless bastard. Screw-ups didn't deserve to freeze solid in the middle of a blizzard, even if they were already dead.

"You've got one twisted sense of humor," Jack muttered to himself, chuckling as he checked over the room, making sure he didn't forget anything. He dug into the black bag and grabbed a couple of bills. He tossed them down for housekeeping and left the room.

First stop was a drive-through car wash. He needed to check the front of his Escalade for damage. Depending on a couple of things, it could be a while before they connected his SUV to the dead bodies at the rest stop. If his luck held, maybe they never would. Jack didn't put a lot of stock in luck, so he bent and examined the clean, shiny grille. In passing, the tiny indent would go unnoticed. Under a nosey cop's scrutiny, the little scrape and bump could become a major deal.

Jack called in another chit. Cleveland was home to several so called *chop shops*. He traded favors with one of the biggest, and a quick call guaranteed his Cadillac would soon have a nice new, untraceable grille, and he'd have something to drive while they took care of his SUV.

Using a legit dealer would leave a trail, and that was something he wanted to avoid. In the meantime, he'd catch up on the local news. A murder near Erie would be easy to track. He stopped on the outskirts of town and grabbed a current *Erie Times News*, then hauled ass west into Ohio. The cash dump went smoothly, and he netted a tidy share.

Now, for the time being, he'd lay low. He knew what had to be done. He wasn't happy about it, but what the hell? His buddy in Bayside would give him a heads up if anything broke he should know about. His primary concern was finding Elaine Delacor.

Chapter Nine

Lanie closed the door behind Corporal Sullivan, leaned her head against its smooth wood, and took a deep breath. The interview had left her drained and set her nerves on edge all over again. The corporal hadn't been cold or demanding. Actually, he'd been very polite. Not once had he given her the impression he doubted her story -- something she'd point out to T.J. McGraw the next time he crossed her path.

Alone at last, she sank into a chair and stared at the yellow notepad on the table in front of her. Earlier, amidst a welcome burst of energy, she'd scribbled a list of goals. A roadmap to get her life back in order. Back to *normal*.

The uncompleted list taunted her. It was visible proof she'd failed to reach her goals.

Head throbbing, she mentally ticked off what she *hadn't* yet accomplished.

No luck with Erie Insurance. She needed transportation until the garage had repaired her car, but the insurance company claimed a shortage of rental cars had created a delay. She'd also been informed that until the police completed their investigation, they couldn't estimate the damage to her Miata.

The remainder of her list, to wash clothes, get groceries, and scrub the floor, would have to wait. Much as she hated to admit it, she needed a damn nap.

She suspected the lingering effects of hypothermia were partly to blame, but leaned more toward her restless sleep. Fragmented nightmares had plagued her throughout the night. On several occasions, she'd awoken soaked in sweat and trembling. Every time she'd closed her eyes, faceless ghoulish figures had floated toward her as she huddled in her car surrounded by swirling snow. Only their cold, dead eyes pierced the night, moving closer and closer... until a jolt sent her careening toward the unearthly corpses. All in all, she'd probably only slept a few hours, at most.

She shoved aside her tepid coffee. Her stomach growled. She'd been unable to finish the soup Jen had left for her, and now she eyed the freshly baked apple muffins her friend had arranged temptingly in a wicker basket on the counter.

What the hell? She rose and grabbed a napkin. She'd burn off the extra calories in no time once she got back to work. As she selected one of the generous, cinnamon laden treats, she glanced out the window. A small, dark, classy-looking SUV rolled into sight. Dropping the muffin, she balled the napkin in her fist. Her breath caught and held as the vehicle

stopped in front of her cabin. The SUV had a small, shiny front grille --
not a large one like the overbearing rows of chrome on the big black one
from the rest stop. That vehicle was huge in comparison to this dark
colored, sleek little machine.

A swift glance assured Lanie the cabin door was locked. Even so, her
heart pounded in her ears, blocking everything as she curled her shaking
fingers around the cell phone in her pocket.

Then T.J. stepped from the SUV and she nearly collapsed in relief.

He closed the door and glanced around. She knew the moment he
spotted her watching him. Though his eyes were hidden behind reflective
sunglasses, heat shot through her the second his gaze locked with hers.

She moved away from the window, blew out a sharp breath, and
went to unlock the door, brushing tears of relief from her eyes as she
crossed the rug.

He paused on the other side of the threshold, his wide shoulders
filling the doorway. Slanted sunlight picked up the coppery highlights in
his hair.

"You're looking better," he remarked. Then he stepped inside.

She closed the door behind him.

He wasn't in uniform, but instead wore snug jeans and a cocoa
brown jacket. He removed his shades and tucked them into his pocket.
The blue hoodie beneath his jacket brought out hints of indigo in his
intense gray eyes.

Lanie struggled to calm her pounding pulse as he did a slow head-to-
toe appraisal of her. She lifted her chin and wondered if her casual cords
and green turtleneck would pass his inspection, and if he'd notice the
dark circles beneath her eyes. His gaze returned to her face and lingered.
If he noticed obvious signs of stress, he kept quiet.

"Have you seen my car?" she demanded. Before he could comment,
she brushed past him, returned to the table, and sat. Her knees were about
to fold, and she didn't want to end up on the floor at his feet.

"I work second shift today, three to eleven. I'll get to your car then."
He shrugged out of his coat, toed off his low-cut boots, and then nodded
toward the coffeemaker on the counter. "May I?"

"Help yourself. Cups are in the cupboard, left side of the sink."

He found one and poured himself a cup, even going so far as to
search out a spoon and add sugar. Once he settled into a chair across from
her, he took a careful sip of the hot brew and asked, "So... how'd the
interview go?"

"Fine. Corporal Sullivan didn't have a problem with my story. In fact,
he said I gave him a lot to go on for his investigation."

"I see." T.J. let the obvious dig slide. "Have you figured out the make
or model of the SUV that hit you?"

"It was a big black one," she retorted, "with an emblem right in the
center of its grille."

Her pithy remark hung in the air. She wasn't stupid about cars, but this nagging fatigue muddled her mind. She pushed away from the table and went in search of the teapot. Maybe a cup of hot tea would help.

"Actually," T.J. remarked, apparently unperturbed, "that narrows it down."

"I'm sure I could identify the one that hit me if I saw it." She turned to put some water on to boil. "I just need to check out how many big SUVs fit the bill."

Leaning against the counter, she closed her eyes and ran a hand through her hair. She looked up and caught T.J. frowning at her.

"Stop looking at me like I'm an invalid. I'm doing the best I can."

"You're damn lucky. Hypothermia isn't a head cold. It knocks the hell out of your system." He tilted his head and studied her. "To be honest, most folks would still be flat on their backs after what you went through. You're handling it well, probably because you're in such good shape. But damn it, Lanie, don't be so hard on yourself. No matter what shape you're in, if you're not sleeping, it's damn well going to show."

"T.J.--" She hated to admit he was right, but suddenly her limbs felt heavy. The room tilted. "Can you pour my tea when it's ready? I-I need to get off my feet."

He helped her back to the table, then strode to the sofa, gathered up a crumpled throw, and draped it around her. He crouched down, took her chin in his hand, and lifted it until she met his steady gaze. "You're white as a sheet. How much have you eaten today?"

"I had some soup," she mumbled, twisting away from his grip. As if on cue, her stomach gave another unladylike growl.

He cocked a brow.

She looked away and pulled the throw closer. "I was about to have a muffin when you showed up."

The shrill whistle of the teapot distracted him. He left her there, located a tea bag, and added hot water to the mug. He smacked the cup down in front of her, grabbed the basket of muffins, and took them to the table. "I'll join you, if you don't mind."

His gruffness didn't surprise her. Her attitude would test a saint.

*****

While she fussed with her tea, T.J. strolled to the window, coffee in hand. He kept reminding himself she'd been through a lot, which probably accounted for her piss poor attitude. Or at least more attitude than usual for Elaine Delacor.

He studied the view outside her kitchen window. The cabin sat on a ridge overlooking vineyards and orchards. Off in the distance, a wide band of ice on Lake Erie stretched several miles from shore. Where the ice ended, bluish-gray water blended with the horizon. If the weather stayed cold, ice dunes would soon form along the shoreline. They protected the beaches throughout the long winter months, and could be deadly for anyone who ventured out to explore their craggy surfaces.

"There's a face on a tree out there," he commented, lifting the cup in his hand toward the window.

"That's tree-face," Lanie said, raising her tired eyes. She smiled. "Jen and I found him at a garden center this fall. When we attached him to the tulip tree, the colored leaves above him made him look like an old man with a waving mane of golden locks."

"Looks like your old man went bald, and his whiskers turned white." T.J. chuckled, studying the stone cast eyes and sweeping mustache. "But I like him. He reminds me of a stoic guardian, watching over forest and field."

She nodded in agreement. Maybe she'd calmed enough for his questions. He searched for a neutral middle ground. "If I dig up some pictures of full-sized SUVs and email them to you, do you think you could pick out the one you saw?"

"I can't say for sure until I see them." Her hands visibly tightened on her cup, and she took a deep breath. Then she lifted one hand and rubbed her eyes. "You can't have missed that I look like death warmed over. Part of the reason is because every time I close my eyes, I see... I see *something*. Sleep doesn't come easy."

When he didn't comment, she picked up her cup and leaned back in her chair. "At this point, I'm not sure what's real and what my mind's conjuring up. I remember being followed, and that after he hit me I lost control of my car. I've relived that moment over and over, and it terrifies me. That's real. Maybe when I see actual pictures, I'll recognize what he drove. I can't say for sure until then."

She stared straight ahead, her soft green eyes unfocused. Their depth and beauty left T.J. speechless. He tracked her line of sight to dust motes dancing in the filtered sunlight.

He cleared his throat and asked softly, "What else do you see, Lanie?"

She blinked, rose, and moved to stand beside him at the window.

"I see dead people." She gave a weak laugh and met his eyes briefly. "And doesn't that sound familiar? The difference being that I'm very much alive. And I can barely stand knowing that while I took a cat nap, then climbed out and cleaned the snow off my car, two dead men sat in another vehicle not forty feet away."

T.J. reached for her, but she shrugged him off. "I know you have questions for me. Let's get this over with. Maybe if I talk about it, get it straight in my mind, I can get some sleep."

He dug into his pocket for his pen and notebook.

She returned to the table, sat, and started her story at the point when she'd driven smack into the snowstorm. Lanie took him through the entire evening. As she talked, her kitten appeared and hopped onto her lap, making a tiny smile tug at the corner of her mouth. She scooped him up and snuggled him beneath her chin. When she buried her face in his soft, dark fur, the kitten's purr rumbled like a well-tuned engine.

T.J. paused and idly flipped through the notes he'd taken, stealing glances as she nestled Sam Cat to her breast. *Damn cat had a good reason to purr.*

He tucked his notes away and went to get his coat.

With Sam cradled in her arms, Lanie walked with him to the door. He opened it to leave, and the hum of an approaching vehicle caught his attention.

"It's Cassi." Lanie stepped past him onto the porch. Clutching Sam with one hand, she waved with the other.

Cassi McGraw parked her CRV behind T.J.'s Toyota RAV 4. She and her aunt, Ada McConnell, got out, arms loaded with what he suspected was enough food for a small army.

"T.J.," Ada reached them first. "Are you coming or going?"

"I'm on my way to work, ladies."

His cousin's wife, Cassi, stretched up and planted a quick kiss on his cheek. He read the question in her eyes and shook his head. Juggling Sam and attempting to help Ada with a huge, unwieldy kettle, Lanie missed their silent exchange. T.J. was glad.

"Is Nick working?" He dug out his keys and turned up the collar of his jacket.

"No. He's freezing his butt off on Pine Shadow Lake ice fishing with your dad and Rich. The ice has barely formed, and they're already down there pokin' and testing. They're not at all upset by winter's early arrival this year."

T.J. laughed. His dad and Rich McConnell had gone ice fishing together for as long as he could remember. He leaned in for Ada's kiss before she disappeared inside with Lanie. Until last year, Ada's last name had been Blaine. She made a living growing the sweetest berries and freshest herbs in Western Pennsylvania. His dad's best friend Rich had fallen for the sassy gardener like a ton of bricks. Rich, a down to earth, ordinary guy, owned a thriving Ace Hardware Store in Pine Bluffs. At least, T.J. had *thought* Rich was ordinary, until someone had set out to make Ada and Rich's life miserable, and T.J. had ended up smack in the middle of the conflict.

Their budding romance had survived, but not before several hair-raising, life threatening near misses had brought in the state police and subsequently, T.J. After they married, Rich moved into Ada's cottage on Pine Shadow Lake, and they were now in the process of enlarging and remodeling it.

Tom McGraw, T.J.'s dad, was handyman extraordinaire. He'd turned over the reins of the top position in the Pine Bluffs Police Department to Cassi's husband when he'd retired as chief of police. Now with time on his hands, and since he was Rich's best friend, he was hip deep in the ongoing project.

"Wait a minute, will you?" Cassi poked T.J.'s arm. "Let me put this inside, and I'll walk out with you." She disappeared inside toting a bulging grocery bag.

Translated, she wanted to pump him for information about the ongoing investigation.

He tossed his keys up into the air and caught them, waiting patiently, staring at the snow-covered tree face across the way. Finally, the door behind him opened and closed softly and Cassi stepped up to his side.

"Is that a face on that tree out there?"

"Yeah, it is, and I like it," he remarked, smiling at her question. He glanced down at her. "Lanie says she and Jen put it up this fall."

He checked the time. "I've got to get movin', Cass. What do you want to ask me?"

"I'll walk you to your car." She glanced back at the door to make sure they wouldn't be followed.

Dark clouds had moved inland from the lake, and they now blocked the sun and cast odd shadows on the snow. Beneath their feet, snow crunched as they walked in silence. T.J. opened his door and turned to face Cassi. Her dark eyes stood out against her pale winter skin. Nick claimed his wife's eyes broadcasted her state of mind like a news flash. His cousin sure knew what he was talking about, because Cassi's concern was unmistakable.

"You're worried about her," T.J. said, chucking her under the chin. The move made her smile, and that had been his plan. He loved Nick's wife like a sister, but considering their rocky beginning, it was a miracle they'd grown so close.

Two years ago, after her parents had died in an accident, Cassi came to Pine Bluffs to meet Ada. Having been adopted as a baby, Cassi wasn't aware she had any blood relatives until Ada had stepped forward. A twist of fate threw suspicion on Cassi when she ended up at a murder scene. Things went south when Nick fell for Cassi while T.J. tried to unravel the whole mess and find out who'd killed the guy she'd found in the bog outside of Pine Bluffs. All in all, things had turned out for the best for everyone.

"Of course I'm worried about her," Cassi retorted. "And quit staring at me with that funny look on your face."

"Sorry." T.J. realized he'd been gazing silently down at her, reliving the past. "Sometimes my face does its own thing when I'm thinking."

Cassi laughed, then sobered and laid her hand on T.J.'s arm. "I am worried. Can you tell me anything new? What they're pulling out on the news is so vague. Two guys were found dead at a rest stop, and there's an ongoing investigation. That's it." She pulled her gloves on tighter and hunched against a sudden gust of wind. "That's where Lanie called me from, T.J. She called for help, and we got cut off. When I think about it -- my God. She must have pulled in right after someone killed those poor guys. Then she noticed that big SUV, the guy gets out and comes her way, and she panics. Thank God she had the good sense to get the hell out of there. In my mind, it's no coincidence she nearly got killed a few miles up the road when that same SUV rammed her and pushed her off the road."

"You didn't get all that from news reports."

"I talked to her early this morning, at length."

"That's why as soon as the storm broke you and Ada hauled your butts up here." T.J. ran his fingers down her arm and took her hand. "You're a good friend, Cass. Lanie needs that now. To be honest, this is the most subdued I've ever seen your friend."

The wind increased, and snow peppered down. Fine, needle-like missals slapped against T.J.'s bare cheeks.

"Get in," He ordered, sliding in behind the wheel. Cassi dashed around to the other side and got inside with him. He slipped the key into the ignition, gave it a twist, and the engine roared to life. He turned to face Cassi. "Soon as I get to work, I'm going to examine Lanie's car. At this point, we don't know for sure she *was* pushed off the road. I'll find evidence if it happened the way she said it did."

"Don't you believe her?" Frowning, Cassi tilted her head.

T.J. pursed his lips. "Gotta' take it one step at a time. Once we have the evidence, then we'll move forward. The crime unit is working on the murders."

"I see." Cassi's eyes darkened. "How were they killed?"

He nodded grimly. "Can't say. The details aren't public knowledge, and that's all I can tell you right now. I'm supposed to contact the barracks and arrange a meeting once I've examined the Miata. After that, I'm pretty much out of it."

The snow picked up as he swung the car close to the porch to let Cassi out. "You and Ada should pay attention to this weather and head back to Pine Bluffs before dark."

"Just keep me updated." Cassi flipped up the hood of her jacket. "And, T.J.? Please don't let anything happen to Lanie."

"Okay." He squeezed her hand. "I'll do my best."

"Nick and I will be home this evening," she said, reaching for the door handle. She hesitated with it in her hand. "Should I take Lanie home with me? Maybe until this is all settled, she'd be safer in Pine Bluffs."

"Do you really think she'd go with you?" T.J. eyed her with one brow quirked. "*Independence* is the woman's middle name. Along with *stubborn.*"

Cassi chuckled. "When are you going to admit you're attracted to that stubborn woman? I think you should ask her out, get to know the Lanie I know and love. She might surprise you." She leaned in and gave him a kiss, then jumped out and ran for the cabin door.

"Right. When hell freezes over," he muttered to himself. Then he headed for the barracks.

Chapter Ten

By the time T.J. got on the road, snow was coming down fast and furious. He hated having to drive clear to Edinboro. He'd called the garage to make sure they'd secured Lanie's car inside because he sure as hell wasn't standing out in this shit to look for damage.

He'd also called Nick on his cell before he left the barracks to fill him in on the latest, and promised to keep him updated. Nick laughed when he mentioned he'd suggested Cassi get Lanie to spend some time with them in Pine Bluffs. His cousin knew Lanie Delacor well.

As T.J. swung into the lot at the wrecker service, he passed a flatbed tow truck heading out toward the thruway. The driver gave him a jaunty wave, sped away, and was soon swallowed up by blowing snow. T.J. pulled in close, locked his unit, and went inside.

The smell of motor oil hung in the air, and the hollow pounding of metal on metal echoed through the high-ceilinged, cavernous building. Lanie's red Miata sat off to his left. He headed in that direction.

"Hey, McGraw," a cheery voice rang out. The tire iron in the man's hand hit the floor with a clang. He pushed a pair of safety glasses up on his head and waved.

T.J. smiled and returned the wave. "I'm here to check out the Miata."

They met halfway across the floor. As the ruddy faced man joined T.J., he pulled off his thick work gloves and stuck them into the pocket of his stained overalls. A name tag identified him as Chet.

He nodded toward the Miata. "She's been here since I got a call from the barracks late yesterday. I was real careful towing her; knew you'd want us to make sure she was exactly like when they brought her in."

"Thanks. We appreciate that," T.J. said. Strange how Chet referred to the little red car as a *she*.

"I made sure to lock her up tight like you asked."

"Thanks, Chet. Now let's take a look at her and see what we can find."

Didn't take T.J. long to find a deep, rounded divot smack between the car's tail lights. The license plate was crimped, too, and the trunk lid was slightly bowed inward and hiked up. The bumper of a big SUV would withstand an impact with a car this size with no trouble, but its grille might show some damage. It all depended on the angle when he hit her, and in T.J.'s mind he now had no doubt that something had kissed the rear end of Lanie's car with enough force to drive her off the road.

He dug a small digital camera from his coat pocket.

"Chet, take a look at that, will you?" He gestured toward the rear of the car while toying with the camera's focus.

Chet hunkered down and studied the bumper. He ran his fingers through his thatch of shaggy brown hair.

"Something smacked her in the ass," he commented. "Pretty high up to have been done by a car. Maybe a truck or SUV?" He shook his head. "If that's the case, ya might have trouble findin' it."

"Why's that?"

"Them new wrap around bumpers pop back out like a rubber ball if the impact isn't too bad. Might leave a scratch on the grille, but you'll pay hell trackin' it down."

T.J. agreed. Real evidence would be next to impossible to find, especially since they didn't have a clue what might have hit her. Unless he counted Lanie's description of the vehicle as having been *big and black* -- and that told them zilch.

He snapped a few pictures of the damage from several angles, including a few close ups, and then turned to Chet. "Is it repairable?"

"Well, that depends. When I got the call from your people telling me to move the car inside and leave it alone, I did just that. I'd have to get it on the rack, take a look underneath to make sure the frame isn't torked."

T.J. stuffed the camera back into his pocket. "Until you hear from us, I'd appreciate it if you'd just leave it right here. Will you make sure no one touches it until we decide if we want to bring it up to Erie?"

"No problem." Chet stepped back and shoved his hands in his pockets. "We've worked with you guys before on accident investigations. I'll surround it with some big old orange cones. That'll keep everyone the hell away."

Including the insurance adjuster, T.J. surmised. Lanie would not be happy, but at this point, he didn't have a choice. Everything was on hold until something turned up to help them.

His cell phone buzzed. "McGraw."

"T.J., Are you about finished there?" The sergeant's tone made T.J.'s gut clutch.

"All done, Sarge. What's up?"

"I need you to return to the barracks, right away."

TJ told him he would and then disconnected, thanked Chet, and strode out into the driving snow. It took a few minutes for the state car's engine to warm and for the defrosters to make a dent. Sergeant Evans had revealed nothing during their clipped conversation, but T.J. suspected something was definitely up.

An hour later, after driving blind through whiteout conditions, T.J. walked into the barracks. He paused to brush snow from his coat before entering Sergeant Evans' office. He nodded to Evans and draped his coat over a vacant chair.

"Long time, no see," Raife Samuels drawled.

T.J. spun around. His eyes landed on the lean, dark-haired man, and then slid to another man slouched in a chair on the other side of the desk. Raife Samuels and his partner, Fred Connors. He'd worked with the two

49

veterans from the Ohio Investigative Unit before. In his opinion, they were top notch undercover agents.

He stepped forward and shook their hands; first Raife, and then Fred.

"Still wearing that beat up leather jacket, I see." He grinned at Raife. "Doesn't OIU pay you guys enough to upgrade your sorry wardrobes every once and a while?"

"Gentlemen," Evans interrupted. "We've got a couple of hours before the next shift change. Then we'll all hit the Park Tavern, have a brew, and catch up on current fashion. In the meantime, T.J., have a seat. As soon as Corporal Sullivan gets here, we'll get started."

T.J. nodded and dropped down next to Raife. Seconds later, the door opened, and Dan Sullivan entered.

Growing dread settled into T.J.'s gut like a rock. Dealing with OIU was not unusual, but their presence signaled a development in the case. One he feared wouldn't bode well for Lanie Delacor.

*****

Sam Cat wound around Lanie's legs, weaving in and out, rubbing, and purring up a storm. She topped off his food bowl and laughed when he stretched up to tap impatiently on her leg. He trotted in front of her, tail waving like a banner, to his spot in the corner and dove in head first when she put down his bowl. He arched his back up when she ran her hand over him, but never lifted his face from his food.

Her cabin smelled delicious, and she drew in the lingering, comforting aromas. Nothing surpassed the yummy scents of Ada's fresh berry cobbler and Cassi's homemade chili. They'd pampered her, stuffing her with food and making her rest. She'd fallen into a coma-like sleep after they'd left and had slept for hours. Now she peered out the window at the steady snow falling from the night sky. Close to one inch an hour, according to *Fox News at Ten*. The snow had already covered the tire tracks from Cassi's Honda, meaning they'd picked up over five inches since Cass and Ada had left.

Lanie loved snow. Since she'd lived near the city most of her life, she'd never experienced the pristine, hushed beauty of freshly fallen snow beneath a moonlit sky. She leaned on the windowsill and squinted into the darkness. On this moonless night, she detected only a grayish haze created by a curtain of falling snow. She noted the temperature on the window gadget stuck to the glass. A perfect thirty-two degrees. Outside, the trees' bare branches all wore a mantel of white. Stark and still, they reached skyward through the pale, cascading curtain.

Restless and her energy restored, Lanie paced the floor. Indecision plagued her. She wanted to walk out into the night, to bundle up and slog through the falling snow. She just needed to *move*.

What harm could come from a solitary walk in the snow?

Snow crunched beneath her feet and fat flakes melted on her cheeks once she bundled up and exited the house. God, how good it felt to savor the beauty surrounding her. She crossed the yard, passed the towering tulip tree, and paused where the ground dropped away to the orchards below. Row upon row of apple trees crowned with white reached all the way to her landlord's sprawling farmhouse on Sidehill Road. Across the road from the Reed's home, barely visible in the snow, loomed the barn they used for storing farm equipment. Off to the west, the sky lightened, thanks to the soft glow from the city of Erie.

A stiff breeze kicked up, and Lanie tugged the hood of her jacket tighter. She glanced back at the cabin. Before leaving, she'd stoked the fire. She'd also left several lights burning. A thick column of smoke rose from the stone chimney and floated south, skirting the treetops of the woods behind the cabin. Her footprints were no longer visible, having been obliterated by the north wind sweeping along the ground.

Pushing on, she followed the ridge and walked, just walked, until her legs grew weak and the moist night air burned her throat. She paused to catch her breath. Movement at the edge of the trees ahead caught her eye, and two deer stepped into a clearing on the hill.

"You're beautiful," she said aloud.

They turned their elegant heads at the sound of her voice and stood poised to run. She stayed still, barely breathing, until they leapt away with a flick of their tails and disappeared down the hill into the orchard.

She yawned, took one last look around, and headed back to the cabin. Overhead, a branch cracked, and she gasped when it fell at her feet. Her wary gaze swept over the vast expanse of fields and forest surrounding her. Sudden unease, tinged with fear, propelled her forward. She tried to retrace her steps back to the cabin, but they'd disappeared among a series of drifts that had erased any sign of her passing. She floundered, and unable to regain her footing, fell into the snow, rolling down a steep incline and coming to rest in a tangle of dried grass.

In near panic, she scrambled up the sharp embankment.

Upon reaching the top, she stopped and gasped for breath. As she bent to dislodge snow packed inside her boot, pounding from the direction of the cabin echoed through the darkness. Her heart slammed against her ribs, and her trembling legs threatened to fold.

Moments ago, only fat, lazy snowflakes had floated down. Now, however, the rising wind had turned them into missals that smacked her face, making it impossible for her to see more than a few feet in front of her. Head bent, she forged ahead until something beneath the snow caught her foot, and she nearly went down. She kicked free of it and discovered she'd unearthed another fallen tree branch. Grasping it with both hands, she pulled on it. Her mind flashed back to the rest stop, and she remembered how she'd clutched the snowbrush and considered using it as a weapon.

Suddenly, the pounding on the cabin door ceased. She clutched the heavy branch and waited, listening.

What choice did she have? If she stayed out here, she'd freeze, and revisiting hypothermia was *not* a viable option. Only the wind rushing through the bare branches overhead broke the stillness of the night as Lanie moved forward one step at a time, her gaze fixed on the faint square of light visible through the trees.

When she finally reached the cabin, she flattened herself against the rough wood. Inch by inch, she worked her way to the corner. From there, she gauged the distance to the door to be about ten feet. She tested the weight of her makeshift weapon and gathered herself for a mad dash. To make sure nothing blocked her path, she glanced down, and her heart stopped dead in her chest.

Oversized footprints led right to the cabin's door, then crossed the porch and disappeared around the corner. The strange footprints barely registered before she detected the crunch of footsteps behind her.

From the corner of her eye, she saw him. Tall and heavy shouldered in a bulky jacket, the man stalked toward her without hesitation. Darkness hid his face, making him appear sinister and foreboding as he closed the distance between them.

She tightened her hold on the heavy branch and waited, gauging his approach, and then turned and swung like hell.

He ducked, and Lanie missed him. She'd come within mere inches of making contact, but the momentum threw her off balance.

"Hey!" he shouted. "Can't you see--"

She recovered, reversed her swing, and caught him waist high. He grunted, stumbled sideways, and then with amazing speed, recovered and ripped the makeshift weapon from her hands and tossed it aside. She tried to turn and run, but he grabbed her arm and yanked her toward him.

"No, no!" she screamed. "Damn you, let me go!"

She twisted free and swung blindly.

"Damn it, Lanie!" Her assailant recaptured her flailing hand and swept her feet from beneath her. The unexpected move took her down. The snow cushioned her fall, yet before she could get her breath, he dropped on top of her. Air whooshed from her lungs. She lunged upward, fighting for breath.

Then it hit her.

Lanie? The pervert knew her name?

He had her pinned, unable to move. His hood dipped sideways and sat cockeyed on his head, half on and half off, revealing one dark, glaring eye. In direct contrast to the barely contained anger evident in her captor's demeanor, an oddly familiar shock of unruly hair stood straight up.

"T.J.?' She squeaked.

"Well, no shit." His terse, irritated response left her weak and trembling. Weak with relief because he wasn't the unknown assailant in the SUV come to finish the job, yet trembling, because T.J. McGraw had his hard body pressed intimately against hers.

"Let me up," Lanie demanded.

He shifted and released the death grip that had pinned her wrists to the ground. Still unable to move, Lanie widened her eyes when he leaned closer and his warm breath fanned her cheeks. "What in the hell possessed you to try and take off my head?"

"Get. Off. Me," she ordered through clenched teeth. She tried to match his angry glare, but falling snow kept getting into her eyes. Simmering, white hot anger replaced her bone-melting fear. Or, maybe it was red hot *lust*. Regardless, her body's unexpected reaction set off alarm bells on so many levels. With the heel of her hand, she shoved T.J.'s shoulder.

He rolled to one side, then sat up and pushed the troublesome hood out of the way. "Are you all right?"

"I'm fine," she snapped. She lay there, her heart beating much too rapidly, and wiped snow from her face. "Just give me a minute. God, McGraw, how much do you weigh?"

"Doesn't matter." He drew up his legs and rested his elbows on his knees. "What possessed you to go gallivanting all over the countryside after midnight in the middle of a blizzard?"

That did it. She jackknifed up, scrambled to her feet, and left him sitting there as she stomped away, ripping off one glove to delve into an inside pocket for her key.

"That," she said, stabbing the key repeatedly at the lock, "is none of your damn business."

T.J. wrenched the key from her and pushed her aside. The key slid in on his first try, and that pissed her off even more. He turned the knob and pushed open the door.

She brushed past him with a mumbled, "Thank you."

A few steps inside, she turned to face him. Her abrupt stop caused another collision of bodies, another heated jolt to her overworked system. When she almost toppled over, he managed to catch her in mid-fall by wrapping his arms around her. He kept her from falling, but shot her imagination sky high.

First fear, then anger, and then... lust, or *whatever*, created a potent blend. Squelching the urge to wrap herself around T.J.'s tall, lanky form, she decided to get as far away from him as possible. She pulled away and moved across the room, unbuttoning her coat as she went. She tossed it onto a chair, squatted down, and poked at the simmering logs until flames erupted.

"You scared the crap out of me tonight."

"It's my choice if I want to... what was it you said? Gallivant?" Another poke, another vicious jab. She stood and brushed wood chips from her jeans. "Where do you come up with these words?"

"Would you just calm down?"

"I am calm." She stopped brushing at her clothes and straightened.

"Calm, but pissed."

"What the hell are you pissed about?" His voice caught, making her pause to shoot him a curious look.

He had a painful grimace on his face. He hugged his side and glanced around, then took several faltering steps and eased onto the sofa.

"Oh, God." She rushed over and dropped to her knees in front of him. "I forgot I nailed you out there."

"Yeah?" Arms crossed, leaning forward, he met her gaze with pain filled eyes. "Just give me a minute."

"Here, let me help you with your coat."

"No." He blocked her eager hands. "I can handle it. Just back off a minute, okay?"

"Fine." Lanie sat back on her heels and waited while he slipped out of his parka. His features hardened, and he paled. "I'll need you to help me with this sweater, though. Damn it."

She nodded and crept forward between his knees. "You're shaking."

Fearing he might injure himself further, she hovered there, not quite knowing what to do.

He took a deep breath and closed his eyes, then opened them slowly and met her gaze.

"Help me with my sweater," he repeated, sucking in a sharp breath when she slid the sweater over his head. Then he unbuttoned his shirt, and his fingers faltered.

She couldn't stand it. She brushed his fingers aside. "Let me. Please."

With a nod, he drew his hands away and sat very still while she finished the job with quick efficiency. The thermal tee-shirt beneath that shirt presented yet another barrier. He pushed her hands away and lifted the shirt gingerly. Along his ribcage, from just beneath his arm to his waist, his skin appeared red and tender. Dark bruising spread outward from what must have been the point of impact. T.J. lifted the shirt further and twisted for a closer look.

"Oh, shit." He leaned back and snapped his eyes shut. "It's worse than I thought."

"Oh, God, T.J." Tears welled in Lanie's eyes. "I'm sorry. I'm *so* sorry."

Eyes still closed, he shook his head and mumbled, "No one to blame but me. I should have warned you."

"Yes, you should have, but maybe I shouldn't have been out uh.... *gallivanting* around in a blizzard." Without thinking, she reached up and smoothed his tousled hair.

His eyes flew open.

The spitting, crackling fire warmed her from behind, and its mesmerizing reflection dancing in his eyes immobilized her. Trapped between his rock hard thighs, she locked her eyes on his. Time slowed, and her blood flowed through her like a river of lava.

T.J. dropped his gaze to her lips, touched one hand to her cheek, and cupped her neck with the other. He pulled her in and brushed his lips over hers. Then he took her mouth, and her pulse soared.

His scent, his taste, overrode everything. In the far reaches of Lanie's mind, a weak, pathetic sliver of common sense shouted *wait, stop,* and the slow moving river of lava exploded, zipping fast and reckless through her veins.

His deep, throaty moan vibrated against her breasts. She pressed forward, nestling closer, winding her arms around his neck.

"Lanie. *Oh, God.* Lanie. Stop!"

Stop?

She jerked away, gasping. A flash of heat climbed her neck and swept over her cheeks, embarrassment struggling with unleashed passion inside her.

Keeping her eyes averted, she scooted back and attempted to free herself from the confines of his lean thighs. His hand closed on her wrist.

"Don't," she stammered, and tried to twist away.

"Elaine, I didn't *want* to stop."

"Then why...?"

He continued to grip her wrist, but laid his free hand across his mid-section. Pain contorted his handsome features.

She feathered her fingers over the back of his hand. "Twice tonight I've hurt you," she whispered. He released her, and she stumbled to her feet, straightening her clothes as she backed away. "I-I'll get something to wrap your ribs. Then I'll call Jen and see if she can run you to the ER."

Before he could respond, she hurried away to retrieve the tiny first aid kit tucked away in her bathroom closet. What had she been thinking? First she walloped him with a big stick, and then she practically crawled into his lap. She dug through a neat stack of towels in the closet, leaving them in an untidy heap when she spied the box holding her emergency supplies. She took a moment and splashed cool water over her face before returning to the living room.

He'd pulled his sweater back on and stood looking out the window.

"I found it." She waited until he turned. "I'm not sure I have enough material to go around you, but I do have an excellent salve for bruising. Here." She set the box on the table. "You can put some on to relieve the pain while I call Jen."

"No." T.J. came over to her. "We're not calling your friend. If I needed to go to the ER, I can drive myself."

Lanie bit her lip and looked up at him. "T.J., I'm responsible for this. Let me help you."

He stared down at her for a very long moment. The expression in his eyes told her nothing, yet the intensity deep within them took her breath away. "Can I stay here tonight?"

She took a step back and bumped into the counter.

A slow smile curved his lips, and he shook his head. "Look outside."

"What is it?" She turned and gaped at the wall of driven snow obliterating everything within sight. Wind howled under the eaves and slammed the bare branches of a leggy forsythia bush against the cabin. She'd been so wrapped up in emotional turmoil that she'd been oblivious to the unmistakable pounding of wind and snow.

He focused on the storm outside the window.

"From the way you stepped back when I asked to stay over," he said slowly, "I think you misunderstood my intentions." He gently took her shoulders and turned her to face him. "If we ever take up where we left off a while ago, I won't stay over because a snowstorm trapped me. I'll only be with you if we both agree it's what we want."

He touched his lips to her forehead. "Plus, I want to be one hundred percent when and if that happens." Dropping both hands, he turned and leaned against the counter beside her. "I'll try some of that salve you mentioned, but by morning I suspect I won't be feelin' too great."

He pushed away, crossed to the fireplace, and knelt stiffly to toss another log onto the fire. Casting one final glance at the driving snow, Lanie joined him.

"Here, let me do that." She handed him the first aid kit. "The salve I mentioned is in here. Use my bathroom and put it on. There are gauze pads in there, too, that might help keep your clothes from getting messy. Take whatever you need."

He rose, took the kit, and without a backward glance, disappeared down the narrow hallway.

Lanie dug out extra bedding for him to use. Fortunately, her sofa converted into a bed, and with little effort she readied it for her overnight guest. She stoked the fire, added yet another log, and came to her feet just as T.J. rejoined her.

She brushed wood chips from her hands. "I hope you'll be comfortable."

Naked from the waist up, he paused on the other side of the room. The mat of gauze pads he'd taped in place looked stark white against his skin. He eyed the neatly made bed, then her, and lifted one brow.

"So do I," he remarked, before crossing to the bed and lowering himself gingerly onto it. With a wince, he bent to pull off his socks.

"It won't work, you know." Lanie paced in front of the fireplace.

T.J. glanced up. "I'm sorry?"

"You and me..." She stopped and stood facing him, hands on her hips. "You're all... all hearth and home." She pointed an accusing finger at him. "You use words like *gallivanting*, for God's sake. Where do you come up with stuff like that?"

"Gallivanting...? Ah, I get that from my mother, I guess." He shrugged, frowning.

"See? You see what I mean," she accused. "You remember quaint expressions, enjoyed warm meals, and fun-filled holidays."

"I don't see the point." T.J. balled up his socks and threw them down. "What the hell does how I talk or what I grew up with have to do with *us?*"

Sam chose that moment to reach out from under the sofa bed, snag one sock, and retreat.

"Sam, come out here." Lanie knelt and half heartedly coaxed her kitten to give up his trophy. Instead, he wrapped his paws around T.J.'s stolen sock and held it safely out of reach.

"Damn it, Lanie. Forget about the cat. What exactly did you mean by that harebrained remark you just made?"

"The expressions I remember weren't cute." Needing to keep a safe distance between them, Lanie rose and moved away. She studied him, sitting there with firelight glistening on his bare shoulders. "They more than likely would have gotten *your* mouth washed out with soap. You and I, T.J., are like night and day."

She crossed her arms, rubbing away the chill she felt despite the roaring fire. The confusion she read in his frowning expression was almost laughable.

Almost.

"I'm going to bed now. If you need anything, just knock on my bedroom door."

Minutes later, Sam Cat scratched at her door. When she opened it, he dashed in, hopped onto the bed, and settled on her pillow to clean his pristine white paws. She stripped down and pulled on heavy sweats. She missed the warmth of the fireplace and repositioned Sam under the covers to help ward off the chill. While wind howled outside her window and Sam snuggled against her, she let the tears flow.

Exhausted, she finally slept until sun pouring in through her window announced a new day. She dragged herself from beneath the covers and pulled on jeans and a sweatshirt. Moving with caution, she crept down the hall to check on her overnight guest, only to discover the living room was empty.

T.J. was gone.

A fire still blazed in the fireplace, and he'd folded the bedding neatly and placed it on the sofa. She opened the door. The newly fallen snow sparkled in the sunlight, and fresh tire tracks disappeared down her driveway.

She quietly closed the door. As she went to make coffee, Sam wound around her legs begging for attention. She loved the little guy, yet was strangely disappointed that besides her quizzical faced kitten, she had no one with whom to share that coffee or the glorious winter morning.

Chapter Eleven

Jack hated driving an ordinary dark sedan, yet an unexpected delay in getting a new grille for his Escalade had put him in that position. He admitted it was necessary, even smart, for the time being, but he sure as hell didn't have to like it. He'd avoided incarceration for years by being cautious, by taking steps he admitted were often overkill. So he figured this little inconvenience overrode the *big* inconvenience of living behind bars.

The car bumped over rough ground as he swung into the lot of Harry's Eats, an out of the way long, low building along Route 5, two miles east of Bayside. He spotted Terry's pickup and pulled in alongside the spotless Chevy Silverado. Beside the gleaming truck, Jack's temporary transportation looked damn sorry.

He got out, slammed the door, and glared at Terry's truck. He'd be glad when this fuckin' mess was behind him. The nondescript, ordinary ride screamed *failure* to him, and he'd be damned if he'd bow to such indignities any longer than necessary. He wrenched open the restaurant's flimsy door and stepped inside. This time, Terry had better have the right address for the elusive Elaine Delacor.

Though the breakfast rush was over, the salty odor of bacon lingered in the air. A long counter stretched the length of the room, opening to a larger area at one end with booths along the wall and several tables in the center. Except for a lone man with his nose buried in the morning paper, Terry was the only customer. He sat at the far end of the counter, opposite from the lone reader who occupied a booth and seemed oblivious to his surroundings.

Jack hooked his coat on a rack by the door. He strolled over and settled on a stool two down from Terry, who glanced up and gave a brief nod. A waitress pushed through a swinging door from the kitchen.

"Hey, there." She smiled, drying her hands on a limp towel as she approached. "What can I get ya'?"

"Hello, darlin'. Just coffee." Jack turned on the charm and winked. "Nice and hot."

Using the same towel, she leaned in and wiped the counter in front of Jack. As far as he could tell, it was already spotless, but her deliberate move gave him a nice view as she bent forward. The once over look the little tart gave him didn't go unnoticed. Any waitress worth her salt knew how to rack up tips. He may be driving a piece of shit car, but he prided himself on his appearance. He grinned at her departing back and let his eyes slide low until the swinging door interrupted his view.

Almost immediately she butted the door back open, using the class act rear he'd admired, and placed a carafe of coffee on the counter along with a filled steaming mug. She reached beneath the counter and produced a small pitcher of cream, providing him with yet another glimpse of black lace and cleavage.

Jack sighed in appreciation. "Thank you, darlin'."

"Oh, you're welcome, handsome." She fluttered her thick dark lashes and fluffed her kinky blond hair with one hand. "Anything else?"

"Nothin' on the menu, sweetheart."

"I'll be in the back." Her cheeks flushed pink. "Y'all call out if you need anything."

With a quick, flirty smile, she sailed through the door and disappeared. Terry waited several beats before sliding a folded piece of paper down the counter. Jack took a fortifying sip of hot black coffee, then reached out and snagged the offered item. After a fast look around, he unfolded the paper. A photocopy of Elaine Delacor's driver's license, complete with photo. Her vivid, challenging green eyes peered up at him from the page. Creamy skin and raven black hair completed her striking, attractive picture. He'd only glimpsed her the night of the storm, but this little lady presented an appealing, compact package.

He took another sip of coffee and turned toward Terry. "You're sure about this?"

"Checked it twice." Terry put his donut aside and wiped his mouth. "Apparently she didn't give up the place in Fox Chapel until recently. Must be the reason for the delay on her registration. The license came due sooner, so she changed it."

Jack studied Terry. He knew more; Jack could feel it. The off duty Bayside cop with his elbows propped on the counter while he ate donuts and sipped coffee knew something else. Otherwise he'd be smirking like a mutt eatin' road kill.

With one more glance at Terry, Jack took his time folding the paper and tucking it into an inside pocket. Lifting the carafe, he topped off his coffee, then cupped his hands around the steaming mug. He tilted his head and looked sideways at Terry. "Okay, let's have the rest."

Terry's mouth tightened. He shot Jack a look, then boosted up on one hip and pulled another piece of paper from his hip pocket. The man in the booth coughed and drew their attention. Terry flattened his hand over the second note. The man rose, tossed down some bills, and ambled toward the door. As soon as it closed behind him, Terry turned to Jack.

"This hit our office shortly after an alert about two shooting victims found off I-79 in Pennsylvania. Not much information, just this." He slid the tightly folded paper to Jack.

Sure as Satan ruled hell, Jack knew he wouldn't like what the second note contained.

He fumbled with its tight folds, cursing silently until the paper lay open before him on the counter. He smoothed out the deep-set creases and read the cryptic release.

The printout had originated from PSP Troop E Headquarters near Erie. It was dated and included a series of addresses indicating distribution to various law enforcement agencies throughout the tri-state area: Ohio, Pennsylvania, and New York. According to the release, authorities were looking for a dark colored, full sized SUV with possible front end damage.

"They don't know what kind of SUV it is," Terry remarked, keeping his voice low. A smirk curved his mouth. "They're only guessing."

Jack's glare wiped the sleazy smile right off Terry's face.

Idiot!

He spoke through clenched teeth, barely above a whisper. "I don't give a rat's ass about the SUV. That's fixable." He reread the neatly typed statement. "Someone pointed them in that direction. This release isn't about the accident. This heads up right on the ass of the one about the bodies. Not a coincidence. Cops aren't about to broadcast details. They start out with basics, then go from there."

He shifted on the stool and rolled his shoulders. Pain radiated up the back of his neck. With methodical care, he refolded the damning note and tucked it away with the first one.

The waitress chose that moment to reappear, but the broad smile on her face fell away when she reached the counter. "Is something wrong?"

"No." Jack managed a smile and shook his head. "May I have my check?"

"Me, too," Terry spoke up. She glanced from one man to the other as she tallied up their tabs. Jack threw down the amount for both checks, adding a nice tip. He grabbed his coat and slid it on as he walked out the door.

Bundled against the cold, he waited between Terry's truck and his car.

When Terry joined him, he almost laughed aloud at the clueless cop's face. Dumb bastard. He snapped up the collar of his coat.

"Don't you get it?" he snarled. "They've got a witness. Sure as hell, someone saw something at that rest stop."

"The woman in the Miata." Terry blew out a long breath. He dug for his keys and shot Jack a nervous glance.

"No shit, Einstein," Jack muttered, as he yanked on black leather gloves. "Keep me posted." This changed the game, so he reconsidered. "On second thought, I'll contact you."

Without another word, he slid into his car and drove away. As he glanced back, Terry stood beside his truck, staring after him.

"Stupid son-of-a-bitch." He shook his throbbing head. Why did he always end up with the stupid ones?

He'd swing by his place to pick up a few essentials. Then as a precaution, he'd check into some out of the way motel for the time being. Drop out of reach for a while. Damn it, he'd been a fool to think that sexy, green-eyed woman remembered nothing. Her misfortune. Jack didn't relish the idea of taking out a woman. It'd be a first.

No, he didn't like the idea one fuckin' bit, but if she put his back to the wall, Elaine Delacor was history.

Chapter Twelve

Hershey's thick, brown tail thumped the leather in T.J.'s compact SUV, her pure excitement about to explode the second T.J. opened the door. He ruffled the dog's fur, earning himself a sloppy kiss.

"I'll just be a couple minutes, girl. And if you're good, you'll get a donut reward."

He lowered the passenger side window enough to allow the dog's broad head to poke out.

"Behave yourself," he warned, and gave the pup's quivering nose a quick, parting rub.

He'd picked up Hershey from his parent's place just after dawn. After spending a restless night on Lanie's sofa, he'd needed to do something physical, something to work off, or at least calm, the restless need pounding inside him.

Hershey's ecstatic greeting and their impromptu romp in the snow had helped, though occasional stabs of pain in his side reminded him to take it easy. For a small woman, Lanie sure packed a wallop. He'd sucked it up, tossed at least a dozen hard packed snowballs far and wide, and then loaded the dog into his RAV 4 and detoured by The Brown Cow.

He planned to spend the morning working at the carriage house he'd purchased from Rich last summer. In order to renovate it, he'd bumped out the entire back wall of the upstairs living quarters. Downstairs, his first priority had been adapting an area for Hershey. He could now work upstairs without frequent interruptions by the energetic dog.

Today he'd move his ongoing project forward by wielding some tools. With luck, he'd soon be able to move in and do the finishing work at a more leisurely pace. Plus, the pure physical exertion might take his mind off the chart topping lip lock he'd shared with Lanie Delacor.

He entered The Brown Cow deep in thought. Familiar scents and sounds surrounded him, and he paused to inhale the sweet tang of butterscotch combined with the enticing aromas of warm baked goods and fresh coffee.

Across the room, Lois Farrell slid a tray of cinnamon buns into the glass display case. She glanced up when the trio of bells over the door announced his arrival.

"Thomas Jacob McGraw." A warm smile lit her face. "Here to protect and serve, or just to snag a couple donuts?"

He'd been coming to The Brown Cow ever since he could remember. Lois and her sister, Millie, had inherited the dairy bar from their parents, and Lois's sparkling smile and quick wit evoked a smile from him this morning. He strolled over to admire the rolls she'd just added to the mouthwatering assortment of muffins, coffee cakes, and donuts.

"I remember when donuts were the only baked goods you offered, Lois." He pulled his gaze from the tempting display and met hers with a grin. "You've expanded, and you're lookin' great. What's your secret?"

Her cheeks flushed. "No secret, just a couple of good friends."

"Oh?"

"Ada and Cassi dragged me to Cassi's fitness classes. Then the next thing I knew, I was driving to some spa in Erie." She fluffed her wavy brown hair. "Cassi's thinking about opening something like that in Pine Bluffs. Her classes keep getting bigger. She'll soon outgrow the room over Rich McConnell's store."

"No kiddin'."

Lois nodded. "Oh, yeah, and, speaking of makeovers, I hear you're making some changes to the carriage house you bought from Rich. Big changes."

"That's where I'm headed this morning. I've got the weekend, and I want to put in some time. Once I reach a certain point, then I can move in and do the finishing work."

"So you're handy with tools like your dad?"

"Between Dad and Rich, I've learned a lot. If I hit a snag, all I have to do is give a yell in their direction. Though I guess Rich is knee deep in his own projects, since he and Ada got married."

"If you haven't been by Ada's cottage, you need to go take a look at the new kitchen he put in for her." Lois smiled and propped her elbows on the tall glass case. "State of the art appliances. He plans to enlarge the master suite, too, but even before the kitchen makeover, Rich put up an impressive garage. Actually, it's more like a barn for storage and a workshop."

"He got help with the garage." T.J. leaned closer to examine the goodies in the case. He winced and clutched his side. "Right?"

"Yes, he did. The framing and siding, he contracted out. Inside, I believe he and Tom completed the work. Between Rich and your dad, they could single-handedly renovate Pine Bluffs."

She frowned when he rubbed his side. "Are you all right, T.J.?"

"What?"

She raised her eyebrows and gestured toward his hand.

"Oh, that. Just clumsiness. I ran into something. I'll live." He dropped his hand and went back to eyeing the tempting assortment.

She shook her head and wiped the case's glass top. "What can I get you?"

He might as well stock up. Nick had promised to stop by later to give him a hand setting a door, and his cousin was a sucker for The Brown Cow's pastries, too.

As Lois boxed his selection, she glanced out the front window. "Your lady friend looks anxious."

"What?" T.J. whipped around. Oh, Hershey. *That lady.*

He needed to get his hands on a hammer and pound something, really hard, regardless of the pain in his side. He turned back to Lois. "I feel guilty dumping my dog with mom so often lately. Once I get moved in, things will improve."

"I noticed the green chain link fence you installed. Fits in nice. It'll give your dog lots of room to run free and safe."

"That's the plan. I'm glad I got it done before the snow hit." He handed Lois his credit card. "Caught us all by surprise."

She finished packing several boxes in The Brown Cow's signature totes and slid the receipt forward for T.J.'s signature. "Heard Cassi's friend got caught in that nasty pile-up on I-79."

"Elaine? Ah... yeah. She's doing okay. I was on scene that night, and it *was* nasty. That stretch of road's a bad one in winter."

He dropped the slip she handed him into the bag and prepared to leave.

"T.J., the news reported police found two men dead in their car at the rest stop. Rumor has it they didn't freeze to death." She crossed her arms and shuddered.

T.J. fished out his keys. Only a matter of time until something leaked. Sooner or later, that story would be all over the news.

"Can't say. They're still gathering facts and looking into possibilities." He picked up the bag and paused. "Lois, you've got a chief of police, an ex-chief of police, and a state trooper addicted to your baked goods, not to mention your coffee and milkshakes. No criminal in their right mind would come into The Brown Cow."

Lois laughed. "Get out of here. Go pound some nails."

When he reached the door, she called out and he halted.

"Thanks, T.J. I know I'm safe here, but it doesn't hurt to be reassured now and then."

"No problem, ma'am." He gave her a little salute and walked out the door.

He secured the goods in the back of the SUV, safe from Hershey's inquisitive nose, and slid behind the wheel.

"Ready to rock and roll, girl?" He gave his dog a brisk rub, started the engine, and pulled away from the curb.

Building clouds hid the sun, and stray flakes came in small bursts as he drove across town. He blinked to erase the gritty feel behind his eyelids. He'd put in a couple of hours, make some headway, then maybe crash for a power nap. After he'd rested and had time to put everything in perspective, maybe he'd give Laine a call. He couldn't ignore what she'd stirred up inside him. A strange mixture of lust and emotion that combated with his solid sense of duty. Somehow he had to separate them. She'd made it clear -- damn clear -- that the heat he'd felt was mutual.

Hershey lifted her nose and sniffed as he swung around in front of their future home.

"You remember, girl? Lots of room to run, and it's all yours."

64

T.J. entered the high-ceilinged foyer, and Hershey dashed ahead through the open laundry room door. She danced in place, whining, as T.J. slid the state-of-the-art doggie door into place. Without hesitation, she nosed through the protective flap over the opening and disappeared.

He stepped to the window as the dog shot across the snow like a rocket. The fencing was top notch and had cost a fortune given the large area he'd chosen to enclose. He studied the perimeter that wove into a stand of trees, then looped around to cover at least fifty feet before it reconnected with the rear of the building. The ground sloped away to where Pine Shadow Lake bordered his property. From his vantage point, due to the heavy snow cover, he couldn't tell where the land ended and the lake began. The early arrival of Arctic air had frozen the shallow lake, and its surface was now covered with snow.

He yawned and ran a hand through his hair, then checked Hershey's oversized water bowl in the corner. Nearby, a dog bed and a small collection of chew toys awaited his pal when she completed her romp.

The rest of the downstairs area had once been Rich's workshop, along with the laundry and lots of storage. T.J. climbed the wide staircase leading to the second floor living quarters. In what had once been Rich's kitchen, a couple of sawhorses and a sturdy work table filled the space. He'd covered the countertops and all of the appliances except the fridge with drop cloths. Off to one side stood a table topped with a coffee maker and a small assortment of cups, paper plates, and utensils.

He unloaded the bag from The Brown Cow, put on some coffee to brew, and switched on the radio perched atop the fridge. Sixties tunes rolled out, and he adjusted the volume to ear splitting. What more could he ask for? Coffee to combat his sleep deprivation, and music for background noise between his bouts of pounding and sawing.

As he strapped on a tool belt, his tender ribs protested. He ignored the pain. He'd work up a sweat, despite the thirty degree temps outside *and* the spreading bruise on his side. Hopefully the work would tamp down his raging hormones and force his mind to envision squares and hard angles instead of sultry eyes and soft curves.

*****

"You actually hit him with a log?" Jen shot Lanie a fast, wide-eyed look and steered around a clump of snow left by the plow.

Lanie stifled a guilty smile and grimaced. "Actually, it was more like a stick. A big one, yeah. But it wasn't a *log*." She adjusted her sunglasses, thankful for the full blast of sun after the past couple of days and for Jen taking the time -- *again* -- to give her a lift. The insurance company had finally tracked down a rental, and since all the car rental places were at the airport, Jen had offered to drive her to Erie's west side to pick up a car.

After a moment, Jen agreed about the stick. "I guess I'd have done the same. Though I'm not sure I'd have been out walking around at midnight all alone."

"Oh, yes, you would. You'd have been just as stir crazy as I was after lying around inside for a couple days."

"Maybe. But damn it, Lanie. Part of the reason you were flat on your back was because someone deliberately forced your car off the road. And that *someone* just may have something to do with those dead bodies found the next day."

"The officer who interviewed me said it's possible that whoever rammed my car doesn't know who I am." Lanie bit her lip and turned her head as row after row of naked grape stakes flashed by. "He said that when all those cars and trucks wrecked at the same time and a gazillion witnesses started showing up, whoever hit me took off. So how could he know where to find me if he doesn't know who I am?"

"You're right, and I don't mean to scare you." Jen reached over and gave Lanie's leg a pat. "But to play devil's advocate, what if he got your license plate number?"

"Wouldn't do him any good." She smiled and tilted her glasses down to look at Jen. "Unless he's a cop."

"How so?"

"I asked T.J. about that, and he said that unless the guy's in law enforcement, he wouldn't have an easy time finding me that way. Said even *he* needs a good reason to look up someone using their plate number. Any time a trooper uses the system to make an ID, they're held accountable."

"That makes me feel a lot better," Jen declared. She signaled and turned onto the Bayfront Parkway. "Plus, there hasn't been anything on the news about you specifically, or any indication you were even at the rest stop. You kind of got lost in the multi-car shuffle headlines. That's good."

She stopped for the light at State Street. "And speaking of T.J... did I see his car leaving your place just after dawn this morning?"

"Wipe that smirk off your face." Lanie yawned and heaved a sigh. "Yes. He slept on my couch. Of course," she added with a sly smile. "I did get a rather hot n' heavy goodnight kiss."

"Holy shit. And then you made hot officer McGraw sleep on the couch? What are you, stupid?"

A sharp honk from behind them made Jen redirect her incredulous look to the road ahead, and they shot forward through the intersection.

"No, but after being whacked with a big stick, he may not have felt quite 'up', if you get my drift."

Jen's laugh made her grin.

They rode in silence past the convention center and up the gradual rise to the intersection with Eighth Street.

"Let's stop at Romolos for some coffee on the way back," Lanie suggested. "I could use a chocolate fix, too."

"Speaking of decadent fixes, when was the last time you had an overnight visitor who didn't sleep on the couch?"

"You know, I thought Cassi was the only person brave enough to jump head first into my personal life. You're just as bad." Lanie tilted her head and eyed Jen, then turned her gaze ahead as they sped across Twelfth Street toward Tom Ridge Field. She didn't mind Jen's question. Her neighbor had earned her trust a while ago, shortly after she'd showed up with the scraggly black kitten. Cassi had been Lanie's roommate in college. During those years, for the first time in her life, Lanie had learned how to trust another woman and to love her like the sister she'd never had.

Had Lanie loved her mother? Hard to say, when all she remembered was a tired, worn out, short tempered woman struggling to make ends meet. Uncle Charley had stepped in after Lanie's mom died, but by then she'd quit asking why she didn't have a father. Her mom had never talked about her dad, except to say he'd hit the road when she was born.

She glanced at Jen and realized her friend had grown awfully quiet. "Thank you."

"For what?" Jen shot her a puzzled look.

"For being a friend who cares, even though her twisted mind wants to hear about my sex life, or the lack thereof."

"All I'm sayin'," Jen replied as she turned into the airport and swung into the lane for rental car drop off, "is that I feel vibes -- *heat* vibes -- whenever you and T.J. McGraw get together. At first I thought 'uh oh, oil and water', but his reaction when you were hurting and scared the other night wasn't the way a man acts when he wants to avoid someone. Now you tell me he kissed you. If I get your drift, it wasn't the kind of kiss he'd give a pal, or someone he wanted to avoid."

Lanie remained silent as Jen parked and shut of the engine. She noticed a light green compact parked nearby and figured this was as good as she'd get. She turned to face her friend.

"Would I like to tumble into the sack with T.J.? You bet. Do I have any illusions about a future with Mr. Hearth and Home?" She shook her head and reached for the door. "No way. His family and extended family would put the Waltons to shame."

"What about Cassi? She loves her aunt Ada and didn't even know she existed until recently. Then she fell in love with Nick and--"

"Cassi came from a loving family before she ever met Ada Blaine, uh... McConnell. *Or* Nick." Lanie kept her head turned away and blinked back bitter tears. "I had Uncle Charley, and that's it. He loved me and made sure I didn't want for anything. But despite his good intentions, I didn't have a mother who talked to me about becoming a woman, who baked cookies or a birthday cake every year. Charley took me out to dinner and handed me a check on my birthday."

"I see your point, but that doesn't mean you don't deserve to fall in love and make a life with someone."

"Jen, the point is that T.J. does. He's a wonderful man who deserves someone who can give him the kind of life he's known. We're too different. Am I attracted to him? You bet your ass -- or maybe I should say *his* class A butt. The heat you mentioned is definitely there. Will I follow through and take a couple of tumbles in the hay with that sexy man? Maybe. Will it go anywhere? Not on your life."

Jen just looked at her.

Lanie unhooked her seatbelt and opened the door. "Now let's go get me a car so you don't have to hall *my* ass around anymore."

*****

T.J. pounded the last nail into place. Sweat poured down his back, and his side throbbed like a son of a bitch. Time for a break. He'd ripped his tee-shirt off a while ago and pressed ice cubes wrapped in a towel against his side. Doing so had helped, but the ice had melted and now needed to be replenished.

He paused, put down his hammer, and glanced around. Where had that silly dog gone? She'd been buggin' T.J. off and on for the past half hour. The last time he'd looked, Hershey had lain on her back like a lazy old cat snoring away in the hallway. Now she'd vanished without a sound. *Shit.* Poor pup had probably gone back outside to get away from the music blasting from the twin speakers.

T.J. unbuckled his tool belt and eased it off. Squeezing his eyes shut tight, he bit his lip against the surge of pain and dropped the belt at his feet. *Oh, yeah.* Time for a break.

"What the hell. Are you deaf?"

His eyes flew open and he spun and reached instinctively for his gun. Of course, it wasn't tucked into his jeans as usual, but lay atop the fridge several feet away.

Nick stomped across the room toward him with Hershey prancing along in his wake.

"Your watch dog greeted me at the door, and I just followed the ear-splitting music." He stopped long enough to turn down the sound to semi-normal. He glanced at the doorframe T.J. had been working on. "I see you're almost ready to--"

Nick broke off, moved in close, and lifted T.J.'s arm. "What the hell happened to you?"

"It's nothing." Yanking his arm from his cousin's grasp, T.J. shoved his hand away. "Just a bruise."

"Right." Nick's eyes narrowed as he took in the deep purple and sickly yellow colors wrapping around T.J.'s waist. The discoloration reached high on his ribcage and disappeared beneath the low slung waistband of his jeans. "Cut the bullshit and tell me what happened."

"Let me put on a shirt and make some fresh coffee." T.J. rolled his eyes. "Then I'll fill you in on my life and times in hell the past twenty-four hours."

A short time later, as Hershey neatly fielded the last bite of donut T.J. tossed her, he couldn't help but smile at Nick's rolling laughter. Wiping tears from his eyes, Nick washed down the last of his cinnamon roll, leaned back, and stretched out his legs.

"Let me get this straight," he said, dabbing away crumbs with his balled up napkin. "Lanie Delacor, who just *might* top five-foot-three with her shoes on, caught you off guard and whacked you with a tree limb?"

"That just about sums it up. Smart ass," T.J. added. He rose and went to refill his cup. "Hell, I never figured she'd have the strength, let alone the guts, to come at me the way she did. She heard me coming, waited, and then whipped around, gripping that big stick as if she were about to knock one out of the park. And she swung like hell."

"Top me off, too." Nick pointed to his mug, then selected another roll. He took a big bite of the pastry, swallowed, and sipped his coffee. "Guess she's all recovered, then. Any progress with the case?"

"Dan Sullivan from the crime unit is working the case. They've managed to keep any connection between Lanie and the bodies under wraps so far, but I figure it's only a matter of time until something leaks."

"How about her car? Did you check it out?"

"I did, and someone definitely hit her from the rear. They're bringing her car to Erie ASAP to check it out."

"Good move." Nick's raised one eyebrow, studied T.J., and then said, "What are you *not* telling me?"

"Damn. I need to take some pain killers." T.J. returned to his seat and eased down slowly. "Anyhow, remember our pals from OIU?"

"Sure, Raife Samuels and... what's his partner's name? Uh... *Fred.* Right?"

"Yeah. They met me at Erie Headquarters when I got back from checking out Lanie's car. It appears they're acquainted with, or rather *were* acquainted with, the two unfortunate guys who met their fate at the Edinboro rest stop. This in turn led them to Erie, and that made them aware of the attempt on Lanie. Seems our old pal Jack LeFavor has loose ties to the victims."

"Loose ties?"

"Yeah, according to Raife Samuels, Jack's as slippery as ever, and the connection is shaky at best. But that's not what concerns me. When we told him about Lanie's description of the vehicle that hit her, things started to jell."

"How so?"

"Turns out good ole' Jack stores his fancy Benz in the winter and drives a great big black Cadillac Escalade."

"Have you sent those pictures of SUVs to Lanie yet?"

"I did. And after talking with Raife, I was sure to include a picture of a black Escalade. Sullivan checked with her soon after I sent them off."

"She chose the Escalade."

"You bet your ass. He said she nailed it the first time through the lineup I sent. Zeroed right in on the emblem centered on the grille."

"Not good." Nick blew out a long breath.

T.J. agreed. He went in search of aspirin. Only three were left in the bottle, so he grabbed a half filled bottle of water, dumped the pills into his palm, and washed them down.

He paced to the window and back. "If LeFavor was at that rest stop, I'll bet my last friggin' dime he took out his buddies. It's not the first time he's killed to save his own ass, and if he finds out Lanie was there that night, she's in real danger."

"One step at a time." Nick stood and gathered up their paper plates and soiled napkins. "If need be, we'll all keep an eye on her until this is settled."

"Let's give setting this door a shot. It'll take my mind off all this shit. Besides, I'm starting to feel kind of useless after last night."

Nick grinned. "Cassi talked to Lanie this morning. Seems she had an overnight guest who not only slept on her couch, but up and disappeared with the sunrise."

"My call," T.J. responded. He stepped to the door propped against the wall and cut away the protective wrapping. "Got a brain-melting goodnight kiss, though."

When Nick didn't respond, he gathered up the wrappings and stuffed them into a big trash bag before facing his cousin.

"She's always set me off. You know that," he admitted. "Getting my hands on her threw me for a loop. I'll just have to deal with it, and--"

Hershey scrambled to her feet, woofed several times, and dashed down the stairs.

T.J. walked over to the window overlooking the drive way. His heartbeat kicked up a notch as Lanie stepped out of a small green Toyota.

With a grin, Nick laid a hand on his shoulder. "Looks like you've got company, pal."

T.J. scowled at him.

Nick dropped his hand and moved away as Lanie headed for the carriage house door. A moment later, a classic Beatles tune echoed through the room.

With a glance at T.J., Nick cranked up the volume and sang along with the music. "I should have known better with a girl like you."

Chapter Thirteen

Jack tucked his Escalade away in his condo's underground parking garage, where it would remain unseen and inaccessible. A huge benefit included in the pricey fees he paid to live at Braten Place, the upscale condo on the lakeshore east of Cleveland. He pulled in next to his Benz. After another quick inspection of the Escalade's new grille, he unpacked a custom made tarp. He waited a few moments for the engine to cool, using the time to make sure the tarp covering his prized Benz hadn't been disturbed.

Once he'd secured the cover on the SUV, Jack took the elevator to the eighth floor. Unless an individual lived in the condo complex or visited a tenant with his or her permission, no one could gain admittance to the grounds surrounding the condo, much less the underground garage. More perks he paid for through the nose.

The whisper soft journey ended, and the elevator doors opened. He didn't pass a soul on the short walk down his private hallway. He inserted his passkey and opened the door. Windows and a full glass door facing Lake Erie took up one entire wall.

He crossed to the door that opened onto his compact patio. In summer, the little stone deck clinging to the side of the building was a perfect spot to watch the sun sink into the lake. A layer of snow coated the lone table and deck chair he'd forgotten to store for the winter. Cash he had laid out for all this fuckin' security and so called *sophisticated elegance* could be put to better use. Yet he deserved the privacy and the luxury, and being shut off from the commoners had saved his ass more than once.

He hoped like hell it worked this time.

His nerves on edge, he glanced at his watch. Better get that ass in gear. Guys from the shop that had repaired the Escalade had agreed to drop off the sedan he'd been using at a rest stop on I-90. All he had to do was walk to the main entrance of Braten Place and meet them. They'd agreed to swing by, pick him up, and take him to the car. He'd already stashed what he'd need for the next few days in a motel near the Pennsylvania line, so he had nothing extra to carry on his short jaunt to the condo's gate.

He did a quick walk through of the place first, just in case some smart-assed judge felt the need to issue a search warrant. Not one damn word had popped up on the news, though, unless he counted the occasional mention of the ongoing investigation into the recent discovery of the two dead bodies. Except for the BOLO Terry had mentioned targeting an Escalade with front end damage, they were keeping a tight lid on the whole mess. Jack had sweated out the delay for the SUV's new grille, and now felt one hell of a lot better with it repaired and out of sight.

Those OIU pricks knew where he lived, he'd bet on that, but they'd be hard pressed to get a warrant. Braten Place owners were well connected and nosy cops, or any law enforcement types, for that matter, had better have a damn good reason to come snooping around.

He buttoned his coat and pulled his hat low on his ride back down to the garage. Not a single person stirred in the shadowy, cool space beneath the sixteen story building. He punched in his code, and the garage door lifted. No sense walking past the lobby attendant. Braten employees were supposed to be discreet, but who the hell knew when a fifty slipped into a willing hand might loosen somebody's tongue?

He jogged up the ramp, head tucked low to avoid security cameras, and disappeared down the winding road to the gated entrance.

The drop off went smoothly. Before the two guys from his buddy's shop pulled away, he slipped each of them a hundred dollar bill. They'd already been paid, but considering the risk, a bit more incentive was cheap insurance.

Jack needed to rest. His head pounded and his gut rumbled as he slipped into his temporary motel room. He tossed his keys onto a table by the window and yanked the heavy curtain closed. As he slipped off his coat, he glanced around the room. Not bad, but a hell of a big change from the digs he'd just left.

He muttered to himself as he dug into the suitcase he'd left there earlier and carried his shaving gear into the little cubicle off the bathroom. Pausing, he glanced in the mirror and rubbed the rough stubble on his face.

"Son of a bitch." He looked like death warmed over. Felt about the same.

After stripping down to boxers and a tee-shirt, he dropped onto the bed and set the alarm for eight p.m. That would give him a couple of much needed hours of rest, then he'd have to make some decisions. He stood and flipped back the covers, but hesitated before he crawled in and turned out the light. Next to his keys lay the folded copy of Elaine Delacor's driver's license. He crossed to the table, grabbed the paper, and returned to sit on the bed. She was a looker, all right. He held the unfolded copy under the circle of light cast by the bedside lamp. Women, in his estimation, were for the most part a pain in the ass. Real bitches.

He slipped his hand beneath his shirt and rubbed his belly. On the other hand, what in hell would he do without them?

He'd put a bullet in more than one man, and on at least one occasion, had jammed a knife between a sorry bastard's ribs. Survival was the name of the game.

Yet could he kill a woman? Could he look into those gorgeous green eyes and watch them go dull and lifeless? For the first time ever, the thought of doing so made Jack's insides coil as tight as a damn spring.

He refolded the paper and laid it aside. The room felt cold and empty. Wind rattled the window, prompting Jack to dig out a warmer top. He stopped and parted the curtain a few inches.

In the gathering darkness, snow already coated his car. His gaze went to the light high above the motel parking lot, its glow blurred by wind-driven snow, and his mind flashed back to that night, to the way that beautiful green-eyed woman had stared at him from within her car. Could she identify him? *Someone* sure as hell had seen enough to have the cops looking for a damaged Escalade.

He dropped the curtain, crossed the room, and crawled beneath the covers.

Sleep finally came, but nightmares of Frankie Johns' blood-streaked face coming at him through the swirling snow brought Jack bolt upright. He was drenched in sweat and threw the tangled blankets aside. The luminous dial of the clock showed it to be just shy of eight p.m. He'd only been out for a few hours, but despite his freakish nightmare, he was ready to move.

"Survival," he murmured, struggling to his feet. That's what it came down to, no matter who had to pay the price.

Chapter Fourteen

Caught by surprise, Lanie jumped back when the door to the carriage house swung open and a furry brown bullet shot out.

"Hershey! Damn it, get back here!" T.J. shouted, his distraught expression in sharp contrast with the overgrown pup's ecstatic face.

Seconds later, the chocolate lab skidded to a stop at Lanie's feet.

T.J. lunged forward to grab Hershey's collar but pulled up short, winced, and held his side. "Damn it."

"Sit, girl," Lanie ordered the dog, then she rushed forward and laid her hand on T.J.'s arm. "Are you all right?"

"I'm fine." He took a long, deep breath, then looked past her to where Hershey sat quivering in place, her tail sweeping the ground. "She listens to everyone *but* me."

"Typical dog." Stifling a grin, Lanie shifted the bag in her arms. "Uh, could we move inside? It's cold out."

"Get inside." T.J. frowned at his dog. Hershey shot past them into the house. "Come on in. I'll put her out back."

She entered the foyer, set the bag aside, and knelt to greet the enthusiastic pup.

"Hey, girl. You're a beauty, aren't you?" She laughed, dodging frantic doggy kisses, rubbing ears soft as silk.

T.J. rattled a jar full of treats, and Hershey bounded to him and plopped her butt down.

"Guess that shows me," Lanie remarked, pushing herself to her feet. "What is she, about six months?"

"A little older. Closer to seven." He tossed a bite-sized biscuit into the air, grinning as his dog snapped it up. "As long as I have treats, she listens. Okay, out you go."

"Don't put her out on my account." Lanie stepped over and reached into the jar. "Here girl, come sit for me."

Hershey complied, and T.J. set the treat jar aside. "I thought you were a cat person."

"Not at all." Lanie rewarded the dog and backtracked to retrieve the bag she'd left by the door. "I'm the one who talked Cassi into getting Rufus. It took a lot longer than six months before that guy would sit and behave himself." Cassi's Rufus was a retriever, too, but gold in color, a sharp contrast to Hershey.

She laughed when Hershey trotted over and nudged her hand for more treats. "Don't be greedy, pretty girl. She's gorgeous, T.J., and smart. Aren't you, Hershey?" she asked the dog, kneeling and giving Hershey a big hug. "Yes, you are. You're gorgeous *and* smart, but that's because you're a female, and we tend to mature much faster than the males of the species."

T.J. rolled his eyes. "I'm outnumbered. What have you got in the bag?"

She held the bag up and gave it a shake. "Something to keep you from wincing every time you move. I saw that look on your face when you tried to catch Hershey."

"I downed some pain killers. They help."

"This will help more."

"You drove all the way to Pine Bluffs to bring *me* something?"

"Not entirely. I came to see Cassi, to catch up with her. I'm back to normal, and I couldn't stand sitting around doing nothing. So after I picked up my rental car and stopped in to let my boss know I'll be back at work next week, I headed for Pine Bluffs."

"How's the car?"

She shrugged. "Okay. It's all they had to give me. Everything's still up in the air about my Miata, though. I don't know if it can be repaired or not. I haven't even seen it."

"Let's go upstairs, and I'll fill you in on what I know."

Lanie nodded and started up the stairs. "When I stopped at the health club, I picked up some salve and ice packs designed to help bruised or injured muscles." She glanced at him over her shoulder. "I figure I owe you for all you've done the past few days, not to mention my whacking you the other night."

They reached the top of the stairs and stepped into the cluttered living area. Despite the mess, the low classic rock playing on the radio and T.J.'s personal clutter created a relaxed, welcoming space.

"You don't owe me anything." T.J. took the bag and peered inside as he crossed the room. "And please excuse the mess. I'm doing a bit of remodeling."

"I'll say." Lanie studied the work in progress. The basic cabinets and what she could see of the earth-toned tile floor had a classy, yet functional appeal. "I was only here once when Rich lived here, and it looks like you're doing more than just a *bit* of remodeling. This is a major makeover."

"Hey, good lookin'." Nick strolled into the room.

Smiling, Lanie walked over to him and stretched up to kiss his cheek. "Hi, handsome. Cassi said you'd be here helping T.J. I saw your truck outside."

"You've had a rough couple of days, kiddo," he said, giving her a once over, "but you look damn good."

"Hey, don't forget you're a married man," T.J. remarked as he dug into the bag Lanie had brought. He held up a large tube. "This'll soothe my poor, battered ribs?"

"Should do the trick."

He pulled his tee-shirt over his head and winked at her. "Wanna play

75

nurse? We'll see if this stuff really works."

Heat shot up Lanie's neck. She turned away and shrugged out of her coat, hoping the two men wouldn't notice her reaction. Heaven help her if he really *did* want her to apply the salve.

She took her time unwinding the scarf from around her neck and tossed it, along with her jacket, over a chair. When she turned to face them, having recovered from the spurt of lust, her eyes flew open wide.

"Oh, God. T.J., did I do that?" She rushed to his side, concern overriding her reaction to his lean, naked torso. The ugly yellow and deep purple tinged bruise covering most of his left side overrode all pleasurable thoughts of rubbing salve onto his hot body.

He stiffened when she placed her hand on him, his skin all but sizzling beneath her fingers. She tilted her head and stared up at him.

His gaze locked with hers. Flecks of blue blended with the gray, turning his eyes dark and secretive. Spellbound by their steely impact, Lanie froze.

Behind her, Nick cleared his throat. "Ah, I think I'll head on home."

Lanie dropped her hand and jumped back. T.J. blinked several times and rubbed his hand over the spot she'd touched.

She blew out a short breath. "I don't want to interrupt your work."

T.J. opened his mouth, then closed it without saying a thing.

She looked around, searching for the tube he'd been holding, surprised when she spotted it on the floor by his feet.

"Here," she said, stooping to pick it up. She held it out to him. "The directions are on the side of the tube."

"I never ravish the nurses who treat me." Humor softened his eyes.

Nick stepped forward and draped his arm over Lanie's shoulder. "I believe T.J.'s work day is over." He glanced at his watch. "Cass and I have plans tonight, so I've got to run." He gave her a light squeeze. "Stick around, play nurse."

While T.J. walked Nick downstairs, Lanie cleared a spot on the table. She unpacked the special heat activated pack and peeked under the tarps until she located a microwave.

Why did she practically melt every time he touched her? And those eyes... *God in heaven.* She'd never seen them so dark, so mesmerizing. The hints of blue had disappeared, swallowed up by shades of gray the color of summer storm clouds. She shivered. Crossing her arms, she rubbed her skin briskly to shake the feeling.

Moments later, Hershey's scrambling feet and T.J.'s measured tread alerted her to their return. She turned from the window where the midday sun peeked through the heavy, snow laden clouds.

"I think it's going to snow again," she said as they entered the room.

Hershey circled and then dropped onto the well worn rug.

"They're calling for it late tonight." T.J. strolled over and eyed the items she'd laid out. "I do appreciate the thought and the time you took to drop off this stuff. I downed some pain killers earlier, and they took the edge off the soreness."

Lanie moved closer, fighting the urge to ogle his bare chest. She'd given herself a good talking to while he'd seen Nick out, and was determined to keep things light, friendly, more in control.

"The salve is a proven product. It penetrates and acts similar to a topical anesthetic. Then we heat this up," she said, lifting the flexible long narrow gel pack, "and place it on the injury. I guarantee you'll feel better."

"Let's hope so." He grinned. "I have a couple days off and want to move the rest of my stuff here so I can continue to work whenever I have time."

This was better. Talking about everyday things, like furniture, lowered the stress and awareness level, at least for Lanie. She'd keep the pace nice and even, and then ease out the door.

She looked around. "You don't seem to have much here now."

"Actually, I had a new bed delivered a few days ago. I took the one I used as a kid when I moved into my duplex after college. That bed's a double. I wanted to upgrade to something more suitable, so the new one is king-sized. The rest of the old set will work with the new bed, and the smaller bed I can use here in the second bedroom. So far I've only brought over a nightstand and a dresser."

Lanie walked to the rough opening leading to the addition, redirecting her attention just in case he wanted to show off that new bed. She pulled a tarp aside and peered into the large room on the other side. The far wall consisted entirely of windows. The tall, wide expanses of glass opened up the room and showcased his property all the way to Pine Shadow Lake. Skylights overhead filled the room with natural light and a feeling of space.

T.J. came to stand beside her. "This doorway used to lead to a raised deck. I wanted more room, so I added a full two story addition. Go on out, take a look. It's only roughed in, but it's sealed to the weather. Once this door's in place, I can work out there and clean up in here."

She stepped through the rough opening.

"This will be a wonderful space. And this counter," she remarked, running her hand over the smooth, variegated green finish. "This counter is beautiful."

The inside wall backed up to the one with the kitchen sink on the other side. Windows over the sink separated the kitchen from the new room. T.J. slid the tarp covering the new counter aside.

"When the door's in, I'll remove all these windows over the sink separating the rooms, then finish the opening on three sides and put in a wide shelf for setting food, drinks, or whatever on so anyone sitting at the counter can reach up and help themselves."

"You're a clever man, McGraw." She took a moment to visualize the scene he'd painted. "Did you design all this yourself?"

"My mom and dad have done lots of remodeling over the years. Not only to their home, but also to the rental cabins they own that needed to be updated initially. I shared my ideas, and they helped pull it all together."

"And on this side, at this counter, you'll have chairs?" Positioning her back to the counter, she looked across the room at all those wonderful windows.

"I've ordered high backed leather stools, bar height. They swivel."

At some point while giving her the grand tour, he'd picked up a sweatshirt and slipped it over his head. Not having to keep averting her eyes from the neat, sand colored triangle of hair on his chest helped her focus on his remodeling talk. Lanie pushed away from the new granite counter and reentered the kitchen. T.J. followed.

"I have to get going soon," she said. "You said earlier you'd fill me in on what you know. I assume that means there's more to tell. I'd like to hear it."

"Have dinner with me."

"I'm entitled to...what?" She glanced around the tarp shrouded kitchen. "You want to fix dinner here?"

T.J. threw back his head and laughed. "No, I'm asking you out to dinner. There's a new place on the way to North East. They opened late this summer, and the view is spectacular from every table. On clear nights, you can see lights in Canada across Lake Erie. They took an old barn, gutted it, shored it up, and then used the original wood to trim it out. The food's great."

Speechless and wide-eyed, she stared at him.

"Don't look so damned shocked."

"I can't help it," She turned and walked away. When she spun back around, his crooked grin appeared. "Stop that."

"What?"

"That... that smirk you get on your face whenever you get me flustered." She crossed her arms and drummed her fingers against her upper arm. "You don't have to take me out to dinner, unless," she said, narrowing her eyes, "what you have to tell me is *really* bad."

T.J. walked over to her, uncrossed her arms, and linked his fingers with hers.

Lanie's heart hammered against her ribs so fast she feared he could hear the rapid thuds.

He gave her hands a gentle squeeze and then held on when she made a weak effort to pull away.

"The invitation for dinner is twofold," he said, "First, you. I have a lot to tell you. Some good, most not so good. A glass of wine and dinner in a quiet spot might take off the edge and give you time to settle. Time to consider all I have to say."

Her insides balled like a lump of play dough. He rubbed his thumbs over her palms, and her knees about folded.

"And second," he continued. "I want to explore, to find out why whenever I get within two feet of you I feel like a grenade someone just pulled the pin on, and I don't know exactly when, or if, we're going to blow sky high."

*****

T.J. had been right about the wonderful cabernet he'd chosen. Franciscan Estate, a 2008 Cabernet Sauvignon and one of her favorites, did the trick to help her feel better. If nothing else, they had good wines in common. He'd been right about the food, too. Although, passing on the caramel crème brule had almost brought tears to her eyes.

"Sure you don't want to change your mind about dessert?" T.J. leaned back and swirled the deep red wine in his glass.

Lanie met his teasing gaze, smiled, and shook her head. For dessert, *he'd* be just about perfect. Clean shaven and wearing a scent designed to drive women dizzy with lust, he'd been right on time. He wore a blue shirt beneath a light gray sports jacket. His dark gray trousers held a razor sharp crease, and yet the soft fabric created a casual, relaxed fit.

She sipped her wine and contemplated the man across from her, thankful he couldn't read her mind. "I'm sure. Until I get back to work, I'm in danger of packing on pounds with all the lounging around I've been doing."

"You needed the rest, so don't beat yourself up." He leaned back, studying her. "Do you have any more questions about the investigation?"

He'd been upfront about the danger. She appreciated that, but she also found the reality of the situation disturbing. Step by step, he had explained a connection they'd uncovered between the two victims and a known drug trafficker. A slippery character. One who'd apparently gotten away with murder more than once. How did they know he'd been the one?

A cold chill chased the warm glow of red wine when T.J. had pointed out that Jack LeFavor owned a black Escalade. One the same color, make, and model as the one she'd identified. *Exactly* the same as the one that had run into her. For the time being, he insisted only law enforcement agencies knew this information. A good sign, he'd emphasized. But -- and she'd been waiting for the *but* -- men like Jack LeFavor had connections.

T.J. looked at her, his quiet gray-blue eyes radiating a calmness she didn't feel. It helped. In the short time they'd been together that evening, laughing and talking about mutual friends and things other than murder, she'd learned a lot about him.

"Lanie?"

She blinked and took a deep breath, breaking the alluring spell of his steady gaze.

The waiter approached and discreetly placed a leather bound holder on the table. T.J. nodded, took his wallet from an inside pocket, and slid a credit card in with the check.

"I spoke with Cassi before you picked me up." She finished the rich cabernet and set her empty glass aside. "I'm sure you noticed my overnight bag."

T.J. shrugged and nodded.

"I'm also sure you're behind her suggestion that I spend the night with her and Nick." Anticipating his response, she held up her hand. "Let me finish."

Leaning back, Lanie removed the napkin from her lap, folded it, and laid it aside. She placed both hands, fingers linked, on the table.

"As you know, I'm a tad independent," she said, raising her brow when he grinned. "However, I'm not stupid. I've listened to everything you've told me, not only tonight, but throughout this whole fiasco."

Her heart stuttered when he reached across the table and cupped both her hands in his. Her reaction made her wonder if he'd been right. *Were* they on the verge of blowing sky high?

Guess it was time to find out.

"Until they find this man, this Jack LeFavor, I need to pay attention. I'm going back to work on Monday. I'm surrounded by people all day at the health club. From what you've told me, it may take a while for him to identify me and then locate me. If he's even trying, because unless he knows for sure I can recognize him, he may decide I'm no threat."

"So far, I agree." He stroked her clenched hands with a gentle caress.

She took a deep breath. "Okay, here's what I know for sure. Those two men were dead when I got there. Looking back, the black SUV must have already been there, too. I didn't see it at first, but I remember following deep tire tracks up the ramp. They cut off to the left, toward the lower parking area, and I pulled up by the building. I remember this because I didn't have any tracks to follow after I veered off, and I was afraid I'd get stuck."

"I came to the same conclusion once I talked to you." T.J. tightened his grip on her hands. "LeFavor's cautious. He won't act rashly. More than likely, he'll wait and see what shakes out in the media. So far we've managed to avoid revealing our interest in your car, other than mentioning it was at the scene of a multi-car pileup. He may figure you were just confused, and he got lucky."

The waiter returned the credit card slip for T.J.'s signature, and Lanie pulled her hands free. She picked up her handbag, excused herself, and retreated to the ladies room. A pleasant flowery scent filled the ladies' lounge as she freshened her makeup and fussed with her hair. Low lighting flattered her reflection in the smoked glass mirrors

She'd made a decision. Giving in to this magnetic attraction, getting involved with a man so totally opposite from her could be a big mistake. She could still change her mind, have him drive her to Cassi and Nick's place, and ignore the delicious tremors low in her belly.

She pursed her lips and smoothed on tinted gloss, ordering herself not to over think what was happening between them, or to tear it apart and try to rationalize it. Some things just needed to *happen*. In her past relationships, or encounters, or whatever else she chose to call them, she hadn't had to talk herself into a situation. Not that there'd been that many. For all her bravado, all her far out, independent attitude, she'd been quite selective and had always managed to walk away unscathed.

She'd walk away this time, too. Because heat and sizzle wasn't enough. In Lanie's mind, she wouldn't have a happily ever after. At least, not the happily ever after T.J. would expect.

With a sigh, she dropped her lip gloss into her bag and snapped it shut. Turning sideways, she studied her reflection. Lush. Cassi envied her lushness, or so she said. Lanie's dark green knit dress hugged her well-proportioned curves. Firm, sculpted curves, the result of her chosen career. Her neckline dipped in the front, and her knee high black boots met the hem of her garment. Her decision to wear this particular dress had come easily. It was her favorite.

Choosing lingerie, soft, delicate scraps of lace to wear beneath the green dress, had taken time, because Lanie had known when she made the choice where this evening would end.

T.J. waited patiently, holding her coat open for her when she returned from the ladies' lounge. Her knees wobbled as she wound her way across room and allowed him to help her into it. Then she took his arm, and he guided her toward the door.

Cold, crisp air awaited them as they stepped outside. Lazy snowflakes drifted down. When T.J. opened his SUV's door for her, she turned to him.

"Wait, T.J." She reached up and brushed stray flakes of snow from his shoulder, then grasped his jacket's lapels and pulled him to her.

Puzzled surprise winged over his face in the second before their lips met. He wrapped his arms around her, and the kiss went hot and deep. Until finally, she pushed against his chest and eased away.

He placed his hand beneath her chin and traced her lower lip with his thumb. "If that was my *thank you* for dinner, how about we stop in Pine Bluffs for dessert?"

"Turns out I know a lovely carriage house not far from here." Lanie placed her hand on his arm. "I was given a limited tour earlier today, and I'd like to return and continue the tour, including seeing the new king-sized bed. I'll consider *that* dessert."

She slipped into the SUV and pulled the door closed. Standing motionless, T.J. stared in through the passenger side window as snow drifted down around him.

Chapter Fifteen

Lanie's decision stunned him. Something deep inside warned him to use caution, to tread carefully when taking this serious step with her. She was different, and having to think about his moves or his response to any woman was new territory for T.J. Her sudden willingness threw him... and also excited him on a whole new level.

Little conversation passed between them on the way to Pine Bluffs. The muted, intermittent clunk of the windshield wipers accompanied the lazy beat of an instrumental oldies station on the radio. Upon arrival, Lanie paused on the curved pathway outside his carriage house and lifted her face to the falling snow. The soft glow from the copper lantern over the entrance cast a circle of light around her. T.J. waited patiently. Had she changed her mind?

He jingled his keys, and the sound caught her attention. She turned.

"Lanie, if you've--"

"I haven't." For one long moment, she looked into his eyes. Then she stepped aside.

He unlocked the door and followed her into the foyer, flipping on miniature copper lanterns to light the high-ceilinged space and curving stairs to the second level.

"Where's Hershey?" Lanie fluffed snow from her dark hair.

"I sent her home with Dad earlier. She's never been here by herself. I want to move in and get a familiar routine in place before I leave her alone."

He helped her off with her coat and hung it nearby.

"Thanks." Her secret smile as she smoothed that clingy little dress over her supple curves damn near stopped his heart. The rest of his body decided *to hell with caution.*

She moved to the oak bench at the foot of the stairs, sat, and unzipped her boots. The soft swish of nylon when she crossed her slim, shapely legs to pull her feet free wiped every sensible, civilized thought of treading carefully right out of his mind. When she stretched out her legs and sighed, his entire body clenched.

"These boots may make a fashion statement, but they're far from warm, and they sure as hell wreak havoc on my poor feet."

"Then let's get you upstairs and warm them up." He toed off his own low cut boots and slipped on his indoor moccasins. He focused on her shapely calves on the way upstairs. She may have chilly feet, but *he'd* broken out in a light sweat by the time they reached the top.

He flicked on the lights, thankful he'd taken time to clean up the mess.

"Wow. You've been busy." Lanie padded on stocking feet into the kitchen. She ran her hand over spotless granite countertop. "How'd you manage to accomplish all this with your injury? This place was a work zone when I left here this afternoon. The stuff I brought you doesn't work *that* well."

"Actually, the lotion worked much better than I had anticipated." T.J. adjusted a thermostat on the wall, and a set of gas logs sprang to life. "I put it on, and then applied heat like the instructions said. The combination seemed to do the trick. However," he continued, "I had help with the room. Dad and Rich stopped by after Nick blabbed about my 'accident'. Of course, they couldn't resist pointing out that I'd let a *girl* get the drop on me."

Lanie laughed. "I'm glad you feel better. I still say you sneaked up on me, but I do apologize for the end result."

"It's okay." T.J. rubbed his side, thankful that so far the pain killers were still working. "Anyhow, while they installed the door and hauled over some boxes from my duplex, I cleaned up the place."

"You're a lucky man, McGraw." Her expression sobered, turning almost sad, and she turned away, directing her attention to the cabinets lining the walls. "This wood is gorgeous, a perfect match for these natural granite countertops. Hickory, aren't they?"

"They are. You've got a good eye."

She opened one of the cabinet doors and peeked inside.

"Would you like some wine?" he asked.

"Love some, but I don't see any glasses."

She seemed edgy, but maybe it was just him. T.J. rubbed a hand over his face.

"I have wine glasses somewhere." He crossed to the small pantry off the kitchen and dug into one of the boxes stacked inside.

"Found the wine," he called out seconds later, relieved when he uncovered a corkscrew along with a bottle of the same favored red they'd shared at dinner. A bit more digging produced a couple of wine glasses as well.

She moved closer when he returned and watched him with interest, leaning back against the counter next to him as he prepared to open the wine. He fumbled and almost dropped the bottle when she lifted one foot and slid it against her other leg. The sensuous slide up and down reignited the craving he'd managed to wrestle under control.

"I love the way you can enjoy the fireplace from two sides." She finally stopped rubbing, *thank God,* and moved closer to the dancing flames. The fireplace divided a section of the kitchen from the adjacent room so he could enjoy it from either one. "Ada and Rich recently installed gas logs in the old fireplace at Ada's cottage. *Rich* and Ada's cottage," she corrected. "This one's unique. Almost like having two fireplaces."

"When I turn that fan on low, it circulates the heat." He pointed at the overhead fan. "It's a great set up. I like the convenience of gas logs, too. Don't have to bust my butt hauling wood up those stairs."

He grasped the corkscrew he'd inserted into the cork and twisted gently. The cork popped free. "Ah, there we go."

He held up the two large-bowled wine glasses to the light and checked for spots while casting covert glances at Lanie. She prowled around the room, touching things and fussing with her hair. When she returned to the kitchen to fidget with a box of odds and ends he'd neglected to put away, it hit him.

Son of a gun. She's nervous.

He'd seen Lanie scared, and on one recent occasion, flustered. Most of the time, however, she came across as self-assured, confident, and even *challenging.* Under no circumstances, starting with their first meeting, had he ever witnessed Elaine Delacor displaying her nerves.

Satisfied with the spotless glasses, he poured the wine.

Lanie crossed to the windows over the sink, leaned forward, and peered through the glass. "It's snowing harder."

"Umm." T.J. moved in behind her. "Are we going to talk weather, or Rich's wood choice for cabinets over wine?"

She swung around to face him and braced her hands on the counter behind her. He placed his hands over hers and leaned in, just short of full body contact. Her breath caught, and she closed her eyes. Her lush, dark lashes brushed her creamy skin.

"Lanie?"

She looked at him. What was going on behind those vivid green eyes? Dark and mysterious, they beckoned him. Two forbidden, fathomless pools he wanted to dive into head first. He breathed in the tantalizing scents of her hair, her skin. The tempting combination swamped his senses and shattered his rigid grip on control.

He took her hands and drew her forward into his arms.

*****

Lanie rose onto her toes to meet him. Heat speared through her, a rush of pure fire. He pressed against her and slid his hands low, lifting her and drawing her closer. His mouth closed over hers, and the taste of him rippled through her like heady champagne. He took her breath away, disarmed her with slow, hungry kisses.

She melted against him, let herself float on the sensation. Need rose inside her. Growing, spreading as everything else around them faded. He took control, and his mouth, his body, his hands holding her to him became her world. His scent, so familiar now, surrounded her.

He broke the kiss, then slid his lips down to nip at her neck.

"I hope you're ready," he rasped, "seeing as the tours about to begin. If you've changed you mind, speak up now, because once we're underway there's no stopping." His body vibrated against hers. He buried his face in the curve of her neck and inched his hands lower and firmly took hold of her behind.

The possessive move nearly sent her over the edge. She shuddered and ground her hips against his, instinctively seeking release. He lifted her and braced her against the counter, and she locked her arms around his neck. Snaking one hand down, he gathered the hem of her dress and slipped his other hand beneath the crumpled knit. He touched her bare skin just above her nylons, and she jerked.

"Easy," he murmured. "Let me touch you."

He glided his hand over her sensitive flesh. Exploring her curves, stopping to gently stroke every silken inch. She squirmed and lifted her leg, clamping it around his, twisting to guide his questing fingers where she wanted them.

He caught the edge of her panties, gave them a tug, and bared her from waist to thigh. Cool air rushed over her burning skin. He lifted her higher and awkwardly dragged off the tiny scrap of black lace and tossed it aside. She wrapped her legs around him. He tightened his grip and drove against her.

Pressing her naked body against his, she met each primal thrust. Until, frustrated, she moaned, thwarted by the barrier keeping her from him. She groped between them and reached for his belt.

"Lanie, wait." He clamped his hand over hers. "Stop."

"Stop? Did you say *stop*? I'm on fire here, McGraw. Don't mess with a woman who's about to melt into a molten pool of lust."

"Pause, then," he gasped out. He closed his eyes, took another deep, shaky breath, and leaned his forehead against hers. "Can we *pause*? Move this somewhere a bit more convenient? You're not the only one on fire here."

He pushed against her to emphasize his point. Humor sneaked past the raw sexual hunger in his eyes. "But it's your lovely ass that'll be bouncing off my granite countertop unless we guide this tour down the hall. I have a perfectly good bed."

He stroked her and cupped her soft behind in his hard, warm hands.

Tilting her head, she narrowed her gaze on him. "Can you carry me?"

"Wrap your legs around me, good and tight." He repositioned his hands, and his fingers slid low. Teasing, exploring. Plundering. Her eyes opened wide, and a lazy grin spread slowly over his face. "Then hold on."

She gasped when he stepped away from the counter and clamped her legs tight against his hips as he careened down the hallway. The movement drove her crazy. With each step, her soft center rubbed against his fully clothed body.

"Hurry," she demanded, panting into his neck. "I want you naked against me when I come."

He gave her one desperate, shocked look, stumbled through the door, and crashed onto his bed. He dropped her there, then rolled to his feet and reached for his belt. The leather snapped as he slid it free.

With a few frenzied tugs, she wriggled out of the clingy knit dress and tossed it aside. When she opened her eyes, he stood beside the bed staring down at her. He'd stripped. His lean body, outlined against the light spilling from the hallway, tapered from his broad shoulders to his trim waist. As she reached for her thigh high nylons, he stopped her.

"Leave the rest for me," he murmured in a low, silky tone.

He came to her slowly, slid his warm fingers beneath the wide band on her thigh, and eased the stocking down her leg. She clutched the cool sheets.

"Oh, God, T.J.," she said with a shiver. "Can't you pick up the pace?"

"I like the pace." He slid the nylon free and trailed his hand up her bare leg. Then he stopped, bent down, and touched his lips to her thigh.

She reached for him, but he drew back. A tidal wave of need rolled over her, through her. She'd never hungered for, or been so responsive to, such mounting deep, dark desires. One thigh high nylon and her black lace bra remained on her body. Nearly naked, she pulsed beneath his gentle, exploring fingers as he trailed his hands over her, skimming her breasts. He touched his lips to her belly, making her quiver, and to where her breasts spilled out of the delicate lace.

His eyes gleamed in the low light. Unable to speak through the flood of emotion, she reached for him, and he kissed her. Wild, hot kisses. Then he dropped his mouth lower and closed his lips over her breast. She cried out, and he nipped at her, using his teeth to pull the lace aside, using his tongue on her nakedness. He ravished her, and she loved the wicked thrill of it. The heat of his lips, the way his breath caught when she touched him.

He rolled to one side, fumbling as she reached for him.

"Please, I need you, T.J. Don't stop." Then the quick rip of foil tore through the room, and she understood.

A moment later, he moved between her knees. She whimpered as his body touched hers and lifted her hips to meet him, craving the feel of him against her. The hot, wet, slide of flesh on flesh primed the tangle of need swirling inside her. She hungered for release, yet sought to ride the storm, to prolong the headlong rush.

Then, hard as steel, he drove into her. She closed around him, matching him stroke for stroke. Time and again, a wild blur of motion as he thrust deeper, harder. Her hands clamped onto his muscled hips, taut beneath her grasp, and held on until her world detonated.

"T.J.," she sobbed his name. With a long, low moan, he shared the explosion.

Chapter Sixteen

Jack cursed aloud. Snow pelted down, and driving the piece of crap car he'd been forced to resort to was a royal pain in the ass. He sure as hell missed driving around unaffected by the whims of nature in his made-to-order Escalade. Being forced to leave his luxurious condo to sleep in a flea bag motel pissed him off, too.

Snow smacked against the windshield as he slowed to study road signs. How could he stand five or six more months of this shit? He rolled to a stop at a crossroad, slammed the car into park, and glanced in the rearview mirror. Not a damn vehicle in sight. Only row upon row of trees bare as dead bones lined the road and covered surrounding landscape.

Why would a broad with any brains move to a place like this? Apparently Elaine Delacor had, and therefore, she was brainless. Beautiful, but dim as a twenty watt bulb when it came to choosing a place to live.

Jack picked up the wrinkled paper from the seat beside him.

"One-and-a-half Hilltop Road," he noted, reading the address from his copy of Elaine Delacor's driver's license. He leaned across the passenger seat to peer up the steep road to his right. This was it. "If you're home tonight, and you're alone, I'll do what has to be done. Then get back to livin' life *my* way."

He shifted and swung onto Hilltop Road. The surface was unplowed and bore no visible car tracks. This could play in Jack's favor. His tires spun, then took hold and he climbed slowly, rising above the orchards and passing a small vineyard as stark as the trees. Higher up the ridge, the road wound through a stand of larger trees. Scattered among them were a few evergreens and twisted clumps of brush coated with snow.

His lights caught the reflective numbers on a mailbox alongside the road, and he hit the brakes. *Shit.* He'd almost missed the turnoff for one and a half Hilltop.

"Home sweet home," he muttered, and then drove on up the hill. The road flattened a short distance above her driveway and disappeared into darkness amid swirls of white. He figured that at some point, the road must cross over I-90.

Executing a cautious u-turn, he backtracked to a small clearing just over the brow of the hill. How in the hell would he know if she was home? Worse yet, what if she was at home but wasn't alone?

He turned off the lights and let the car idle as he considered his dilemma. Snow came down at a fast clip, quickly covering the car and coating the windshield. He rolled down the passenger side window. His tire tracks were fast disappearing on the snow-packed pavement. Not a soul in sight, either.

Good.

He leaned forward and rested both arms atop the steering wheel. Damn, he needed a drink. Something strong. Scotch maybe, straight up. Liquid gold that would burn all the way down and help settle the fuckin' nerves dancing in his belly.

The windshield wipers' intermittent swipes broke the ghostly stillness.

He ruled out the small caliber weapon he'd used on Skinny and his pal. That would be foolish. Cops weren't stupid. He'd have to find another way, something different. Because if Miss Delacor had already blabbed about what she'd seen and then turned up with a thirty eight slug between those gorgeous green eyes, he'd be in deep shit.

He switched on the radio.

The announcer's voice droned on about the storm. Jack turned up the volume.

"We're asking everyone to please stay indoors throughout the duration of the storm. Dangerous winds, heavy snow, and dropping temperatures are imminent. Any one of these could cause death to unprepared individuals who venture out alone."

He then predicted large amounts of snow and overnight temperatures bound to set records. Jack flipped off the chatter.

"Who says fate never smiles on old Jack?" He grinned. How hard would it be to make it look as if the woman had just wandered out and gotten lost in the storm? He chuckled to himself, dragged a heavy down jacket from the rear seat, and prepared to meet the elements. Not a single car had passed the whole time he'd been parked here.

He got out and crossed the road. Angling through the woods toward Miss Delacor's place, he followed what appeared to be some kind of farm access road. He plowed through knee deep snow until he stood at the edge of a clearing overlooking a low slung log cabin. A single light burned in the window. Otherwise, the place looked deserted. No tire tracks, no smoke from the chimney.

Insides knotted, he trudged back to his car. Wind howled through the naked branches high above him, as if Mother Nature laughed at his failure. He wasn't about to freeze his ass off waiting for the lovely Miss Delacor to show up. Now he knew where to find her, and sooner or later she'd be here. Alone.

He needed to discipline himself, make plans, and not rush it. He wouldn't return to his condo, not yet. He'd lay low and monitor the situation. Wouldn't hurt to find out where Elaine Delacor worked. The old lady in Fox Chapel had said Miss Delacor had moved to Erie for a new job and had also implied that she still taught fitness classes. He'd make some calls, see what he could turn up.

He emerged from the woods and hustled across the road to his car. Just as he slid behind the wheel, approaching headlights broke through the driving snow.

"Shit. A fuckin' cop car," he muttered. He'd already turned on the lights, and that left him no choice but to pull out and head down the hill. The patrol car slowed and rolled to a stop in front of the driveway at one and a half Hilltop.

Damn, the cop was checking out her place. What the hell should Jack do now? This was not good news. If the cops were keeping tabs on the lady, they had a reason.

If Jack turned around now, he'd sure as hell catch the cop's attention. So while the cruiser idled in place, he continued on down the hill. As he passed, the trooper inside stared right at him.

Jack lifted a hand and waved, then gritted his teeth and kept a slow, steady pace all the way to the bottom.

His heart jumped into his throat when the patrol car suddenly swung around and started after him, lights flashing. They were alone, the only two cars on the road. Jack slid his hand into his pocket, palmed the compact revolver, and eased onto the berm.

In a whirl of white, the marked cruiser blew past him, hung a hard left, and dipped out of sight. Briefly, the faint wail of his siren cut the air. Then *nothing*.

Jack sat there in sub zero temperatures, sweat trickling down his back.

Chapter Seventeen

Warm and soft beneath T.J., Lanie stretched and sighed like a satisfied cat. He moved to one side, propped his head on one hand, and stared down at her. He swept his gaze over her naked body. Well, her almost naked body. He grinned and eyed her one slim, sexy leg still encased in nylon from her sexy red toes to her luscious thigh.

She stirred when he traced a slow path from her belly up her body. He cupped her breast, savoring its fullness and silky texture against the palm of his hand.

A lazy smile curved her lips. "What am I doing here with a man like you?"

"If you have to ask, maybe I should do it again to help you figure it out."

"Oh, T.J." She reached up and placed her hand against his cheek. "You know what I mean. Up until a short while ago, we avoided one another. Now here I am, naked in your new bed, and I can't quite figure out how it all happened."

He slid his hand down her body, over the curve of one lush hip, and tipped her toward him. He pulled her in until they were skin to skin, and her eyes went soft with desire.

"You're more than I bargained for, Lanie. I didn't have a plan or a type in mind for a woman. I wasn't looking. But you're more," he repeated. "Much more."

"I'm not your type, T.J." She settled in against him, her emerald eyes intent as if delving into his soul, searching for answers. "What we've got are raging hormones that run amuck when we're together. Things were fine until you touched me, and I touched you back."

"I outgrew raging hormones a while ago. I like touching you." He toyed with the silky strands of her dark, tousled hair. "No, I *love* touching you."

He pressed his lips to her cheek, her brow, and lingered when they met her sexy mouth.

She broke the kiss. Her fingers played over his chest, stroked up his arm, and threaded lightly through his hair. She fussed with his cowlick.

"You can't tame this, no matter what you do, right?"

"What?" Puzzled, he raised his eyes to see what she meant.

"This enticing little swirl right here in front." She gave it a tug. "I shouldn't tell you this, but from the first time I met you, I've wanted to get my hands in your hair to explore that little bit of wildness on straight and narrow T.J. McGraw."

"My cowlick? Wild?"

"Turns me inside out." She gave a little wiggle.

The wiggle did it.

He rolled her over and settled between her silky thighs.

She surged against him and trembled. "See what I mean?"

"You didn't touch. You wiggled. *This* is a touch." He trailed his hand over her breasts, her belly, and lower.

Her breath caught. "I have another confession," she whispered. "The cowlick's second."

"To what?" he managed to choke out as he covered himself. He slid a hand beneath her thigh and pulled it up so her knee was bent.

"Your prime butt," she purred in his ear.

He buried his face in her sweet smelling hair and slid inside her. Lost in the thunder of his own rapid heartbeat, he hung onto his control by a thin thread. Her wiggles became thrusts, and he gave in, catching the rhythm.

No stopping now.

He pounded into her, spurred on by the urgent sounds humming in her throat. She came hard, and the sensation of her body squeezing around him sent him over the edge.

When his mind cleared enough for him to think, T.J. covered Lanie with a quilt and slipped away to the bathroom. She was sound asleep when he returned, lying on her side with both hands pillowed beneath her head. He slipped in behind her, pulled her against him, and fell dead asleep.

*****

"T.J., wake up."

"Hmm?"

"I said 'wake up'." Lanie nudged his shoulder. "Let go of me. I need to get up."

He released her and rolled onto his back. Pain shot up his side. "Ouch. Oh, shit."

"What is it? What's wrong?"

"Pain killers wore off," he muttered. His eyes adjusted, and light from the hallway outlined Lanie sitting bolt upright beside him. Her breasts jutted out as she turned, presenting the most erotic silhouette he'd ever seen.

Her hand flew to her mouth. "Oh, oh, your side."

He nodded.

"Did I hurt you?" She drew away the quilt, knelt beside him, and ran her cool fingers over his bruised ribs. "How could I have forgotten?"

"Well, actually..." He managed a grin. "I think I forgot my name a few times when we--"

"Where's the light?"

"Ah, well, there's a lamp on the dresser," he answered, surprised by her abrupt tone.

She crawled off the bed and stalked across the room. When she turned on the light, his gaze flew to that single nylon stocking. The creamy flesh above the band on her thigh sent a jolt to his midsection. Unconcerned with her naked state, she hurried back and sat on the side of the bed. "Let me take a look."

He rested his head on his bent arm, giving her free access to his naked torso. When she bent over him, he whispered, "Maybe now we can play nurse."

Her concerned expression vanished, only to be replaced by anger and hurt. She jerked back, leapt to her feet, and lunged away.

He grabbed her wrist.

"Let go!" she cried out.

Before she could break free, he hooked his arm around her waist and hauled her back onto the bed. He flipped her over and pinned her to the mattress. As she twisted and pushed against him, she almost slipped away.

"Stop it," he ordered, tightening his hold on her until she went limp. She glared up at him, her defiant eyes moist and bright, and then looked away.

"Hey, I was only kidding. I--"

"You *play* with toys. I'm not a damn toy."

Beyond words, T.J. just stared at her. What the hell? First she couldn't get enough of him, then she's fussing over him like a mother hen, and now all of a sudden she's ready to bolt out the door. They'd had incredible sex, *off the charts* sex -- *two times, damn it* -- and they'd connected more than just physically. More than simply sharing a roll between the sheets.

She had admitted an attraction to him since day one, and that had surprised the hell out of him, since she'd always made a point to avoid him like the friggin' plague. His head spun. Why the sudden turn around?

He eased his grip. She averted her eyes and folded her arms over her breasts. He reached for her, but reconsidered when she stiffened.

"I'm not sure what set you off," he said, carefully choosing his words. "If I offended you, I apologize. We were teasing, enjoying each other on a lot of levels here, Lanie. What went wrong?"

*****

The tiny lamp cast a lone shadow on the wall. Lanie fixed her gaze on it and fought back bitter tears. She'd overreacted big time and was at a loss as to what to do next.

Heat radiated from the man beside her, and a part of her longed to curl against him and let the chips fall where they may. She knew better. Sleeping with him had been a whim, an itch she'd scratched -- and the sooner she made that clear to T.J., the better. Whether it had been a one night stand or a moment of madness, or both, she must make him understand it ended here.

His calm, compassionate eyes locked on hers when she turned to face him. She took a careful breath. "I shouldn't have let this happen."

"Lanie." He touched her cheek. "I admit, you caught me off guard, but I sure as heck didn't back off. We didn't do anything wrong."

"Oh, God." She rubbed her hands over her face. "I sound like some whiny female claiming she *got carried away* and regrets what she's done. That's not true. I'll never regret tonight."

The truth of her words almost shattered her heart. She blew out a long breath.

"I don't know why I snapped at you. Sometimes words come out of my mouth, and I wonder where they come from. Don't you see? I'm a loose cannon, a volcano about to erupt. You know that. How many times have you called me *difficult?*"

He smoothed a spiky strand of hair behind her ear.

"And I'm perfect?" he asked. "You're passionate and tend to grab the world by the ass. Quite frankly, your hell bent, get-out-of-my-way style made you top my list of women to avoid."

"See?" she broke in. "I was right. Why don't you just admit it? Naked woman trumped difficult. *That's* why you didn't back off tonight."

"Earlier, you called me *straight and narrow.*" His jaw tightened, and his eyes turned stone cold. "I'm not sure what that means, Lanie, but don't insult or demean what I feel or how I choose to treat you as a woman. I haven't been into one night stands since college. Even then, I didn't use and then discard anyone once I got my rocks off."

"That's crude, T.J. I don't appreciate or deserve to be--"

"Shut up, Lanie. Let me finish. I'm not going to apologize for what happened tonight. Nor am I going to forget about it and walk away." His voice softened, but his eyes remained ice cold.

"In my book, *straight and narrow* isn't a flaw. It's a responsibility. People depend on me and trust me on so damn many levels it sometimes scares the shit out of me. As for relationships, I don't lie, and if I'm involved intimately with a woman, I don't cheat."

Taken aback by his passion and indignity, Lanie's breathing hitched. "Are you sorry you've become involved intimately with me?"

"I enjoyed our evening together, although I still believe you're difficult." He angled his head and the chill in his eyes faded. "But I've discovered you have an infectious laugh, a soft spot for strays, and you're fearless to a fault in the face of adversity. I want to know more."

With a grim smile, he gave her cheek a gentle pat. "Like it or not, Lanie, everything changed between us."

She couldn't force words around the huge lump in her throat.

T.J. sat up and swung his feet out of bed, grabbed his discarded shorts, and pulled them on. Seconds later, a two-toned chime echoed down the hall.

Lanie took hold of the sheet and hauled it up to her chin. "What's that?"

"Shit," T.J. mumbled. He picked up his crumpled slacks and stepped into them. "That's my doorbell. Who the hell...?" He spun around, facing her. "Did you ask Cassi to pick you up here?"

"No, I was supposed to call her." She yanked the sheet free and used it to cover her nakedness as she scrambled to find her clothes. "Then I got distracted."

She tossed the quilt aside and found her dress in a heap at the foot of the bed. She spied her bra on the floor and snatched the single nylon hanging from the iron headboard. Scooping up the bra, she gave T.J. a furious look when he burst out laughing.

"What's so damn funny?" she ranted, grappling with her clothes and clutching the sheet like a lopsided toga.

"What's funny," he gasped, wiping his eyes, "is you trying to cover up everything I've been admiring throughout this evening's... ah, *tour.*"

"Oh, shut up. Just shut the hell up." The bell chimed again. Giving up, Lanie dropped the sheet and shook out her wrinkled dress. She slipped on her bra and hooked it in place, then pulled the dress over her head. "Aren't you going to get that?"

She shot him a swift, accusing look. He appeared unruffled. Slacks zipped, but unhooked; barefoot, and naked from the waist up. If she had the damn time, she'd drool.

"Just enjoying the view."

She plopped down onto the bed and pulled on her single nylon. When she straightened. he'd disappeared down the hallway. She rushed into the bathroom, flicked on the light, and almost screamed aloud at her reflection.

Her hair stood up in spikes, and she'd put the stupid dress on backwards. With a couple of clumsy contortions, she righted it, then grabbed a stiff, bristled brush and took a stab at taming her wild hair.

Seconds later, she emerged, and feeling a bit more put together, made her way down the hall. The door leading to the downstairs foyer burst open. Nick and T.J. followed Cassi into the room, and Cassi's dog, Rufus, clamored up the steps behind them.

Cassi stopped, causing Nick to bump into her. A tense moment of silence followed.

Lanie sucked in a deep breath and pasted on a wide, wooden smile. "Hi. I was about to call you. We stopped after dinner so I could see more of T.J.'s place, and I forgot about the time."

Behind them, T.J. rolled his eyes. Somehow he'd managed to find a shirt and put it on, but it hung open revealing his bare chest.

Nick's strangled cough sounded suspiciously like a muffled laugh. He recovered and nudged his wife forward. "We had dinner with some friends," he offered. "On the way home, we decided to drive past and when we saw lights... we, ah figured you were here and stopped."

"Well, I'm glad you did. I was just about to call you, so this will save you a trip. I'll just get my bag, and we can get going."

She shifted her gaze to T.J. "If you'll just give me your keys, I'll go down and..." Frowning at the look on his face, she let her words trail off.

His eyes grew wide and focused on something behind her. Rufus brushed past her, his golden tail waving like a flag. With head held high, he trotted straight to Nick.

"What ya' got there, fella?" Nick asked, kneeling down. The dog plopped his butt on the floor and dropped something dark and tangled at Nick's feet. A wide grin spread over his handsome face as he rose.

"Hmm. Are these yours, cousin?" he asked, looking at T.J. and holding up Lanie's black lace bikini panties.

Chapter Eighteen

T.J. stared at the two full glasses of red wine on the counter. He lifted one, sniffed it, and swirled the liquid around in the glass. Then he sipped it. The soft Cabernet went down smooth as silk. He took another sip, relaxing as the warmth spread.

He polished off the first glass while leaning against the counter and mulling over the past few hours. With a careless shrug, he set the empty aside and picked up the second glass. What the hell? His head was already buzzing, and his bruised side throbbed like a son of a bitch. Why waste a perfectly good bottle of wine?

He dragged a chair close to the fireplace, positioning it so he could prop his feet on the raised hearth. Still clutching the glass, he retrieved the half filled bottle and dropped into the chair. He'd just kick back and drink enough to dull the pain. Maybe then he'd be able to sort out this whole bloody evening. Or maybe he'd just drink until he forgot all about it.

He settled in, slouching down until his head rested on the chair's well worn cushion. The fire's warmth wrapped around him. He polished off the wine and tried to pin down what had made a truly spectacular evening turn to shit.

After Rufus had showed off his retrieving skills, things had kind of gone downhill. He gave Lanie credit, though. She'd handled the situation with style.

Even Nick had appeared surprised when she'd stepped forward and claimed the tiny scrap of lace. They'd shared no small talk, no *how was dinner?* Hadn't even asked the question more appropriate for this circumstance: *How was the sex?*

She'd tucked the panties into her bag and turned to him with a raised brow. Her message had been clear, and he'd gone to get her overnight bag. She, Cassie, and Nick were all in the lower foyer when he had returned. He'd hoped to have a few words with Lanie in private before they left, but Nick and Cassi had herded Rufus out the door, and Lanie had looked ready to follow them.

Then she'd stopped and turned to face him. The raw emotion in her eyes had almost brought him to his knees. They were open wide, fringed with sooty, black lashes, and her potent green gaze had shot straight to his heart.

She came to him, rose on tiptoe, touched her lips to his. He reached for her, but she backed away and slipped out into the night, closing the door behind her.

So here he sat, alone. Sipping and drifting, until the familiar two-toned chime interrupted his mental replay of lush breasts, creamy thighs, and soft sighs of pleasure.

Ignoring the repeating musical sound, he finished off the second glass of wine.

"Hey, I know you're up there. Open the damn door!"

T.J. heaved a weary sigh and stumbled to his feet. He held on to the smooth oak railing as he made his way downstairs. Damn legs just weren't cooperating. Out of habit, he'd tucked his off duty weapon into the waistband of his trousers. The compact Bersa dug into his side, and his pants slid lower with each cautious step. He flipped on the outside light and pressed one eye to the tiny hole in the middle of the door. He drew back, rubbed his eye, and tried again. This time, he came eye to eye with Nick's irritated scowl.

"It's me again, you idiot. Open the door."

"Gimme a damn minute, will ya?" he mumbled, fumbling with the deadbolt.

The lock clicked, and Nick pushed the door open. A fine layer of snow covered his head and shoulders. Wind whipped across the stoop, sending a shower of white through the open door

T.J. stepped back, cursing, as Nick swiped away the icy layers before stepping inside.

Off balance, T.J. shot out a hand and braced himself against the wall to keep from landing on his ass.

Nick eyed him closely while shrugging out of his heavy parka.

"What the hell?" he asked, leaning in close to T.J. and sniffing. A slow smile spread across his face. "Well, I'll be damned. You're toasted."

"Am not," T.J. muttered. "I had a little wine. Nothing I can't handle." He adjusted the slipping gun and pulled his gaping shirt together. "Whadda you want? It's snowin' like a bitch out there. You should be home snuggled up with your wife."

Swaying a bit, he grabbed Nick by the arm. Nick guided him toward the steps, and they made their way to the top. T.J.'s feet were freezing. They'd been all toasty until he'd tromped downstairs barefoot to let his hair brained cousin in out of the damn blizzard.

"What are you doing here, Nick?"

"Just stopping back by." Grinning, Nick lifted the bottle of cabernet and eyed the two empty glasses. "Not a good sign, drinking alone."

"Up yours. I'll drink whenever I damn well please."

Without a word, Nick rummaged around until he located some coffee. T.J. laid his gun on the counter and stalked off to find some warm socks and a sweater. When he returned, Nick shoved a steaming cup of coffee into his hands.

"Here. Sit the hell down and drink that." He'd also found a box of leftover pastries from The Brown Cow and slapped them down at T.J.'s elbow.

T.J. just looked at them.

"Won't hurt you to put something on your stomach, either," Nick growled, and went to pour a cup for himself.

With a sigh, T.J. sipped the hot brew. Now that his toes weren't freezing, his frame of mind had improved considerably, and the wine buzz had settled to a pleasant hum. He broke off a piece of donut, chewed it slowly, and studied his cousin.

"Get everyone settled in?" he mumbled around a mouthful of crumbs.

Nick pulled out a chair and sat across from T.J. "I did. Cass was making tea when I left. I'm sure they have a lot to talk about." He raised the cup, sipped, and shook his head when T.J. pushed the box of leftovers across the table. "You feelin' better?"

T.J. shrugged. "I'll live. This helps." He raised his cup. "Thanks."

"I stopped back by for a couple of reasons," Nick said. "Your lovely, gregarious Lanie clamped her mouth shut and didn't say a word on the drive to our place. Now I've know Elaine Delacor almost as long as I've known my wife, and Lanie being so quiet is not friggin' natural."

"Yeah?" T.J. slumped into his chair. "Seems she's full of surprises all of a sudden."

Nick chuckled. He shifted, and drank some more coffee. "I'm goin' out on a limb here, but, I'm guessing that sexy little lace number didn't just fall off Lanie's curvy little bottom."

T.J. should have figured his cousin would shoot straight for the jugular. No subtle hints, no dancing around, just point and shoot.

He stared into his half-filled cup, gave it a slow spin between his hands. "A minute ago, you referred to her as 'my' gregarious Lanie. Far from it, my friend. I lay no claim on the woman."

"So tonight was what? A quickie? A one-nighter?"

"Whoa, just a damn minute." He scooped a hand through his hair. "Are you trying to piss me off?" Before Nick could respond, T.J. pushed away from the table and stood. Annoyed when the room tilted, he hesitated, then paced across the room.

"You know damned well I don't treat women that way, especially ones I care about. God, it's like déjà vu. Only now I'm defending myself to *you* instead of to Lanie. Naked woman trumps difficult, my ass." He paused long enough to refill his cup. Damn the caffeine, he wasn't about to sleep tonight anyway.

"T.J., sit down before you fall down. I have no doubt I'll get the story from Cassi, but I'd sure as hell like to hear your side of what happened here tonight. And for Pete's sake, don't leave out the déjà vu part about the naked woman."

He glared at Nick, then joined him at the table. Setting the coffee aside, he propped his elbows on the tabletop and cradled his head between his hands. "I'm going to have one mother of a headache come morning." Then he leaned back and relayed, blow by blow, the past few days leading up to the 'grand tour', the term he used to refer to his encounter with Lanie.

Nick listened, asking a few questions on occasion, but mostly he just let T.J. ramble.

Before too long, the coffee pot was bone dry, and aside from a few crumbs, the Brown Cow box was empty. Wrung out, both physically and mentally, T.J. propped his feet on the hearth. At some point, he and Nick had hunted up another chair and settled side by side in front of the fireplace.

Nick yawned and scraped a hand over his rough cheek. He glanced at the time. "You have to work tomorrow?"

Eyes closed, T.J. nodded. "On at two. I'm supposed to meet with the guys from OIU on Monday for an update. Actually, Sullivan, the crime corporal on the case, arranged to have the meeting early that morning. He extended the invitation for me to sit in."

"Sounds like a descent guy."

"He's fair, and he's thorough. One of the reasons I'm glad he's on the case."

"I'd better head on home. I'm not so lucky. My alarm will go off at six a.m., a little over four hours from now."

T.J. rose, gathered up their empty cups, and tossed the empty donut container into the trash. "You haven't said much."

Nick finished rinsing out the coffee pot. He grabbed a paper towel, dried his hands, and wiped the counter. "I was here to listen. If you want to hear what I have to say, you'll ask."

"Then I'm asking."

"I'm going to make this clean and simple." Nick looked at the time again. "To begin with, you and I are damn lucky. We have parents who love us. They kept us in line when we needed it, made sure we had food to eat and a roof over our heads. You agree so far?"

"Yeah." T.J. reversed a chair, sat, and propped his arms on the back. "But I don't recall ever hearing that Lanie ever went without the basics. Granted, her mom died when she was pretty young, and her dad took a hike from responsibility, but she didn't grow up in poverty."

"All true. I'm playing the devil's advocate here, and I want you to think about what I'm saying."

T.J. lifted a hand and nodded.

"What did we do on snowy days? On holidays, birthdays, lazy summer nights?"

"Well..." Memories rolled, sweet and strong, through T.J.'s head. "Not enough time to fill all the gaps." He grinned at Nick, knowing their minds were in sync. "I'll give it a shot, though. We drove my mom nuts sledding like maniacs down the hill. Holidays were, and still are, filled with enough food to feed an army and people spilling out the doors. Same goes for birthdays, graduations, and every one of life's little goals we accomplished."

"How about summer nights?"

"Ah, fireflies and the Fourth of July." A crooked grin broke through.

"Until we became teenagers, then it was dark corners and fast hands."

Nick laughed aloud. "Those were the days." He drew in a deep breath and turned sober. "Now what do you think Lanie remembers about her childhood?"

"I'm not sure I follow you."

"Lanie and Cassi were roommates in college. At first, Cass thought she'd drawn the roommate from hell. Time proved otherwise. Elaine Delacor turned out to be not only a bright, straight, four-point-oh student all four years, but she was -- and is -- one hell of a good friend. When the folks who adopted Cassi died in a plane crash, Lanie was the one who pulled her through. And Lanie insisted Cassie follow up when Ada contacted her."

"All right," T.J. agreed. "I've no doubt she's a good friend."

"Good friends share their deepest secrets, and what Cassi learned from Lanie almost broke her heart. There had been no parties, no relatives spilling out the door in Lanie's life. According to Cassi, the man Lanie called Uncle Charley is responsible for every bit of happiness and security she ever knew. He put food on the table and made sure she did her homework. I imagine he footed most of the bill for college, too. Although Lanie worked her butt off to help."

T.J. rubbed a thumb between his eyes. The expected headache crept across his brow. "I get the picture, but why would that make her feel unworthy of having a happy life of her own now? She's strong and smart. I don't get it."

"Here's my theory." Nick said. "Lanie feels quite capable of taking care of herself, of dealing with the basics. Her uncle loved her, and she loved him, yet all the extras that come with families, all the clutter and confusion, are as foreign to her as a walk on the moon."

"She's afraid of failing," T.J. muttered, the answer finally coming to him. "As long as she's only responsible for her own life, she's comfortable. She said I was a lucky man when I mentioned how Dad and Rich helped me out, and more than once lately she labeled me as 'straight and narrow' or 'hearth and home'. She also had the nerve to suggest we ended up in bed because of raging hormones. She ran hot and cold. One minute telling me I wasn't her type, and the next crawling all over me."

"See?" Nick laid a hand on T.J.'s shoulder. "Sounds to me like a woman who's falling for a man she doesn't think she can measure up to, but she still can't quite resist the fall."

T.J. followed Nick to the door. The snow had stopped, but had left behind at least another five inches on top of what already covered the ground.

"Sure you're up to working tomorrow?" Nick pulled on his thick gloves and dug out his keys. "That's a nasty bruise."

"Have to be. I may be getting tangled up with Lanie on a personal level, but that doesn't mean I can back away from my job. Even if it crosses the line when it comes to keeping her safe. I have a bad feeling about this LeFavor character. I'll try to keep it middle of the road for Lanie, while at the same time, make her aware of the danger. It's a fine line."

"If there's anything I can do to help, just ask. You know that."

"Thanks." T.J.'s insides knotted, and he met Nick's quiet gaze. "For tonight, and for the offer."

With a nod, Nick trudged through the snow to his Ridgeline, and T.J. closed the door.

By his calculations, he'd be able to get a solid eight hours of sleep and still have time to stop by and exercise Hershey before he had to leave for work. He'd shower in the morning.

He grabbed his toothbrush from the jar on the bathroom counter. After brushing, he sloshed some water on his face. He reached for a towel, and his hairbrush clattered to the floor. Where had that come from? He picked it up and was about to stow it away when he noticed several dark pieces of hair clinging to the stiff bristles. He pulled several free. Deep in thought, T.J. slowly rubbed the soft, silky strands between his fingers.

*****

On the drive from T.J.'s carriage house, Lanie clamped her mouth shut and stared out the widow. Gentleman that he was, Nick had never questioned how her black bikini panties had ended up on T.J.'s kitchen floor.

She excused herself and hurried off to shower as soon as they arrived at Nick and Cassi's.

Feeling calmer, she emerged to find Cassi lounging in flannel pajamas by a crackling fire. Nick was nowhere in sight.

Lanie crossed to the window and peered out at the fresh blanket of snow. Frosted in white, naked tree branches outlined against the night sky created a timeless winter landscape. Woods surrounded the cabin on all sides. A path to Pine Shadow Lake cut away to the east, and a wide, meandering drive led in from the road on the west.

"Feeling better?" Cassi approached Lanie and ran a hand down her arm. "I brewed a fresh pot of tea. Get some and come join me by the fire."

Once Lanie had settled onto the deep-cushioned sofa, the hard knot in her belly eased. Rufus ambled over, turned in a circle, and plopped down with a thud. He'd been a gangly, half-grown pup when she'd helped Cassi pick him out. He'd matured into a handsome golden retriever, and tonight had lived up to his retriever bloodline.

"Was it good sex, great sex, or blow-the-roof-off sex?"

Lanie gave her friend a cool, considering look. "I'd say about average for first time, get-to-know-one-another sex. Too bad about T.J.'s roof, though."

Cassi thought for a moment. Then she got it and laughed, and Lanie's lingering headache faded. Cassi propped a cushion in the corner and angled to face Lanie.

"It's been a while for you, hasn't it?"

"That's a very personal question."

"Not really, but now you know if T.J.'s red hair is an all over kind of thing, right?"

Lanie chuckled. "Now *that's* personal." She took a deep sip of tea and leaned back. "I remember the night I made that rather risqué remark about red-headed men. We were in Ada's cottage. You'd just admitted you'd fallen for Nick, and I admitted I'd checked out T.J.'s sexy ass. You accused me of being a shameless *ass checker*."

Nodding, Cassi toyed with the tie of her pajama bottoms. "You told me not to overanalyze everything, to wait and see where things went with Nick. Maybe you should take your own advice, see where things go with T.J."

Lanie shook her head. "That's different." She rose and moved closer to the fire. "*We're* different."

"Do you mean you and me, or you and T.J.?" Cassi asked.

Lanie blew out a hard breath. "Both. I love you like a sister, Cass. When you fell in love with Nick and married him, I was over the moon happy for both of you. I knew it would work."

"And you don't think it would work with you and T.J.?"

"Doesn't matter what I think." She turned and faced Cassi. "This sudden, crazy urge to get my hands on him is pure sexual fantasy. Great while it lasts, but it'll end eventually."

She bent to pet Rufus. He rolled over, exposing his belly, and gave a contented moan when she rubbed his chest.

"Ah. So you're going to have a hot affair for as long as it lasts and then walk away?"

Lanie sat back on her heals and studied the look on Cassi's face. Her heart ached. "I hate it when I disappoint you."

"I'm not disappointed, Lanie."

"Your face says otherwise." Lanie gave Rufus a parting rub and rejoined Cassi. "I wasn't ready to like him, much less tumble into bed with him. There's always been a kind of... heat generated when I'm around T.J., but ever since the night of the accident, little by little, things have changed."

She raked a hand through her damp hair and chose her words with care. Making Cassi understand was vital. "I'd wait for him to stop by or call, telling myself it was about the case. Then on the night he came by late and I whacked him with the stick, he kissed me."

"Really? He kissed you? I would have thought he'd have been pissed off."

"He was at first, then I helped him take off his shirt to check the injury. Next thing I know, I'm plastered against his naked chest and he's kissing me brainless."

"I can see how that happened. Didn't he stay over that night?"

"He did. He slept on the couch; I slept in my bed. I really slammed him, Cass. He was a hurtin' puppy. I figure that's why we stopped after the kiss."

"I take it he's all healed?"

"Oh, yeah. Dinner out, great wine, another kiss. Then I lost my head and all but propositioned the man."

"You?" A slow smile spread over Cassi's face. "I thought *he* seduced *you*. Well, well, well. You almost snuck that by me. What really happened?"

"This tea's cold," Lanie grumbled. She stared into the cup, frowning. "If we're going to talk about my misadventures in T.J.'s new bed, I need a more potent drink. What I'd really like is the glass of cabernet I never even tasted at T.J.'s."

"I'm afraid if we open wine now, we'll both regret it tomorrow." Cassi stood and stretched.

Lanie joined her friend and hugged her. "I'll have enough regrets to face tomorrow. By the way, where's Nick?"

"He ran out to check something at the station."

"Did he say anything about the panty episode? God, I felt like an idiot."

"He didn't say one word to me. Just kept grinning like a fool and muttering something about payback." She picked up her cup, and together they moved into the kitchen. "The first time I went out with Nick, T.J. stopped by and caught us in a similar compromising situation."

"They're almost like brothers," Lanie mused. "Always ribbing one another."

"The McGraws are a tight family."

Lanie stepped in and rubbed her hand over Cassi's back. "That's why there's no future for T.J. and me."

Cassi smacked her empty cup onto the counter. "That's ridiculous. Why do you persist in believing you're no good for any man?"

She raised her hand when Lanie started to respond. "Don't say it," she warned. "I've known you since college. You're one of the warmest, smartest people I've ever met. I don't know what I would have done without you when I lost Mom and Dad."

A single tear traced down Cassi's cheek. She wiped it away with a furious swipe. "Yet every time a man gets too close, you shove him away. Why, Lanie?"

Her tone brought Rufus to his feet. Whining, he shoved between them, his feathery tail batting against their legs.

Lanie nudged him aside and wrapped her arms around Cassi. "Please. I can't stand seeing you so upset. Not over me." Her voice hitched. Her throat burned like fire. "You fit in, Cassi. Don't you see? You grew up surrounded by love, and even when fate tried to rip you apart, you survived. All those years you didn't know Ada, she loved you and watched you from afar. Now you're surrounded by family. In the years to come, you'll draw from old traditions and blend with Nick and his family. Meld traditions and create new ones."

She let go, fighting back tears, and turned away. "If I let myself fall in love, I'm not sure I'll have anything to give."

Cassi's head whipped around when the door opened, and Nick strode in from outside.

"God, it's cold as a bitch out there." He yanked off his coat. "I thought you two would--"

"We were having some tea before we turn in."

He gave a slow nod, tugged his scarf free, and shot cautious looks between the two women.

"I'm really beat." Lanie captured Cassi's hand and gave it a gentle squeeze. "Thanks for the tea. I'll be all right."

She kissed Cassi's cheek, then turned to Nick. "I love you both."

Without saying another word, she hurried out of the room.

Chapter Nineteen

By the time T.J. crawled out of bed, took time to stop and toss a few snowballs for Hershey, and drove to work, he felt as if he'd already put in a full day. He faced eight hours in uniform, and his head felt two sizes too big. Guys around him prepared for the second shift, and each time a locker slammed it damn near brought him to his knees.

Les Andrews paused by T.J.'s locker to clip his tie in place. "Hey, T.J. Have a rough night?"

T.J. straightened and eased his locker closed. "I look that bad?"

"Hell, you look like death warmed over."

Together they walked upstairs to the patrol room. The barracks was quiet. On Sundays, civilian office personnel and most officers weren't around. Voices from the front desk filtered down the hall, confirming the location of an abandoned vehicle and the dispatcher's promise to send the next available patrol unit to check it out.

T.J. and Andrews checked out keys for their assigned vehicles.

"How was last night?" T.J. stuck the key in his pocket. "I wasn't on, had a date, but it was nasty out there."

"Ah, so that's where she was." Les grinned and settled his hat into place.

"Who?'

"What's her name? Ah... Delacor. The one who lives on Hilltop we're supposed to check up on."

"Maybe." T.J. busied himself checking out his gear. Rumors spread fast among the men, and somehow his connection with Lanie had leaked out. He adjusted his holster. "Not that it's anyone's business."

He met Andrews knowing smirk with a stone cold stare.

Les raised a hand and backed away. "No problem. I did make a note on my log about the car parked near her place. Catch you later," he said, then turned and walked away.

"Hey, hold on." T.J. strode after Les. "Tell me about the car."

"Not much to tell, T.J. It was snowing like hell, and for once things were quiet. I took a detour off Route 20 and drove up to Sidehill, just to kill some time before my shift ended."

"What time was that?"

"Ten o'clock?" Les screwed up his face, shrugged. "Maybe a little before." He rubbed his hand against his cheek. "No, come to think of it, it was a couple minutes after. I ended up working overtime when I caught a bad accident right about then."

"So you saw a car parked on Hilltop near Lanie's place?"

"I stopped at the end of the driveway at one-and-a-half Hilltop. The place looked deserted. No smoke from the chimney, and only a small light in the window. Didn't see any tire tracks in the snow, so I figured she'd gone out for the night."

"Did you drive in, check for sure?"

"Thought about it, but I'd been checking the place pretty regularly, and when someone's home there's always been smoke from the chimney and lots of lights on. Besides, I had second thoughts about getting stuck trying to do a house check."

T.J. understood. Sometimes they had to make choices. "Where exactly was the car?"

"I noticed his lights when I topped the hill and stopped. He was heading down toward me and slowed down when I pulled over. Kinda strange, I thought, someone driving around on a night like that on a barely passable side road. I was prepared to pull him over, find out who he was, and ask what the hell he was doing there when I got a call."

"Did you get his plate number?"

Les shook his head. "He drove right past me, even had the balls to wave. I tried to eyeball his plate, but the damn thing was covered with snow. I was about to stop him and get his registration when headquarters called. Bad one on Route 20 with injuries and a possible fatality. I had to go."

"Shit." T.J. didn't like the whole deal. Too many unknowns. "What make was the vehicle?"

"Dark colored Ford Taurus, either blue or black. The one with the straight, narrow grille across the front. Musta been a 2008 model. I could hardly see because of the snow."

"You're sure the driver was a man?"

"Positive."

"Thanks, Les. I'll pass the info along to Sullivan."

"Glad to help." Andrews started to leave, then turned back. "She's one sharp woman, T.J. Can't say I blame you."

T.J. smiled, tipped his hand to his hat. "Thanks."

He wouldn't see Sullivan until Monday, yet he felt the corporal should be informed about the Taurus, so he called and left the man a brief message, including what Andrews had told him. He checked his car and dumped his gear inside. Though the air had a sharp chill, the sun beat down from a cloudless blue sky. A nice break in the weather.

If things remained calm, he'd grab dinner early. He was assigned the east side of the county, including the Borough of North East. Michael's Pizzeria sounded like a good bet for something hot and quick.

Would Lanie be home yet? Maybe when he stopped to eat, he'd give Nick a call and see when they had driven her back to her place. She should have planned to stay with them again tonight, but he hadn't said anything because she was going back to work tomorrow and he knew she'd balk at the idea. He'd tell her about the unknown car as soon as possible. Hated to do it, but she had to know. Besides, he really wanted to talk to her, and to see her.

Last night stuck in his mind. The way her lush, naked body had moved under his replayed at the damnedest times, the image vivid as hell. Now he had more to remember than just her green eyes. A *hell* of a lot more.

As the sun dipped low, he circled round off I-90 and took Route 89 into North East. He'd used his cell and called ahead for a honey mustard chicken pizza. Maybe he'd drive down to Freeport Beach and catch the sunset while he ate. Ice dunes along the shore had formed early this year due to the cold air and the wind driving the water. They were pretty to look at, downright gorgeous when the sky cleared and the sun reflected off the icy waves frozen in place.

Natures sculptures, often six feet high. Beautiful, but deadly. He'd helped pull a guy out years ago after he'd broken through the crust and fallen into the ice cold lake water below. One minute the guy had been climbing the dunes, waving to his buddies on shore -- and the next, he was gone. His buddies had tossed a rope one of them had in his trunk and pulled him out.

God, what a mess. He'd been half frozen and cut all to hell from the jagged ice. Not pretty. He'd lived, though, after spending some time recovering from severe hypothermia, a broken ankle, and gashes deep enough for stitches.

T.J. spied a slot right in front of Michael's, parked, and went inside. The tempting smell of the restaurant's famous homemade sauce filled the compact waiting area.

"Trooper T.J.," Michael called out from the back. "I'll have your pizza right out."

Seconds later, he came through the door from the kitchen carrying a flat, square box. "Good to see you." He rang up the sale and slid the box across the counter. "Are you eating in?"

"No." T.J. glanced out the window. Light bounced off the buildings across the street, and shadows deepened along South Lake Street. "Thought I'd run down to Freeport and catch the sunset. Who knows when the snow will start again? I could use a Lake Erie sunset fix."

"I hear ya." Mike smiled, wiping the counter by the register. "Today's the first day I haven't been bustin' my butt shoveling the sidewalk out front. We've been busy, though. Cold weather makes 'em crave pizza."

"Works for me." T.J. smiled and lifted his pizza. "Catch you later."

He returned to his patrol car, shot down Route 89, and crossed Route 5. The sun was low in the sky as he parked at Freeport Beach. Things remained calm, and the pizza hit the spot. A few other brave souls parked nearby to watch the sunset. They waved at him as they strolled past the deserted playground along the creek.

The dunes were the largest T.J. had ever seen. They towered above the shoreline, weaving along where water met land. Some were smooth and curved; others, ragged and rough. All were enticing death traps for anyone foolish enough to venture beyond the safety of land.

The rest of his shift passed without serious incident. He made a couple of traffic stops and dealt with one minor fender bender. If one car hadn't slid into the guard rail and had to be towed, the accident would have been non-reportable.

He yawned and headed back to the barracks, then decided he might as well do a quick drive past Lanie's place on the way. Detouring, he drove south to Sidehill Road and turned west. She'd been on his mind off and on all evening. Would she be glad to see him if he stopped in?

The Reed farm came into view up ahead. Jen's familiar Jeep sat at the end of the driveway, waiting to turn onto the road as he approached. He flashed his lights and pulled over.

Leaving her Jeep idling, Jen hopped out and jogged over to his car. He lowered the window, and she stooped down to eye level.

"Jen, I'm glad I caught you."

"What's up, T.J.?"

He relayed the incident about the car. She didn't know anyone nearby who drove a Taurus and agreed to ask her parents if they did.

"Kinda weird, isn't it?" she added. "Why would someone cruise up Hilltop in a snowstorm?"

"Crossed my mind, too," T.J. agreed. "Have you seen Lanie today?"

"Talked to her on the phone a while ago. She's been busy getting ready to go back to work tomorrow. House stuff, groceries, getting things in order to make it easy when she works every day. We didn't talk long. She seemed a little distracted, so I didn't push. Though she did mention she'd like to talk with you about something."

T.J. checked his cell phone. Maybe she'd left a message. He had a voicemail, but it wasn't from Lanie. Just a brief message from Sullivan acknowledging T.J.'s message and reminding him about their meeting first thing Monday morning. T.J. turned back to Jen. "We've got patrols checking on her whenever possible. It's the best we can do."

"I think I might head up there, maybe see if she'd like some company tonight." Jen straightened and scuffed one foot in the snow with the toe of her boot. "Does she know about the car from last night?"

"It's possible Sullivan called her. If she knows, she might welcome your company. Another vehicle in her driveway would be a deterrent."

Jen nodded agreement. "Then I'll just slip back inside and grab a change of clothes."

"You're a good friend, Jen." T.J. slid the car into gear. "Tell her you ran into me, and I said I'll be in touch tomorrow. I'm off duty in about twenty minutes, but I'm on first shift tomorrow. Otherwise I'd stop by tonight myself."

"I'll let her know." She smiled and stepped back.

He checked the road and then pulled away. A fast glance in his rearview mirror caught Jen getting into her Jeep and backing up the driveway to her parent's house. At least for tonight, Lanie wouldn't be alone, and from now on he'd make damn sure she remained safe until Jack LeFavor was out of commission.

*****

Lanie did her best to make up for leaving her little guy alone overnight. Sam pestered her, underfoot from the moment she'd walked in the door, following her around, meowing, and snaking between her legs, even though Jen had stopped in to feed and take care of him. Even left a note saying how she'd spent time playing with the young cat, tossing him his favorite catnip mouse. Didn't seem to count. He wanted nonstop attention *now*.

Once Lanie had put her things away and made a cup of tea, she'd settled by the fire and given Sam her undivided attention. He now lay sprawled across her lap dead asleep. She had the rest of the evening to herself, allowing her time to do some serious thinking.

She'd made a lot of mistakes in her life, most driven by her own hard-headedness. When Uncle Charley had stepped in after her mother died, he'd brought her stability, security, and a set of rules she'd fought tooth and nail. He'd threatened the freewheeling lifestyle she'd become accustomed to spending time alone with little or no supervision while her mother worked endless hours. Uncle Charley had done the best he could. Lanie hadn't been easy, but he'd made sure she'd gotten the necessities. She'd known he loved her, but back then his efforts to do the right thing just weren't enough for a self-centered teenager. She blamed her mother for not planning ahead and making sure Lanie's father would take care of her.

Lanie's mother's lack of preparedness had made Lanie an avid planner. Once she'd learned Uncle Charley, a stern man with a soft heart, really did care about her and wasn't just out to wreck her life, things had gradually changed. He'd taught her to work for things she wanted and to look out for herself. The reward, he had assured her, would be her independence and a future where her dreams became reality. He'd stood behind her, propped her up, and watched with pride the day she'd gripped her college diploma and sent her graduation cap sailing skyward with a wild whoop of joy.

Many birthdays and holidays had come and gone since then, but she'd never forgotten their last Christmas together. Charley had dug out a box of ornaments, ones passed down through family members long gone by the time Lanie came under his care, unpacked the delicate decorations, and together, they had trimmed a tiny tree. As they hung the shiny balls, he'd talked about his family. She'd learned of grandparents she'd never known, and the way her mother had been before life had smacked her down.

Not long after that memorable holiday, Charley had died, and Lanie had suddenly found herself alone. He must have known his days were numbered that Christmas. He was gone, but his words had stuck with her and spurred her on to follow her life's plan.

Serious involvement with T.J. McGraw wasn't part of her plan.

A flash of headlights through the window set her heart racing. Carrying Sam, she went to investigate her late night visitor and welcomed the sight of Jen's familiar Jeep.

Sam skittered off when she released him to open the door.

"Hi, neighbor," she greeted Jen, "What you got there?"

"We're having a sleep over." Jen locked her Jeep and slung a duffle over her shoulder. She grinned and slid right by Lanie into the cabin.

Lanie closed the door, and her cell phone chimed. She held up a finger and answered.

"Miss Delacor, its Corporal Sullivan. Do you happen to know anyone who owns a late model, dark colored Ford Taurus?" The corporal got right to the point, but his calm, steady voice didn't fool Lanie. This wasn't a social call.

She drew in a deep breath and took a moment to decipher his question. "No, Corporal. Off hand, I can't think of anyone who drives a Taurus. Why?"

Jen dropped her duffle and came to stand beside Lanie.

"Last night, a patrol checking your residence spotted a Taurus parked along Hilltop," Sullivan explained. "The car moved off when Trooper Andrews arrived, but the trooper got called away before he could follow up and identify the driver."

"I see." Lanie cleared her throat. "I, uh... wasn't home last night."

"When you returned, did you notice if anything had been disturbed or was out of place?"

"No, everything was as I'd left it."

"Good. If you notice a car matching that description, be sure and contact PSP right away."

"I'll do that, and thank you for calling."

She ended the call and stuffed the phone back into her pocket. "That was the corporal who's working the case. I take it you heard about last night?"

"Yes." Jen placed her hand on Lanie's arm. "I ran into T.J. a while ago. He asked me if I know anyone around here who has a Ford Taurus, like one seen up here last night. I don't," she added, before Lanie could ask. "So, here I am."

"Is it safe for you to be here?" Lanie asked, shifting the cushions on the fold out sofa "Let's get you settled. I have to work tomorrow, so it's got to be an early night."

"Not a problem." Moving close, Jen helped her fold out the bed. "They figure any indication you're not alone will give unwelcome visitors second thoughts. T.J. assured me patrols are driving by when time allows. He also seemed relieved when I offered to come and stay over."

"Really?" Lanie punched the cushions into place on the makeshift bed. "Humph. Too bad he couldn't drive by himself."

"He was on his way off duty. My guess is he'd planned a quick run by since he was headed in your direction. When I spoke with you earlier, you didn't seem too anxious to see him again anytime soon. Did you change your mind?"

"I think I've *lost* my mind." Lanie lifted the lid on the storage ottoman and tossed a pillow at her friend. "Here, help me make your bed."

She dumped sheets and a blanket on the fold down mattress. They worked in silence until they finished making the bed. Sam leapt up to check things out. He stretched and settled down on top of the covers, making himself at home. Jen scratched his head, causing him to purr and roll over, exposing his white belly.

"How's my buddy," she crooned. "Goin' to sleep with me tonight?"

Lanie smoother a corner of the quilt. "You know I slept with him."

"With Sam?"

"No, smart ass. With T.J."

"I kind of figured that. You want to talk?"

"Eventually. I talked my brains out with Cassi last night. She's not happy with me."

"For sleeping with her husband's cousin? That surprises me."

"No. I honestly think she's thrilled about the whole situation. She's not happy I'm dead set against anything serious, though. I told her I'll be happy with a nice, hot affair. Nothing more. She doesn't understand why."

"Uh huh." Jen plumped a pillow, stretched out, and pulled Sam against her. "When you're ready, I'd like to hear why myself."

Lanie glanced at the clock. No sense trying to sleep now. She poked the hot embers in the fireplace to life, grabbed another pillow, and joined Jen on the bed.

"It all started," she said, "when I foolishly agreed to have dinner with him."

Chapter Twenty

The clatter of keyboards, the insistent ring of multiple phones, and an underlying hum of conversation greeted T.J. the minute he entered the barracks. Atypical for a Monday morning at Troop E Headquarters. Several messages awaited him in his mailbox. He sifted through them, tossing the ones he'd already addressed, keeping ones that needed his attention.

He'd called Sullivan before leaving for work. As usual, Dan had sounded wide awake and on top of things. They'd briefly covered the incident from Saturday night. Sullivan had spoken with Andrews and instructed him to follow up and ask around to determine if someone living near Lanie owned a dark colored Ford Taurus.

Based on what Jen had told him the night before, T.J. doubted they'd find anything.

Sullivan had arranged to meet him and Raife Samuels from OIU around eight a.m. in the barracks this morning. He'd already contacted T.J.'s supervisor, Sergeant Evans, with the request. The sergeant had agreed to have other patrols cover T.J.'s assigned area until after the meeting. That way he wouldn't get tied up with an incident. Evans was decent in that respect. He not only worked with his own department, but also granted other law enforcement agencies the courtesy of cooperation. In the meantime, T.J. would catch up on paperwork.

When the morning staff meeting broke up and first shift patrols headed out, T.J. had the conference room to himself. He went for coffee and returned, settling at one of the long work tables to tackle backlogged reports until the meeting with Sullivan.

Sergeant Evans opened the door and leaned in. "Got time to fill me in on this case?"

"You bet, sir. Come on in." T.J. slid his paperwork back into a file. "There's fresh coffee out on the desk if you're interested."

Evans grimaced and shook his head. "Gotta cut back on caffeine. I'll just grab a bottle of water. Better for me in the long run."

T.J. dug through his files and located everything he'd been working on in regard to the case while his boss was gone. On top lay the damage report for Lanie's car.

"I see her car's out back in the garage," Evans said.

T.J. nodded. "They brought it up from Edinboro as soon as they had a flatbed available. With this weather, it took a bit longer than usual."

"How about her personal belongings?"

"I retrieved her handbag the night of the accident. There were a couple of sealed boxes in the back. I checked over the weekend, and they've been itemized and secured until she can pick them up."

"How's she doing?"

"She's back to work today," T.J. offered.

The sergeant's question seemed innocent enough. T.J. figured he'd managed to keep his personal interest in Lanie separate from the case. He wondered if the sergeant agreed.

Mark held his gaze a long moment, then said, "We're doing our best to look out for her. I've instructed every patrol in that section to try and swing by during their shift."

"Good to know," T.J. responded. "If the guy Andrews spotted Saturday night was up to no good, I figure he got the hell out when a marked car showed up. Sullivan didn't say much when we spoke this morning, but I suspect Raife Samuels isn't driving over from Ohio for a social visit. He's gotta have something new."

"I agree." Mark glanced at the clock. "They should be here soon. I'll let you get back to your paperwork." He pushed out of his chair. "If I'm not tied up, I'll sit in on the meeting."

At 8:03, Dan Sullivan and Raife Samuels burst through the door. Sullivan's close cropped hair and clean shaven face contrasted sharply with Raife's shaggy, jet black hair and shadowed cheeks. His disreputable leather jacket was the exact opposite of the corporal's dark suit. They both carried steaming cups of coffee and simultaneously dumped their files and folders onto the table. Raife had his in a ratty leather binder; Dan's were contained in a neat stack of manila folders.

"Mornin', gentlemen." T.J. tipped back his chair on two legs and lifted his hand to shake Raife's. "How's life treating Ohio's top notch investigator?"

Raife slipped off his jacket and sat. He took a careful sip of coffee and lifted one shoulder in a careless shrug. "Eh, some days you eat the bear, some days the bear eats you."

"Ain't that the friggin' truth." Dan flipped open his first folder and glanced at T.J. "I've spoken with Les Andrews and updated Raife about the car incident, which, by the way, may turn out to be nothing. We'll know more later today. As I've mentioned, Andrews is checking with residents who live on Sidehill and south of I-90 where Hilltop Drive turns into Ridge Road."

"There aren't many houses once you cross the thruway," T.J. pointed out. "I only know of one other place on Hilltop. Shouldn't take Les long to cover the area."

"Don't be so sure, or too quick to discount the Taurus." Raife tapped a rapid beat the table with a stubby pencil. "I'm pretty certain both vehicles registered to LeFavor are tucked away beneath his condo east of Cleveland."

"Interesting." Sullivan scowled into his coffee. "Have you seen either of the vehicles, or the man himself?"

Raife shook his head. "Jack LeFavor's MIA. Has been since right after you found those two stiffs at the rest stop. Braten Place, the condo I mentioned, is private with a capital P. The complex is gated, and only tenants and their invited guests are welcome. They're not about to let a guy who looks like me anywhere near their precious tenants, and I don't want to go flashing any ID around.

"Yet," he added. "After receiving the release about an Escalade with front-end damage, the state guys have been keeping a close eye on Braten Place. I've given them a head's up about a possible connection to LeFavor. Last week, a late night patrol got lucky. He observed LeFavor's black Escalade entering the complex."

"Did they see any damage?" T.J. asked.

"They weren't close enough. Late at night, black vehicle." Raife shook his head and added, "Rumor has it old Jack stores his Benz there during the winter, too. Since that night, there's been no sign of either vehicle."

"So the man and his usual modes of transportation have disappeared?"

"That's right, T.J." He tossed down the pencil and picked up his coffee. "I'm sure Jack would frown on driving a lowly Ford, but don't let that fool ya." Raife slid down in his chair. "The guy's slick as shit, and he's not above doing what's necessary to accomplish his dirty work."

"Crap." Corporal Sullivan muttered. He scrubbed both hands over his face. "Any more good news, Samuels?"

Raife laughed. "Oh, it gets better. We're positive the latest upsurge of cocaine in the area is tied to LeFavor's network. He calls the shots, and his underlings jump through the hoops. Unless, like the two unfortunate guys at your rest stop, they screw something up and pay the price with their lives."

T.J. flipped through a couple of pages. "Cocaine residue was found in the victim's car." He read on, "Trace amounts in the vehicle, and on the clothing of one victim."

"Pulls it all together." Sullivan studied his copy of the same report. "Makes a neat little circle, except we still don't know why they ended up so far from their normal drop sites."

"Here's our take," Raife spoke up. "We've got a fairly reliable snitch in Ohio who reported something went wrong with a big exchange. Drugs for cold, hard cash. The drug drop got screwed up when two guys took off with the money *and* a hefty bundle of cocaine."

"I'm assuming the two met their maker off I-79 in Pennsylvania that night, but why LeFavor?" T.J. cut in, puzzled by the story oo far. "Why, when he's so damned anal about getting his hands dirty, would he take it upon himself to drive here from Ohio and take out two screw-ups? Why not let someone else do the dirty work?"

"Good point," Raife shot back. "Except Jack LeFavor's a fuckin' control freak. He'd take it upon himself to handle things. The storm that night provided what he'd consider perfect cover. Hell, he's driving this top of the line SUV, more ego fuel, when he meets these guys at the rest stop. I'm guessing, but I'd say one of them contacted Jack and wanted to meet. He would've chosen the location, and he'd consider the rotten weather to be in his favor."

"He's one smart son-of-a bitch." T.J. mimicked Raife and tapped his pen on the table. He shot Sullivan and Raife a sly grin. "He didn't count on a multi-car pileup screwing up his plan though, did he?"

"Can't trust Mother Nature." Raife chuckled, then added, "Ended up taking out both guys. He's done it before. Somebody screws up -- he eliminates 'em. Now he's got the cash *and* the drugs, and all that's left is for him to hightail it back to Ohio, sort out the mess, and move on."

"Then Lanie pulled in off the thruway," T.J. said, silently cursing the implication he'd just visualized. "And Jack's perfect plan just got complicated."

"A witness," Raife agreed. "Just what he *didn't* need."

"And the rest," Sullivan concluded, "we know. When Lanie left, he followed her and forced her off the road at the Edinboro exit. He was about to finish what he started when all hell broke loose. He knew that unless he got the fuck out of there, he'd end up on the evening news. Not the kind of recognition Jack craves."

T.J. pushed his cold coffee aside. Now what? Drive bys weren't going to stop LeFavor. Sooner or later, Lanie's status as a witness would become public knowledge, putting the man's back to the wall. He'd have to stop her from talking.

Shoving back from the table, T.J. grabbed a recent picture of LeFavor from his file. He needed to stretch. To move and work off the nervous energy pumping through him. He looked up from the picture when someone tapped on the door and Sergeant Evans entered.

"Sorry I'm late," he said. "I'd planned to be here on time, but something came up."

He closed the door and cast an uneasy look at T.J. as he took a seat at the table and offered, "If there's anything I can do in regard to your investigation, Dan, I'll be glad to help. McGraw, quit pacing and plant your ass. We'll work things out, one way or another."

They put their heads together, updating Sergeant Evans and deciding on a course of action. Once they heard from Trooper Andrews, they'd know whether or not the owner of the Taurus had a legitimate reason to be on Hilltop Saturday night.

Based on those findings, Sergeant Evans agreed to alert all patrol units to watch for a dark Ford Taurus anywhere in the surrounding area. He'd advise his men to conduct a routine stop, with caution, if they spotted one. Troopers would have LeFavor's picture, but headquarters would not release an official BOLO. They walked a fine line between tipping off the guy or getting lucky and catching him. Enough evidence existed to at least bring him in for questioning.

Raife promised to keep in touch, and then headed back to Ohio. Sullivan went to see if Andrews was having any luck.

T.J. glanced at the time. "I'm heading out now, Sarge. I'll let Elaine Delacor know she can pick up her belongings whenever she wants."

Mark paused outside his office door. "T.J., can you keep this case separate from your personal life?"

"I've basically done all I can on the case, besides following up on what we discussed. Looking for the Taurus and keeping an eye out for LeFavor." He'd been expecting the question, but he sure as hell didn't know the answer. He shifted his files and stepped aside for two other troopers to pass. "You're right about my personal life, though. I may be involved with our witness."

"*May* be?"

"Sarge--" T.J. searched for the right words. How the hell was he supposed to answer his boss when he didn't know himself? He took a deep breath. "When I'm on duty, my job takes priority. She's important to me, though, so I'm going to do whatever's necessary on a personal level to keep her safe."

Evans nodded. "Fair enough. Your part in the investigation is mostly to just follow up, at this point, anyway. So I don't have a problem with that. If you were working in crime, I'd have to pull you. Corporal Sullivan needs all the help he can get right now. I imagine having someone, shall we say, working undercover, will be an asset."

Evans walked into his office and closed the door.

Huh. T.J. stood there a full minute staring at the closed door. The guy had some radar. Guess that's what made him a damn good supervisor.

T.J. hit the road. He'd already formulated a plan for the immediate future. He got off at two p.m., leaving him plenty of time to go home and get in some play time with Hershey. Then he'd sweet talk his mom into acting as a full time puppy sitter for the next few days. Wouldn't take much. She had a soft spot for the dog, and for her son.

To be fair, he'd have to tell her about the change of status with Lanie. Unless blabbermouth Nick had already beaten him to it. Regardless, his mother wouldn't be surprised. She had a sixth sense when it came to those she loved.

Fortunately, he was high on the list, but he hoped she'd understand when he told her he planned to spend his nights at one and a half Hilltop for the foreseeable future.

*****

Sweat dampened Lanie's tank top and her muscles screamed, but God it felt good to push her physical limits. She'd come in early to lap the track and spend time getting reacquainted with free weights. After hitting the shower, she'd check up front and see what was on the agenda this morning. Her primary function was to act as a personal trainer and an advisor. New members of Erie-sistable Fitness Center were entitled to a single one-on-one evaluation free with their membership. After that, they could set up a schedule for follow-ups or regular sessions.

She spotted Kitty and waved on the way to the employees' private locker room. Kathleen Atkins was a fair woman, and Lanie liked working with her. As manager, she ran a tight organization, and they'd hit it off right away.

Lanie missed working for Cassi, though. She'd managed Fox Chapel fitness for her friend and been forced to look elsewhere for work after the fire had destroyed Cassi's business. Cassi had been the one to prod Lanie into searching for a new job in Erie.

Kitty, part owner and manager at the center, had offered Lanie a position right away. The starting salary could have been better, but after some research, Lanie discovered it was average for the area. She'd been careful while working for Cassi, and had been surprised when Uncle Charley had left her a nice little nest egg. For the time being, money wasn't an issue.

Kitty had increased her salary after a few months, and more than once had mentioned she needed an assistant manager. She'd also hinted that Lanie stood a good chance when it came time for her to select someone.

"Hi, welcome back!" Kitty shouted over the pounding water.

Lanie shouted back, "Thanks! It's good to be moving again. I avoided the scales this morning. Too much down time and comfort food."

Kitty's laughter echoed through the locker room. "I saw you on the track earlier. I don't think you have to worry."

Lanie shut off the water and grabbed her two towels. She twined one around her body and used another to squeeze moisture from her hair. Kitty sat propped against the wall at the end of the bench between the lockers. She held a clipboard and flipped through several attached pages. She had her sleek dark hair pulled back in a neat ponytail, and a frown creased her brow.

"Problem?" Lanie pumped a dab of styling foam out and skimmed it through her hair.

Kitty continued to scowl at the list on her board. "I'm going to push for an assistant at our next board meeting. I'm part owner, and that should count for something," she muttered. Lifting her gaze, she broke into a smile.

Lanie returned the smile and sat to smooth on body lotion. "What's on tap for today?"

"I shouldn't complain, but we've got a slew of new members, all clamoring for attention. Everybody wants to start sculpting that perfect body as soon as they sign the agreement."

"I'm up to helping a few new members today." Lanie slathered on face cream and then pulled out her sports bra and briefs. "Let me finish dressing and dry my hair. I'll come to your office, and we can work up a schedule."

"Thanks, Elaine. You always come through for me." She clipped her pen to the board. "How are things? I haven't seen much on the news about your accident."

How much should she tell Kitty? The corporal had suggested she keep things low key until they sorted out details. She hadn't mention how she'd been pushed off the road, but everyone knew her car was out of commission. Several girls she worked with, as well as Kitty, were clearly envious of her Miata.

She'd keep it simple. "Not much to tell. I still don't know if my cars repairable since the state police have it under wraps."

"The state police?" Kitty's eyes widened. "They don't blame you for all those cars smacking into one another, do they?"

Lanie laughed. "No, they don't." She realized her slip, but it was too late now. "Ah, one of the cars that hit me is causing problems." She grabbed her dryer. "Enough about me. Go organize that list," she said, nodding at the clipboard. "I'll be there in a couple of minutes."

The morning flew past. New members were a challenge, and Kitty hadn't been kidding when she'd said they had a slew of them. Lanie glanced over their information sheets. Most were in their mid-to-late thirties. Most were women. Several men worked at the center, but held other jobs as well, so they usually scheduled their training sessions in the evenings.

Two men were on the list for assessments. The older of the two would be in tomorrow. He'd requested one of the guys on the evening shift. The second man had conveniently left his age off the form. Lanie took note of the weight and height he'd put down.

Kitty looked over her shoulder. "That one called over the weekend. One of the girls took most of his info over the phone. Claims he's new to the area." Kitty tapped the second man's form. "He asked for you."

"How does he know me, or that I work here?" A little skitter of nerves made Lanie take a closer look at the man's information.

"He's moving here from near Pittsburgh." Kitty bent closer and searched the form. "Here it is. Just the town, no street address. Are you familiar with Oakmont, Pennsylvania?"

"Yeah. It's a little north and across the Allegheny River from Fox Chapel."

"Well, maybe he knows you from there."

Lanie studied the name. "Jonathon Atherton," she murmured, then shook her head. "Doesn't ring a bell. But there were a lot of members at Fox Chapel. I'll ask Cassi. Maybe when I see him, I'll recognize him. Funny he left off his age, though. Did he make an appointment?"

"No, just gave the information and said he'd be in touch when he got to town."

Lanie tucked it under the other forms. "We'll just have to wait, then."

"Don't forget next week's a short one," Kitty said.

"Next week?"

"Thanksgiving?"

"Oh, my God. I'd forgotten all about it." Lanie covered her face with both hands. How could she have forgotten? Last year, she'd gone to Nick and Cassi's to help them celebrate their first big holiday as a married couple. Tom and Mary McGraw, as well as Rich and Ada McConnell, had been there. The day had been picture perfect, with great food, great friends, and a touch of snow to kick off the holiday season.

She glanced out the window. Holidays were mixed blessings in her life. What would this one hold? Last year, T.J. had worked and come to Nick and Cassi's late. Her stomach did a little dip, remembering the tall, leggy blond he'd brought along that evening. Lanie had been on her way out the door when they had arrived. The woman's name escaped her now, but not the way she'd clung to T.J. That image rushed back like a bad dream, along with the way everyone had greeted them when they'd walked through the door. All so hearth and home, so perfect.

"Woo-hoo." Kitty waved her hand in front of Lanie's face.

Lanie blinked. "Sorry. Fantasy trip."

"You look beat," Kitty said. "Go home and get some rest."

A short time later, Lanie slipped on her coat and trudged to her rental car. Snow was coming down again, a fine mist leaving a light coating on the ground. Her drive home would take about twenty-five minutes. Street lights winked on as she crossed town. Presque Isle Bay was white, probably not frozen, but covered by a skim of ice that held fresh snow.

A steady stream of traffic moved along, building as shifts changed and stores closed.

She flicked on the heater, relieved when heat poured forth in a steady stream. She'd cut through Lawrence Park and work her way through Harborcreek to Sidehill, then home. Warmed over soup and crusty bread would do for dinner. Then she'd curl up with Sam Cat and just wallow in front of the fireplace.

Her own little hearth. Her own little home.

The snow increased as she crested the ridge, and she caught glimpses of the sturdy little cabin between the trees. She parked and gathered her things. Sam Cat's sleek outline in the window caught her attention. At least someone missed her. Although he'd more than likely been watching the rabbits that had scurried away when she'd driven up.

He greeted her at the door.

"How ya doin', Sammy?" she crooned. He trotted ahead of her into the tiny laundry room off the kitchen, where she dumped her gear. Snapping on two small lamps as she went, she returned to the combination kitchen-living area. A low counter separated the two areas, and light glowing through colorful lampshades warmed the room.

A floor to ceiling stone fireplace took up most of the wall opposite the kitchen. She paused and lifted a recent picture of Sam from the heavy beam that protruded from the stone to serve as a mantel. In the shot, his bewhiskered face peered around the tulip tree as he gazed up quizzically at the tree face.

She replaced the framed print, knelt, and lit the kindling she'd prepared that morning. When it whooshed to life, she waited a few seconds, then nestled a couple of small logs on top of the crackling flames. Brushing wood chips from her legs, she rose and went to heat the leftover soup for her dinner. Then she changed into soft lounging sweats and pulled on a pair of thick, warm socks.

Upon returning to the kitchen, she was about to open some wine when headlights appeared through the gathering dusk and falling snow. She recognized the sleek little SUV that pulled into her driveway as belonging to T.J. A heated rush of annoyance, a weak-kneed surge of relief, and a sharp, quick quiver in her belly made her heart pound.

He looked up in surprise when she threw open the door.

"Hi. I brought dinner." His crooked grin disarmed her.

She stepped back and waved him in.

"Thanks," he said, and stepped into the cabin. Juggling a couple of bags, he slipped out of his low cut boots and dumped a ratty looking duffle by the door. He crossed the room and set the bags on the counter. "Hope you like rigatoni with meatballs."

She inhaled the spicy aroma. "Smells wonderful."

He unwrapped the food and opened several take-out boxes while she turned off the heat under the soup and set it aside.

"Get some plates, will ya?" He shot her another grin. "I'll unload our gourmet meal."

"I was about to open some wine."

"Perfect." He glanced across the room. The fire she'd built crackled, shooting sparks up the chimney. "How about we eat by the fire?"

"Perfect," she responded, making him laugh, and went to get the wine. This seemed so... normal. He moved about her kitchen in sock clad feet and worn jeans. She sneaked glances at him and remembered the night they'd spent together. Her cheeks flushed hot.

Yet he hadn't so much as kissed her since he'd walked in the door, and that kind of pissed her off. She glanced up when he dropped a couple napkins and bent to pick them up. His denim jeans stretched and clung to his taut backside.

He straightened and swung around.

"Need any help?" he asked, nodding at the wine bottle she clutched in her hand. He grinned again.

"Uh, no." She pulled open a drawer and fumbled for a corkscrew. He'd caught her looking when he'd bent over, and he damn well knew what she'd been gawking at.

Dinner was unbelievable. She'd had pizza from Michael's Pizzeria before, but had no idea his Italian dinners were so delicious. The warmth from the wine and the fire slid over, around, and through her. She sank into the sofa's deep cushions and propped her feet on an oversized ottoman. He refilled her glass. Once he was done, she lifted it and gazed through the rich color at the fire. The glass distorted the blaze. Dancing tongues of flame appeared to rise from the rich colored wine, creating a strange effect.

She took a careful sip. "What are you doing, T.J.?"

Beside her, he swirled his wine and sipped from his glass. "I'm enjoying a glass of wine with a gorgeous woman."

He reached out and took her hand. She glanced down at his their joined hands.

"Maybe I need to rephrase that. *Why* are you here?"

"Same goes," he replied. Keeping a grip on her hand, he relaxed into the soft cushions and tilted his head to meet her solemn gaze. "We can't ignore Saturday night, Lanie, and pretend it didn't happen. I imagine you're a little pissed because I didn't call or contact you until now."

He slid his hand up her arm, then back down to twine their fingers. "I apologize. A gentleman shouldn't enjoy a woman and then leave her hanging."

"So, I repeat, why are you here? Is it to pick up where we left off, or to apologize? Because," she continued, "I'm not sure I want to continue, even though I *enjoyed* you just as thoroughly, and I'm not so insecure as to need an apology if we stop after one night."

A delightful shiver ran through her when he leaned in and touched his lips to hers. "I want to get this right," he said, "because I need to say several things. Come here."

He wrapped his arm around her and pulled her against his side.

She sank into his warmth and rested her head on his shoulder. He'd showered recently, and the underlying scent of his soap surrounded her. Not flowery, not spicy, but something enticing like a flickering sandalwood candle coating the air with its warm fragrance.

"Six months ago, if someone had told me I'd be involved with you on such a personal level, I'd have laughed my ass off." His voice rumbled in her ear as he talked. "But here we are. I don't know where we're heading. All I know is that when I'm around you, I have to touch you. Even when you irritate me, I want to touch you."

"I admit I like for you to touch me." She rubbed her cheek against his soft sweater, then eased back and gave him a wicked grin. "I can ratchet up the irritation."

"How am I going to finish talking when you say things like that?"

"It's the wine, T.J. The wine, the fire, and a handsome man. I'm a healthy, normal woman. We're on the brink of an affair, and we have to decide if we're going to continue it or end it."

"There are many kinds of affairs. I can't say I've never been involved with anyone else."

An image of the tall blonde clinging to his arm last Thanksgiving flashed through Lanie's mind, and the picture hurt more than she ever would have imagined.

She pushed the memory aside. "You said there are things you want to say. Do any of them have to do with the ongoing investigation?"

"Yes, and although they're important, I first want to talk about us." He kissed her again. "I'm staying here tonight. It's up to you whether I sleep on the sofa, or in your bed. The reason I'm here is twofold. First, I can't get you out of my mind. I've discovered there's more to you than I ever imagined. More than soft skin and lush curves."

He emphasized his words with another kiss. This time he lingered, his lips moving over hers, teasing, promising. "Whenever I think about you, about making love to you, I know I want to do it again. This time, slower. You stir my blood, and I want to stir yours in return."

"Consider me well stirred." She sighed when he kissed her yet again.

He pulled back. "As for the case. I met with Corporal Sullivan and Raife Samuels this morning."

"Samuels?"

"He's from the Ohio Investigative Unit. The one who linked Jack LeFavor and the murder victims."

"LeFavor. He's the one who's after me." She grasped T.J.'s hand more tightly.

"That's something we don't know for sure," he emphasized. "Sullivan said he informed you about the car from Saturday night."

"He did. A Ford Taurus at the end of my driveway." She smiled up at him. "I looked up a Taurus on Google. I know what they look like."

"Good girl." He squeezed her hand and chuckled.

He finished updating her about the case. Making her aware with gentle touches and strokes to her arms, her hands, and the sensitive spot on her neck.

"I have to work shifts," he emphasized. "That means you'll be here alone during some large gaps of time. I'd like to contact Jen, see if she can stay with you when I'm working."

"You asked her to come here last night night, didn't you?"

"I told her the situation. Didn't have to ask. She's a good friend."

Tears stung her eyes. Why did she have such a hard time accepting help from friends?

She cleared her throat. "I don't want to put anyone out. I also don't want to take any chances. My nightmares about those two men haven't gone away. I suspect they won't until the man responsible for their deaths is caught."

She turned to face him, looked into his blue-gray eyes, and couldn't resist smoothing his cowlick. "We'll work things out. I plan to put in some long hours at work, too, so I can catch up. Seems I'm the personal trainer of the hour recently. Some guy from Pittsburgh who's moving to the area asked for me specifically."

"Really?" T.J. frowned. "How did he know about you?"

"He comes from the Fox Chapel area. Must have met me when I worked at Cassi's place."

"Get me his name and address. I'll check him out."

"He hasn't moved to Erie yet. I'll let you know when he does and get you what you need. Anyhow," she continued, "I'm surrounded by people all day at work. Business has picked up."

He seemed satisfied. "We'll talk to Jen and coordinate our schedules. I don't think LeFavor will try anything if someone else is here. Even another vehicle in your driveway will deter a man like him. He's cautious. He's also sneaky, and is an opportunist. Don't give him a chance to get you alone."

"What about my car?"

"Thanks for reminding me. I almost forgot. Your car is at headquarters. Once the crime unit has documented the damage, they'll release it to your insurance company. The good news is that one of the guys who works with Sullivan looked it over. He's a bit of a mechanic, and in his opinion, it's fixable. Probably needs a new trunk lid. The wrap around bumper sits low, and before the Escalade hit you, it was much higher."

She couldn't stop her spreading smile. "I thought I'd never drive my Miata again."

"One more thing. You had some boxes in the vehicle. They're locked up nice and safe. They weren't pertinent to our investigation, so you can pick them up any time. Let me know when you can stop by the barracks, and I'll make sure someone's there to release them to you."

She'd forgotten all about them. They mostly contained odds and ends she'd stored. Things she'd packed up before heading off to college when she lived with Uncle Charley. She'd have to go through them, probably throw a lot of stuff away.

T.J. eased away and got up. He poked the fire, tossed on another log, and gathered their dishes.

Lanie rinsed their wine glasses and helped load the dishwasher. As she stood at the sink and peered out the window, T.J. came behind her and wrapped his arms around her.

She didn't question whether he was staying over; that was a given. He'd put the ball in her court as to where he would sleep, however, so that decision was hers. Was that the act of a clever man or a gentleman? She suspected a little of both.

Her decision made, she turned in his arms. His unreadable expression didn't fool her. The fire in his eyes, in sharp contrast with his rigid jaw, revealed his barely leashed desire. He wanted her. And she wanted him. No games, no promises. Just *now*.

"Let's go to bed," she whispered, wrapping her arms around him more tightly when his eyes went deep and dark. "In *my* bed."

*****

Needs T.J. had locked down with ruthless will burst free upon hearing her words. She molded her body to his, and he kissed her. Deep

123

and hard, then tender and soft. He wanted to sample her this time, to taste her like fine wine. Savor her.

His blood fired hot. His body craved her. And to his delight, she matched him kiss for kiss, stroke for stroke. The lure of her scent and the fire in her provocative emerald eyes took him to the edge of pure lust.

"Come on," she coaxed, her throaty voice filled with forbidden promises. "I want you to touch me. I want to touch you."

She took his hand and led him down the darkened hallway. Her bedroom was cool and dark, and it smelled of her. For a moment, she left him alone by the door. Then a soft click, followed by a flicker of light, cast her captivating smile in the glow of candlelight.

He moved to her side. Her eagerness and unabashed need excited him. She took his face between her cool hands and pressed her lips to his. She tasted wild and bewitching, willing and tame. A jumbled, delightful contrast that made him delirious with need.

"Lanie," he murmured. "Let me."

He caught the hem of her sweatshirt, and she helped him peel it off over her head. Her breath caught when he pulled it free and tossed it aside. He covered her breasts with both hands, molding the lushness, making her gasp. She was beautiful. Her skin was like silk; her body, toned and firm. He hooked his thumbs beneath the band of her sweats and slid them down.

"My turn," she said softly, her tone a teasing, seductive whisper. He breathed in the heated scent of her and hungrily ran his hands over her sleek shoulders, her smooth back. Touching, sliding beneath her lacy undergarments to arouse her, taking greedy pleasure when she writhed beneath his searching fingers.

She took hold of his sweater, rose on tiptoe, and struggled to pull it off. He yanked it free, and followed it with his tee-shirt.

At last, they tumbled onto her bed. Naked skin to naked skin. Heated bodies sliding together, seeking release, yet pausing to enjoy. He swept his hand over the soft curve of her hip and explored her delicate skin, moist with desire.

Between them, they shared quiet murmurs, whispered needs, and sudden gasps. Unable to wait any longer, he prepared himself and slid inside her. She sighed in pleasure, wrapped her arms and legs around him, and drew him in deeper.

In the wavering candlelight, her mysterious green eyes, so soft and sensuous, held him in their enigmatic spell. His mind emptied. The thunder of his heartbeat erased all thought except the thrill of her body rising to meet his measured strokes.

He sought to draw out the pleasure for her, and for him. This was no headlong race to the finish; only the sensuous glide and plunge of their bodies moving together.

Her breathing quickened, and her body bowed beneath him. The rush of release sent him pounding against her, and she cried out.

Together they fell, his long, low moan blending with her sobbing release.

*****

T.J.'s eyes flew open when a sudden gust of wind rattled the window in Lanie's bedroom. He must have dozed off. Lanie lay snuggled against him; one arm draped across his chest, and one leg hooked over him. Her lush curves were pressed against his body.

Very slowly he turned and met her sleepy gaze. "Hi."

"Hi, back."

Welcoming the sweet feel of her naked body, he drew a quilt over them.

"Are you cold?" she teased, stroking her hand over his chest.

He choked out a laugh and snaked his hand up to close over her breast. "I'm not, but let me cover you and keep you warm."

"Good idea," she purred, her hand leaving his chest and sliding lower. She closed her soft fingers around him. "Let me know when you're warmed up."

He toyed with her, and the tip of her breast hardened and thrust against the palm of his hand. His body responded to the glide of her teasing strokes. He gazed into her eyes until she sensed his arousal.

Close to losing control, T.J. could wait no longer. This time wouldn't be slow and easy. He slid into her and she clamped around him, crying out her pleasure. A few quick thrusts, and his world exploded.

Afterwards, still wrapped in Lanie's silken embrace, he fell into dreamless sleep, only to be jolted awake hours later by the Beach Boys' song, *California Dreaming*. Well, it was a winter's day, but Lanie wasn't beside him in bed.

The rush of water from the shower across the hall competed with the music.

He fumbled with the volume and turned down the band's pitiful lament of being stuck in New York City, then swung out of bed.

It took him a few seconds to locate his briefs and pull them on. He found his jeans folded on a chair, and his Bersa on the bedside stand. He vaguely remembered removing it from the holster attached to his belt and placing it there right before he'd tumbled into bed with Lanie.

The bathroom door opened, and a cloud of steam poured out. Wrapped in a huge towel, Lanie dashed into the bedroom and yanked open one of her dresser drawers.

"Morning," she said. Clutching clean undergarments, she shot him an engaging smile. "Did you sleep well?" Her lilting voice assured him she certainly had.

"Oh, yeah," he answered, then seized the edge of her towel and ripped it off.

She grabbed for it. "Give me that," she yelped. "It's freezing and..."

Her voice dwindled and her eyes widened right before he closed his mouth over hers.

Her struggles ceased, and she melted against him. When the kiss ended, she hung limp in his arms.

"I have to get ready for work." Her breathless protest packed little punch.

He let his hands roam over her back, then settled them on her smooth rear. He gave her a gentle squeeze. "Just my way of saying good morning."

"Nice tradition," she remarked. She put her arms around him, slipped them into his shorts, and returned the squeeze. With one final pat, she pushed him away, stooped down, and retrieved her towel.

Cursing the fact that he had to go to work, too, he gathered his clothes and stepped into the bathroom, leaving her to finish drying herself off and dressing.

When he emerged, she sat on the bed fully clothed, pulling on socks.

"I didn't see you put that there last night," she said, indicating his Bersa with a tilt of her head. "It's not the same kind Nick carries."

"No, Nick's off duty weapon is a Walther. Mine's a Bersa 380."

"So this isn't the one you use on duty?"

"No, we carry Glock .45 caliber semi-automatics."

"Go ahead," T.J. urged. "You can hold it."

She wasn't shy about touching the weapon. He chuckled. Apparently, she wasn't shy about touching a lot of things.

He tamped down his lascivious thoughts and sat beside her on the bed.

"It's light." She turned the weapon over and hefted it gently. "I'm sure it does the job. I've seen the one you carry on duty. It's bigger and more impressive."

"This one's called the Bersa Thunder." T.J. leaned in. "It's designed for accuracy and ready for immediate action. It's light, weighs just over a pound, and holds seven rounds."

"Nice." Her brow furrowed, and she handed him the gun. "What did LeFavor use to kill those men?"

"A snub-nosed .38." He hated to see her relaxed, teasing mood disappear. That had been an abrupt change from curiosity to apprehension. "A garden variety gun that works well at close range. An easy one to obtain and dispose of."

He stood and slipped the Bersa into the clip-on holster at his waist. Taking both of Lanie's hands, he pulled her up so she faced him. "I'm not going to let him get to you."

"I know you'll try, and that's all I'll ask of you." Her eyes, no longer teasing and sparkling with humor or liquid and lazy with desire, turned serious. He didn't like the shadow of fear tainting those beautiful emerald green pools. Nick had always claimed that Cassi's eyes broadcast her emotions; T.J. believed Lanie's were a window to her soul.

She pulled her hands away. "I need to dry my hair. I made coffee, and I have a selection of cereals in the cupboard to the left of the sink. Help yourself. I'll only be a few minutes."

T.J. found the cereal and topped it with fresh blueberries from a bowl on the counter. When he heard her approaching, he poured another cup of coffee and handed it to her when she entered the room.

"Thanks. I see you found the berries."

"They're good." He slid his empty bowl aside and refilled his coffee. He'd grab a shower and shave after she left, but he had a few things to say first. He sat across from her. "I'll talk while you eat."

"Okay." She scooped cereal and fruit into her mouth. She chewed, swallowed, and took a sip of coffee. "Are you working today?"

"Yes." He glanced at the clock. "But not for over an hour. If you don't mind, I'll make use of your shower after you leave."

"That's fine." She scooped up another spoonful. "What do you want to talk about?"

"The first time we made love," he said.

Her eyes grew wary, and she furrowed her brow.

He reached across to caress her hand. "*After* the first time we made love, you asked what you were doing with a man like me. Then last night, *before* we made love, you asked me what I was doing here."

"Guess I ask a lot of questions about us." She looked down and touched his hand.

When she lifted her eyes, he continued. "I believe you're questioning where we're heading. To be honest, I can't answer that right now."

"T.J., I don't want any promises from you."

"Here's how I see things." He took a minute to gather his thoughts in silence. "I'm not sure I understand what you mean by 'a man like you'. Frankly, I don't think you know what kind of man I am, at least not on a personal level. I'm learning more about you each time I see you. Sooner or later, you'll decide if you want to learn more about me. Or not. It's your decision. As far as what I'm doing here, my straight forward, honest answer is that I want to make sure you're safe. Not because of my job, although that's a given in the whole mix, but because I *want* to be here. I won't let anything happen to you. That's a promise I intend to keep."

T.J. waited. He had nothing more to say. Only the soft jingling bell on Sam Cat's mouse toy as he played beneath the table broke the prolonged silence. Did Lanie realize how tight her hold on his hand had become? Or that the look in her eyes had changed?

Maybe they would have a chance after all, when all this mess with LeFavor ended.

Chapter Twenty-One

Jack figured the small green compact parked at Elaine Delacor's cabin must be a rental. The Miata was either totaled or in for repairs. A couple of phone calls had helped him nail down the health club where she worked. She'd gone upscale. No surprise there. Fox Chapel Fitness had been a classy joint, and he knew Elaine had once worked there thanks to her chatty old neighbor lady. Erie had a couple of clubs, and he'd gotten lucky on the second call. He needed Elaine's work schedule, needed to pin down details. This living like a bum and slinking around town was a pain in the ass.

He'd checked out of the motel near the Ohio line and moved closer to Erie. The new place was off the beaten path, and according to the desk clerk, was a popular place for fishermen. He had warned Jack their guests came and went at odd hours, and that suited him just fine. He doubted they paid much attention to their transient neighbors.

He swung into his new digs, parked, and let himself into the cramped, run of the mill motel room. Before he even took off his coat, he checked the phone messages at his condo. No request from cops or anyone else for a face to face.

That pleased him, and more than likely meant they didn't have shit on him. He smirked. He knew how to outsmart stiff-necked cops.

He scanned the room and then did a careful overall check of the place. Though it was nothing fancy, the room appeared normal. The bed was made, the bathroom sported clean towels and new soap, but still it was nothing out of the ordinary.

He yanked off his coat and threw it aside. Then he crossed the room, eased back the curtain, and looked out the window. Satisfied by the nearly deserted parking lot, he opened his bag and pulled out his Glenlivet. He held up the distinctive bottle.

"My pal," he muttered. "Top shelf, single malt. Best damn scotch ever made."

He deserved the best, by God. He'd hit the ice machine down the hall, then kick back with his old pal and think things over.

His hand shook as he poured. He lifted the glass and waited, watching the amber liquid wind through the ice, crackling and settling. He tossed back a hefty slug and hissed a sharp breath between his clenched teeth. The scotch burned all the way down and hit the bottom of his gut like a ball of fire. He topped off the glass and sprawled into a lumpy side chair. After a few more sips, the knotted muscles in his neck began to loosen.

He needed to sort through all this shit and get the hell moving, because his current situation was fast becoming intolerable. That close call with the cops the other night had rattled him and made him pull back, rethink his approach. He wouldn't have hesitated to shoot the state trooper he'd encountered, and that could have screwed up everything.

He hadn't heard anything more on the news about the dead bodies. He caught an occasional mention of the ongoing investigation, maddening hints, little bits and pieces that dribbled out every once and a while. They were driving him bat shit crazy. He *hated* being kept in the dark. What did they know?

To ease the tension building with each passing hour, he'd splurged tonight and treated himself to dinner out. A couple of miles east of the motel, he'd found a cozy spot. Joe Root's, a bustling little bar and restaurant where he'd had a nice, thick steak. Nobody had paid him any attention, except for the waitress, and he figured all she wanted was a big tip. As long as he kept a low profile, this little section on the west side of Erie would do just fine.

The restaurant sat on the corner of West Eighth Street and Peninsula Drive. Erie-sistable Fitness was only a short drive south, and then east toward Erie. Damn convenient. He'd work on getting a handle on Elaine Delacor's schedule, and then he'd map out a plan.

After returning to his motel room, he flipped on the TV. A homey movie, complete with a made to order family and one big-assed turkey, reminded him of the fast approaching holiday. Big holidays wreaked havoc, and people got distracted. A perfect opportunity for him to blend in with all the confusion.

He frowned and rattled the ice in his glass. He'd have hell to pay if the Delacor woman recognized him. He had no clue if she'd gotten a good look at his face that night or not. He'd been bundled up against the cold, and it'd been snowing like hell. Yet they were still looking for his SUV, and they were watching her like damn hawks.

She knew something.

He got up and roamed the room. His connection to the deceased didn't help. He rubbed his hand over rough stubble on his face and again cursed the two idiots responsible for the whole damn mess. Too many odd pieces of information could tie it all together and fuck up his life. A twinge of alarm overrode his pleasant alcohol buzz.

No, she knew too much. *Way* too much for comfort. He'd be taking a chance if he went after her, but he couldn't see an alternative. He had to find her. What happened then would remain to be seen.

He tossed back the rest of his drink. He wanted this done. All the crap he'd endured since that snowy night infuriated him. Why had everything gone so wrong?

He took a deep breath. Risks be damned. Elaine Delacor had to die.

Chapter Twenty-Two

Lanie stuck her head into Kitty's office. "Morning."

"You're here early." Kitty swiveled around at her desk. "Come on in. We have a few minutes before the madness begins."

"Madness? I'd kind of hoped today would be a slow one, you know, with everyone out shopping for the big holiday tomorrow."

"No such luck. I swear they all think that if they come in today and sweat like pigs, they can eat like pigs tomorrow." She grinned when Lanie burst out laughing. "Want some coffee?"

"No, I had my quota this morning." She dug into her bag and dragged out a bottle of water. "I'll stick to this for now, but if you want to talk, I have time before my first session."

"Nothing about work, but I'd like to know how things are with you on a personal level. And please, if I'm overstepping, just say so."

Lanie dropped her bag and pulled up a chair. She uncapped her water and drank before responding. "The search for the man who threatened me has come to a standstill. They're still looking for him, but as T.J. says, he's dropped off the radar."

She stretched out her legs, relaxed back in the chair, and sipped more water. The longer he stayed out of sight, the better. She'd already let her boss in on the details, including her connection with the murders. Kitty was responsible for the safety and well-being of the members of Erie-sistable Fitness, and Lanie thought it made sense to have her boss aware of her current circumstances. Since Corporal Sullivan and T.J. had agreed for her to talk to Kitty, she'd informed her boss of the situation when she'd returned to work last week. She'd even offered to take time off if Kitty was uncomfortable, but so far that hadn't come to pass.

The trim, lithe, dark-haired woman had merely thanked her and emphasized that she appreciated Lanie's trust and consideration. She had no problem whatsoever with Lanie coming in to work and had quietly set a few safety measures in place. At first, Lanie had felt a little silly walking to her car at the end of the day flanked by two burly fellow employees. The guys didn't ask any questions, however. They just made sure she made it safely to her car. If anyone had noticed, they hadn't said a word.

Kitty tilted back in her chair. "If it's none of my business, just say so. This isn't employee to employee, Lanie. Consider it friend to friend. I'll understand if discussing personal matters makes you uncomfortable."

"You're a fair employer, Kitty, and you've become a good friend. I respect you, and I trust you. Usually I avoid getting close to people. Now I find myself with a number of new friends, you included." She hesitated and tipped her water bottle toward Kitty. "I'm also having a rather steamy affair."

"That's not news to me." Kitty smiled swiveled her chair from side to side and tilted her head. Her smile slid into a knowing grin. "You've got a relaxed, loose look about you now. Especially this morning. I take it Trooper McGraw was on bodyguard duty again last night?"

"He takes my body very seriously," Lanie replied, with a solemn nod.

Kitty laughed, and she joined in.

When their laughter subsided, Lanie stood and prepared to leave. "I appreciate your concern and support regarding both the case and my own personal dilemma."

"I'm not sure I'd refer to your relationship as a *dilemma.*"

"I'm having an *affair*. A rather hot affair, with no-strings." Lanie shouldered her duffle bag and tucked the bottle inside. "*Relationships* lead somewhere; this affair will eventually burn itself out and end."

"I see the look on your face whenever he calls." Kitty stood and came around her desk, stopping when she was face to face with Lanie. "The bounce in your step when you walk through that door every morning. You're kidding yourself if you think what's going on between you and the hot cop is going to burn out anytime soon."

"A lot is going on for me right now, and it's all foreign to anything I've ever known. I never thought I'd be afraid. I mean *really* scared shitless. It sounds like a bad cliché, but my life flashed before my eyes when that big assed SUV rammed into me. Fear took hold, and for the most part, it hasn't let go. At times my life hasn't been easy, but I've always faced things head on. You might say I've been fearless, or maybe even reckless, at times."

"This has shaken you more than I realized." Kitty touched her arm and gave it a little rub.

Lanie covered her friend's hand with one of her own. "The fear is finally easing. I jumped at every shadow for those first couple of days. Each one that passes safely helps me to relax a little more. And as for the affair, it's just as foreign as the fear." She chuckled. "I've had affairs before. Not a parade of men through my life, but a few entanglements. Why this one's so different, I'm not sure.

"It just kind of... exploded." She threw up both hands with her fingers spread. "I've always kept my distance from T.J. because we irritated one another to no end. Then all of a sudden, on the night of the accident, we were thrown together. Maybe my being the lady in distress and T.J. acting as my knight in shining armor -- or in this case, as my sexy trooper in uniform -- had something to do with it. Anyway, *kaboom!* Next thing I know, my hero's sharing my bed, and I'm not in any hurry to push him out."

A group of patrons burst through the main entrance, their voices ringing out. Laughter accompanied their pounding feet as they set out on the track outside Kitty's office.

Kitty glanced up as they ran past.

"Don't be in such a hurry to push him away," she advised. "We'll talk later. Maybe do lunch next week after the holiday."

Lanie nodded.

Kitty walked Lanie to the door. "By the way, where are you going for your turkey fix?"

"To Rich and Ada McConnell's. Remember, I told you about them? She's my friend Cassi's aunt, and she and Rich got married this past summer. Ada's dying to show off the new kitchen he designed for her, so they're hosting the holiday. Cassi and T.J.'s cousin, Nick, will be there, too, along with Tom and Mary McGraw, T.J.'s parents. T.J. works that day then has to go out again at midnight that night. I'll probably only see him when we all sit down to eat. Today after work, I'm heading to Cassi's to help with all the preparations. I'll stay there and go to Rich and Ada's with her and Nick on Thanksgiving Day."

"Too bad T.J.'s on duty. Sounds like he pulled a rough schedule."

"He says it goes with the territory. Also gives me a chance to get a solid night's sleep," Lanie added with a parting grin.

As Kitty headed for the front reception area, more people poured in through the doors. She'd been right about this being a busy day. Lanie headed for the locker to change for her first session. Once she was ready, she checked her list of clients for the day. Several girls were new. The rest were familiar and were making good progress.

The club would close early today. She wanted to check in on Sam Cat before heading to Pine Bluffs, and she couldn't help feeling a tiny stab of guilt. Jen would look after him until Lanie returned, and the little guy seemed to deal well with her coming and going, but still... she promised herself she'd spend the weekend making up for neglecting her furry little pal.

She'd also promised to call T.J. if the weather turned bad. If the slow moving storm predicted for Erie hit by the time she got off work, he'd said he'd drive her to Cassi's house.

Leaving the locker room, she glanced out the window. Heavy dark clouds rolled by. She stopped and rubbed her arms when a sudden ominous chill overrode her buoyant mood.

*****

The stone-faced young man behind the wheel of the red hatchback signed the ticket and handed the clipboard back to T J

"Slow down," T.J. advised him, then added, "and keep your eye on the weather."

The man nodded and closed the window with a snap.

T.J. stepped away from the vehicle and waited until the fellow pulled away before slipping back into his state car.

A steady stream of travelers moved past him on I-90, down a long gradual slope and across Wintergreen Gorge Bridge. He hated to ruin anyone's holiday, but that jerk in the overloaded hatchback weaving in and out of traffic deserved the pricey summons he'd just received.

Cars continued to roll past him at a steady clip. Many held families headed home for Thanksgiving. He smiled and waved at two kids staring wide-eyed out the back window of a loaded minivan. He remained parked on the berm just west of the bridge for a short while. Sometimes just the presence of a visible marked patrol car slowed people down.

So far, they had experienced no major accidents. If the snow held off, those on the road would have a chance to reach their destinations in plenty of time. He glanced at his watch and noted his shift was half over. Once it was done, he'd head home and catch a couple hours sleep before reporting back for duty at eleven p.m.

Lanie was staying with Cassi and Nick tonight. She'd offered to let him crash at her cabin since she wouldn't be there, to save him the drive to Pine Bluffs. He might just do that, though he'd feel weird sleeping in Lanie's bed all alone. Remembering her little cat, he chuckled. Maybe he wouldn't have to sleep alone after all.

After checking the traffic, he pulled back onto the thruway. A few miles east near the Harborcreek Exit, he looked out over the lake. Sheets of falling snow were already visible in the distance. If the wind shifted, he might have to make that drive to Pine Bluffs regardless. He wasn't about to let Lanie drive that rental south in a snowstorm.

Leaving the interstate, he looped back around to head west. He was halfway up the westbound ramp when a red Toyota Prius shot past him on the thruway like a bullet. He hit the lights, sped up, and merged into traffic.

Idiot. This ticket would cancel out anything the jerk hoped to save on fuel.

After writing a ticket for the driver of the Prius, T.J. stopped for a quick sandwich at Arby's for lunch, then got back on the road. Traffic worsened as the day went on. A couple of hours before his shift ended, he got tied up with an accident. Between having the cars towed and rerouting the backed up traffic, he'd been unable to call Lanie. As he finally headed in to the barracks, the wind picked up and snow began to fall. Not what he wanted to see.

"T.J., I need to talk to you," Sergeant Evans called out as T.J. entered the building.

He changed course and followed Mark into his office where Corporal Sullivan waited. Something was up. He just hoped for once, the news was good.

"I know you're in a hurry to get going." Mark sat down behind his desk. "So we'll make this quick. Dan, have a seat. You too, T.J."

"I just wanted to let you know we've alerted other agencies to the LeFavor situation." Dan pulled up a chair and laid a folder on the corner of Mark's desk. "We've not making any headway, and getting the information to more people might turn up something. A brief release identifying LeFavor and the vehicle he's suspected of driving went out to Millcreek PD and the City of Erie about an hour ago."

"All right." T.J. dropped into a chair. This *was* good news. He'd agreed with the cautious approach initially. However, the lack of results and not knowing where the hell the guy had gone had weighed on everyone. "What made you decide to do this now?"

"A couple of things." Dan flipped open the folder and held up a picture of a late model Ford Taurus. "Do you have any idea how many of these damn things are driving around out there? We don't have the time or the manpower to pull them all over and check them out. Departments like Millcreek and Erie see them, too, but they're more likely to spot one at a restaurant, or maybe a motel in town, if we get lucky. That bastard doesn't know we're on to the fact that he may be driving something besides his Escalade. He might get sloppy. From what I've heard, he's a smug son of a bitch who thinks all police are brainless idiots. I want to nail this guy's ass."

T.J. glanced at his watch. "I'm going to check the weather, and if it's getting bad south of here, I'll meet Lanie when she leaves work and drive her to my cousin's place."

"Check with dispatch," Mark suggested. "The south patrols will give you a better idea about the conditions than any news report."

"Good idea. Where are you guys heading for Thanksgiving?"

"Home," Dan replied, gathering up is paperwork.

"I'm staying right here in good old Harborcreek." Mark stood and stretched. "My wife's family is in town, and they'll all be there. About fifteen all together. How about you?"

"Between bouts of sleep, I'll eat with friends and family in Pine Bluffs." T.J. told them goodbye, and then headed up to the front desk.

He'd catch up with the weather and then give Lanie a call.

*****

"You lucked out," Kitty murmured. She tilted head her and indicated Sue, another fitness trainer, and a stocky, middle aged man dressed in matching workout gear. "Mr. Atherton, the new member from Oakmont."

Lanie took a closer look. Something about the way he stood with his hands on his hips while he took a break from lifting weights caught her attention.

He wasn't tall. She guessed he was a hair under six feet and solid, not bulked up like some of the older guys were. He probably only worked out occasionally. He stood angled away from her, so she couldn't get a good look at his face.

Kitty touched her arm. "Elaine? Do you know him?"

Lanie shook her head. "I can't be sure. There's something familiar about him, so maybe I did work with him in Fox Chapel."

"Well, we're going to find out." Kitty turned with a smile as Sue and

John Atherton ambled toward them, their heads bent, laughing. He'd thrown a towel around his neck and patted away perspiration as they approached the reception desk.

"How'd the workout go, Mr. Atherton?" Kitty asked.

"Good. You've got a great place here. This little lady knows her stuff. As well as Miss Delacor here," he said, directing a broad smile at Lanie.

Something about him, his smarmy smile and the overabundance of fake charm that oozed from him made Lanie take a step back. She forced a polite smile. "I'm sorry, but I don't remember you, Mr. Atherton."

"John. Call me John."

Lanie swore he changed before her eyes.

The stiffness of his stance eased. He heaved a quick sigh and wiped his sweaty brow. "You never worked with me at Fox Chapel. One of the other ladies did. I knew about your excellent reputation as a trainer, though, and that you'd moved north after that tragic fire. So..." He shrugged and kept his hard assessing gaze on her. "When I moved here, I tracked you down. Figured you'd work for a class act place here, too. And I was right."

He gave Sue a companionable elbow bump.

"Well, I'm glad you're satisfied with our staff," Kitty said. She turned to Lanie. "We're wrapping up here. Why don't you head on out and beat the storm?"

"I think I will." She turned to John Atherton. "Sorry I don't remember you, but welcome to Erie-sistable Fitness."

A couple of the other trainers approached the desk. They were laughing and talking.

"Lanie, you live around here. Have you seen the ice dunes at Freeport Beach?" Tall, trim Alice Moore lived in North East. Lanie liked her and admired her rapport with clients.

Lanie turned her attention to the group of her fellow workers, relieved that Mr. Atherton had turned his so called charm on poor Sue for the moment. "No. I haven't seen them yet, but I've heard they're really spectacular."

"You should stop and see them. The word *spectacular* pretty much nails it." Alice's enthusiasm was catching. "But they can be dangerous. They formed early this season, and open water isn't far from shore. The dunes look like waves frozen in place, yet they're hollow, and if someone stepped on them, they'd break right through."

"If I were heading that way, I'd stop," Lanie said, "but I want to swing home and check on my cat before I head to Pine Bluffs for the holiday."

Kitty looked up from her paperwork. "Lanie, you might be smarter to take the Bayfront Parkway across town and head out Route 5 to North East."

"Why?"

"The snow along the ridge in Harborcreek is getting bad. I checked

Doppler radar on my computer, and bands are already setting up all along the lakeshore. They're moving inland and curving southwest."

"How about North East and Pine Bluffs?" Alice asked.

"If you stick close to the lake until you reach North East and then head inland, you might miss the worst of the snow." Kitty turned to Lanie. "Why don't you get going?"

"Sounds like a good idea. I'll take your advice. If it's not snowing too hard, I'll even take a peek at those ice dunes at Freeport Beach." She smiled at Alice, and together they moved away toward the locker room.

Lanie paused to wish Sue a nice holiday.

"Let me know how the dunes look if you stop," Sue said. "I'm a bit of a camera buff and would love to get some shots of them."

"You have a nice holiday, too, Miss Delacor." Mr. Atherton said. "And take your friend's advice. Stay off the ice dunes. They could be deadly."

Lanie nodded and hurried away, fuming about John Atherton's creepy remark.

"Conceited jerk," she muttered later, after grabbing her things from her locker and going outside. She brushed snow from her car. Quite a few vehicles were still in the lot, and all of them were covered with a fresh layer. Once she was done, she tossed the long-handled brush into the back and slid inside.

As she crossed Erie's Bayfront, the tension in her body melted away. She wouldn't let an offhand remark by a total stranger ruin her holiday mood. In a few hours, she'd be sipping wine at Cassi and Nick's. They'd planned a pie baking marathon, and she couldn't wait.

She tried calling T.J. and got his voicemail. Figuring he must be busy, she left a message on his cell explaining her change of plans. A call to Jen confirmed the heavy snow on the ridge, and her friend agreed to check on Sam Cat. She also promised to let Jen know as soon as possible if T.J. planned to stay the night at Lanie's cabin.

The road to North East was in fine shape. Brief snow squalls slowed her down a couple of times, but by the time she reached Route 89, the sun peeked through to brighten the overcast late afternoon sky. She hesitated, then turned north and headed for Freeport Beach. Those ice dunes would be stunning at sunset. She'd only take a minute to look at them, and then head south to Pine Bluffs.

*****

On his way to change out of uniform, T.J. tried to reach Lanie by cell phone.

Huh, she'd left a message. Must have been when he was in Mark's office. He listened to it, enjoying the smooth, easy sound of her voice, irritated he had to work tonight instead of snuggling up in bed with her.

He replayed the message twice. She sounded relaxed, even

mentioned she might stop and check out the dunes. Although he was a bit disappointed she didn't need him to drive her to Pine Bluffs, he was glad she'd been smart enough to monitor the weather and change her plans accordingly. He just hoped she wouldn't linger at the beach. The road to Pine Bluffs looked okay for now, but any shift in the wind could change that in a matter of minutes.

"T.J.!" Mark Evans voice rang down the hallway. "My office, now."

A bit irritated, T.J. turned around and hurried back down the hall. When he reached the open door to Mark's office, Dan was on the phone.

His boss raked his hand through his hair, nodded briskly, and snapped into the receiver, "How long ago? Where?"

T.J. waited in the doorway. Behind him a few troopers walked by, their laughter echoing down the hall. Their fading footsteps echoed in obscene cadence with the thoughts pounding through his head. *Not good, not good, not good.*

Dan hung up the phone, his mouth set in a grim line.

Mark motioned T.J. into the room. "Close the door."

T.J. stepped inside and did as his superior asked. His brain scrambled ahead, and a sick parade of *what ifs* threatened to bring him to his knees.

Dan jerked his tie loose. Resting one hip on the sergeant's desk, he rolled up his sleeves.

"That was Millcreek PD," he said. "One of their officers remembers a blue Ford Taurus parked at a motel just west of Peninsula Drive. They've been keeping an eye on the bar across the street from the motel, and after seeing the fax today he mentioned it to his sergeant."

"Are they checking it out?" T.J. did a rough calculation. "Lanie works a couple of blocks east of Peninsula, on Twelfth Street."

"I'm aware of that." Dan nodded. "The officer's on his way to the motel now. This could be nothing, T.J. The only reason we're taking a closer than average look at it is because most of the clientele at that motel drives trucks. The officer said the cars only there during the day, and it kind of stands out when the lot empties each morning. He wouldn't have thought twice about it if we hadn't sent out that fax. Good cops take notice and remember what they see. We'll just wait and--"

The phone shrilled, and every muscle in T.J.'s body tightened.

Dan answered it. He listened for a moment, then lowered the receiver and turned to T.J. "The Taurus is gone, but they showed LeFavor's picture to the motel clerk. It's our man."

T.J. shot to his feet.

"Damn," Mark muttered, pointing a finger at T.J. "Stay put until we know what we're dealing with here."

Dan covered the receiver. "The officer just arrived where Lanie works. The Taurus isn't there. He's going inside to see if anyone's seen LeFavor."

"Lanie's on her way to Pine Bluffs," T.J. paced to the door and back.

He checked his cell phone, noted the time of her call. "She's probably almost to North East by now."

He tried her cell again, but it went right to voicemail. Damn. Where the hell was she? Why didn't she answer?

"Okay, we'll handle it from here. Thanks." Dan slammed down the phone. "He was there, and he left a little over a half hour ago. Calls himself John Atherton."

T.J.'s heartbeat hammered in his ears. He started for the door.

"McGraw," Evans said. "Do you know which way she went?"

"She took the parkway across town, then Route 5 to North East." His mind raced as he remembered her words. "She mentioned maybe stopping at Freeport Beach."

The sergeant swung around and pointed out the window. "The beach? In this weather?"

"She wanted to see the frickin' ice dunes." T.J. slammed his fist against the wall. "I gotta go find her."

T.J.'s outburst stopped Dan halfway out the door.

He glanced back. "Sarge?"

"Go grab someone and get the hell to North East," Sergeant Evans ordered.

Sullivan gave him a curt nod and took off down the hall.

The sergeant nudged T.J. roughly toward the door and tossed him a set of keys. "T.J., you're with me. Go get my car and pull around front. I'll get another car rolling toward Freeport and put out a BOLO on the Taurus and on Lanie. Move!"

Chapter Twenty-Three

Lanie promised herself she'd only take a quick peek at the dunes to see what all the excitement was about. She'd been to Freeport Beach before at a different time of year, when the waves were rolling in and crashing on the beach, the sun beating down, gulls screaming.

None of that compared to the stark beauty and eerie silence of the frozen waves.

She left her car and crossed the barren, deserted beach for a closer look. Hunching her shoulders against the steady gale off the lake, she turned right and followed the meandering curve of craggy ice along the shore. She must be crazy to walk down a snow coated beach in winter, trudging over the hard packed ground while tendrils of white swirled and wound around her feet. The barren landscape forewarned her to keep away, yet its raw beauty captivated her and drew her closer.

Further from shore, a thin coat of ice rode atop the waves, heaving and rolling with languid dips and swells, fighting the icy grip of winter. For unknown reasons, the wildness, the total sense of being alone, didn't bother her. Instead, the sensation energized her. Embracing the moment, she spread her arms and faced the wind.

She hadn't been alone, totally alone, for a while, and she wanted to savor this brief respite from the tangled mess her life had become.

Further along the beach and off to her right, the fast moving water of Sixteen Mile Creek slid past and disappeared beneath the ice at the mouth of the creek. She gazed out over the lake, past the craggy dunes and the undulating ice. Open water the color of burnished steel kissed the dark underbelly of clouds on the horizon. Tiny pinpricks of ice peppered her cheeks. She squinted against a sudden assault of wind driven snow, a sign that the wind had shifted.

T.J. had been right about the dunes. They were spectacular. She wanted to call him, *needed* to call him. To share her feelings. To not be alone anymore. She wanted him there with her. Now. Wanted him to wrap his strong arms around her, until their bodies pressed together as one against the driving wind. She longed for someone to understand her needs and to chase away the loneliness. Couldn't that someone be T.J.?

She slipped off one glove, unzipped her coat, and searched for her cell phone. Where had she tucked it? The wind caught her jacket, and the bitter cold air bit at her fingers.

God, she was freezing.

She'd ask him to bring her something hot, and they'd snuggle in the car and... *damn.* That's were her phone was -- in her stupid car. She attempted to zip up, but her stiff fingers failed to cooperate. She dropped her glove.

She lunged for it, and the wind skimming the ground ripped it from within her grasp. Her bare knuckles scraped solid ice. Cursing, she whirled around, rubbing her injured hand. Then she straightened, and froze

"Hello, Elaine. Is this what you're looking for?"

The bottom dropped out of her world.

*****

Sergeant Evans yanked open the car door and leaned down until he was eye to eye with T.J. "I still have a few calls to make, so I need you to drive. Are you okay with that?"

T.J. nodded. "Let's go."

In full pursuit mode, he barreled north on Nagle Road. He slowed to thirty-five as he neared the light at Route 5, then snapped into a tight right hand turn and headed east.

Mark Evans slapped a hand on the dash. "Holy shit, McGraw. I'd like to get there in one piece." He gave his seatbelt a vicious tug and pulled out his cell phone. "When we get close, cut the siren. I'm calling North East for backup. I'll bring them up to speed and advise them to shut down 89 from Route 5 to the beach."

Streets and houses flashed by as indistinct blurs on the roadside. Startled motorists dove for the berm as T.J. pushed the limit, siren blaring, lights flashing. He drove focused, using every damn skill he'd ever learned. They'd get the hell there in one piece, but would they get to Lanie in time?

The road plunged down a ravine. Never faltering, the powerful engine roared as he climbed a steep winding hill. Then up ahead, snow swallowed the road. He entered North East Township hampered by low visibility and had to force himself to slow down.

"We're all set." Mark broke the connection and blew out a loud breath. He glanced from side to side and then leaned forward and peered out the front windshield. "I can't see a damned thing. Where in hell are we?"

"North East Township. Do we have anyone there yet?"

"Trooper Andrews is about two miles south of Freeport Beach on 89, and North East PD is right behind him. We'll soon know if LeFavor's there."

They burst out of the blinding snow onto the flats. Vineyards lined the road, row upon perfect row of grapevines, an artist's dream frosted in white. T.J. barely noticed. The rolling vineyards only meant they were getting closer.

He didn't agree with Mark. To him, the key wasn't *if* the man were there. He knew in his gut that Jack LeFavor would be at that beach. He'd stalked Lanie, watched her place, and found out where she worked. The bold bastard had walked right into the fitness center. Her boss had confirmed he had arrived a couple hours before Lanie had gotten off work. He'd be at the beach all right, because T.J. knew in his gut that LeFavor had followed her when she'd left.

Heaven help the son of a bitch if he hurts her.

When they passed North Mill Street, T.J. killed the siren. They started down the hill just as Mark's phone buzzed. He answered and listened, his lips clamped together.

T.J. eased off the road and inhaled deep, quiet breaths till his nerves settled. *By the book, McGraw, do this by the book. Do it the way you've been trained.*

His hand went to the butt of his weapon, seeking to touch something tangible and solid to help calm his racing heart. Don't let it be too late, he prayed silently, knowing that despite his training, sometimes nothing would stop a determined killer's bullet.

Mark ended the call. "Lanie's car and the Taurus are parked at the end of the road. Sullivan backed off after confirming the identity of both vehicles. At this point, we have to assume they don't know we're here, but they can't be far away."

T.J. spotted Dan Sullivan and his partner in civvies huddled together with Andrews. An unmarked car was parked alongside the cruiser beside Freeport Restaurant, a local eating spot at the northeast corner of the intersection of Routes 5 and 89. The dinner rush hadn't yet begun, and the restaurant's parking lot was almost empty. A good thing, considering.

Mark turned to T.J. "Let's do this together."

They swung into the lot, and Mark motioned for the three men to get into their car. Sullivan and his partner hustled into the back seat, followed by Trooper Andrews.

"God, it's a bitch out there," Andrews muttered, brushing snow off his coat.

T.J. and the sergeant angled to face them, and Mark asked, "How far down are the vehicles?"

"Just short of the restrooms on the right." Sullivan coughed and cleared his throat. "As soon as I verified they were the vehicles we were looking for, I backed up and turned around."

"Did you see anyone on the beach or inside the vehicles?" Mark asked.

"Not that I could tell. Both appeared to be unoccupied, but without getting any closer, I could only see part of the beach."

"Okay." The sergeant drummed a nervous hand on the dashboard. "We've got to assume they're somewhere on the beach, then. My guess is that they're closer to the creek, or you'd have seen them." He swept his intense gaze over each man. "Is everyone familiar with that area?"

"I'm not," Sullivan's partner said. "Give me a brief rundown."

Mark turned and pointed toward the beach. "At the end of the road on the left, there's a local yacht club. It's a long, low building, and it's closed for the winter. This time of year, there's no beach in front of the club. To the right, the beach goes all the way to Sixteen Mile Creek. If you approach it from here, on the right just past the restrooms, you'll find a small parking lot next to a picnic area and playground."

T.J. shifted and blew out a hard breath. All this damn talking was taking precious time. Time Lanie didn't have.

Sullivan reached over and laid a hand on T.J.'s shoulder. "We're going to get her, T.J. That bastard won't get away this time."

T.J. could only nod. He hoped to God the sergeant was right. In less than an hour, darkness would fall, and the damn snow just kept coming down.

"Andrews," Mark ordered. "I want you in there first. Pull up to the right of the Taurus. That will put a marked car between LeFavor and his only means of escape. It will also announce our presence. That son of a bitch is *not* walking away."

His meaning came through loud and clear. They'd do what had to be done.

"T.J. and I will follow Andrews and park on the left," he continued. "Sullivan, you two hang back out of sight and block the road, just in case. Any questions?"

"What if they're not on the beach?" T.J. yanked on his gloves and eyed the lone North East PD car blocking the road. They needed more time, more back up.

Mark stared toward the lake. "They're there, T.J., and we're gonna nail him."

Every muscle in T.J.'s body tightened.

Turning around, Mark scanned the face of each man. "Andrews, once you're in place, let us know what you see. T.J. and I will hang back until you report, in case LeFavor spots you and tries to slip past. Once you've established a visual, we'll move into place."

Les Andrews secured his hat and gloves. "I'll be in contact."

The three men dashed to their cars, leaving T.J. and the sergeant alone. T.J. folded his arms on the steering wheel, leaned in, and waited for each man to move into position.

He stared down the long, straight stretch of road to the lake. In all probability, Lanie was alone and helpless somewhere on that beach. If that bastard did anything to her hurt her...

No, don't go there. We have a solid plan, a good plan. He trusted these men with his life. Now he had to trust them with Lanie's.

"Are you in love with her?"

T.J. jerked. "What did you say?"

"I asked if you were in love with her."

"I care about her." T.J. leaned back and pressed the heels of his hands to his eyes, then dropped his hands and stared straight ahead. "Yeah, I love her."

"T.J." Mark shook his head. "There's a difference. Whichever applies, don't let it fuck with your mind when this goes down."

The radio crackled, and Trooper Andrews reported, "I have a visual. They're on the beach near the mouth of the creek."

"We're on our way," Mark responded.

T.J. threw the car into gear and headed for the beach.

Chapter Twenty-Four

Lanie recognized the man with sickening clarity. The bulky coat. His wide legged stance. The looming threat. John Atherton, from the fitness center. Only… *not John Atherton.* His name was Jack LeFavor, and the night she'd first seen him came back to her in a rush, slamming into her as hard as the driving wind.

He held out her glove.

Lanie ignored him and tucked her bare hand beneath her arm even though her fingers stung like fire where she'd scraped them on the ice. The muscles in her legs quivered.

Should I run?

"Don't want it?" He shrugged and tucked her glove into his pocket. Then he withdrew a small handgun and pointed it at her belly. "Guess you have bigger problems, anyway."

Lanie eased back a step and glanced up the beach. How far would she get before a bullet slammed into her back?

"Go ahead. Run. I didn't plan to shoot you, but I will." He curved his mouth in a vicious smile. His eyes remained flat. Cold. *Calculating.*

She shivered, her thoughts scrambling.

"Not feelin' so friendly now, are you? I saw past that 'business smile' earlier at the fitness center when you looked down your pretty little nose at me. Couldn't wait to get away."

Lanie's stomach knotted. She'd known, damn it. Why hadn't she paid attention to her instincts? His sleazy smile, the way he'd looked at her. She shook off that vision and focused on the here and now. Struggled to slow her rapid breathing, to think. He wanted her dead. He'd stalked her, and he'd waited. Then he'd taken a big chance by showing up at the club.

He was a desperate man.

"Trying to decide what to do, Elaine? Pitiful." He laughed, shook his head, and gestured with the gun. "To be honest, I don't want to use this. So here's the deal--"

"You've already killed two men with that gun," she blurted, unable to stand the suspense. Her voice sounded hollow and throaty. Weak. And she *hated* that. Hated feeling helpless and so damned vulnerable. This man stood for every miserable moment she'd endured since the night of the accident. She drew herself up, flexed her numb, bare fingers. "So… why stop now?"

"I don't want to shoot you." He narrowed his eyes. "But I will."

"If you shoot me, they'll know it was you," she shot back.

His jaw tightened, and anger glittered in his eyes. He wasn't laughing now.

"That's a thirty-eight snub nose," she continued, lifting her shoulder in a casual shrug, even as her pulse roared in her ears. "You used that gun to kill those two men at that rest stop. So if you shoot me with it, too, the police will know. Trust me. And they'll hunt you down like a dog."

His mood turned. Jack LeFavor, a cruel, dangerous man, had a gun pointed at her, and yet she felt oddly calm. He took a step toward her.

"You're a brave woman, Elaine. A smart one." He sneered. "What you said about the gun tells me you know more than I thought."

She eased back another step, and then another, until her foot bumped a sold wall of ice behind her.

"Go on. Run. And if you run that way," he said, jerking his head to the left, "Then I'll have no choice but to put a bullet in your back. Ever been shot, Elaine?"

His cold stare never left her face. "They tell me it hurts like hell."

She looked away and stared down the beach. The wind roared in her ears. Bone chilling cold numbed her limbs, and slick nausea rose up her throat. He wanted her dead.

She had nothing to lose.

Just as she started to dart away, he lunged toward her.

Lanie turned and scrambled onto the dunes. She stumbled once, almost going down. Clawing at ice that crumbled and broke, she pulled herself up and regained her footing, righted herself, and pushed aside the reality of what lay beneath her feet. Blood dripped from her bare hand onto the ice. A bright red splash against the cold white wave, spreading like spidery fingers. The ice cracked and moaned beneath her feet.

She ignored the warning, dug in, and moved higher.

"Good girl." LeFavor's voice stopped her in mid-flight.

She faced the lake. To the west, a fast moving band of snow moved onshore. Pouring from heavy clouds, the wide sheets undulated and fell in lazy waves.

Slowly, cautiously, she turned to face LeFavor.

He now held the gun at his side instead of pointing it at her. He eased forward, and suddenly she knew his game.

Like he'd said, he'd never intended to shoot her, and she'd fallen right into his trap. He'd planned to force her onto the dunes all along. He'd gambled, and he'd won. When the ice beneath her feet gave way and she plunged into the frigid lake, he'd just walk away.

Jack studied the approaching snow. The rising wind had flipped off his hood. He yanked it back into place and tightened it around his face. Then he just stood there, watching her and the falling snow, calmly waiting for her to fall into the water and die.

Anger surged through Lanie, and she lifted her chin. "What if I don't break through the ice?" she taunted. "Are you brave enough to come after me?"

He didn't even flinch.

The bastard.

Still gripping the gun, he crossed his arms and shook his head. "Has nothing to do with being brave. I'm not that stupid."

More thin sheets of falling snow moved across the beach.

"The ice will give way soon," he said. His cheeks were red, raw from the icy wind. He shivered and hunched deeper into his heavy down jacket. "Or maybe you'll just freeze where you stand. I'm a patient man. It's just you and me, Elaine. We're all alone out here."

Behind him, a flash of light and movement filtered through the curtain of white.

Hope flickered inside her, and she tilted her head toward the parking lot. "Not anymore, Jack. Not anymore."

He whipped around as a marked state police cruiser rolled to a stop.

*****

T.J. swung in next to the marked car. His heart hammered in his chest as the sergeant spoke with Andrews.

"What's the status?" the sergeant asked.

Andrews replied, "Looks like the girl's trying to get away. She's out on the ice. LeFavor's still on the beach."

T.J. unfastened his seatbelt and reached for the door handle.

"Hold it." Sergeant Evans clamped his hand on T.J.'s arm. "Do you see a weapon, Andrews?"

"Negative. I can't see shit through this snow. He knows we're here, though."

"Shit." Evans scanned the beach in front of them. "We can't get a car any closer with all of these damn boulders in the way. Let's see what our friend has in mind. We're coming over, Andrews."

They used the marked car as cover, and within seconds, T.J. and the sergeant slid into the back seat of Andrews' cruiser. Wind whipping off the lake rocked the car.

Now T.J. could see Lanie out on the dunes and LeFavor about ten feet away. T.J. clenched his fists and his blood pounded hot, even as ice cold fear slammed into his gut. He set his jaw. Giving in to either the fear or the anger would hamper his judgment. He had to stay focused. *Think McGraw, damn it. Think.*

Evans slid to the edge of his seat and held out his hand. "Give me the mike. Let's give our boy a head's up."

T.J. gripped the butt of his weapon, then let it go, only to do it all over again. The beach faded in and out. One second it was veiled in white, and the next it was a deadly tableau.

"Should I kill the lights?" Les asked.

"No. It'll distract him. I want that." The sergeant brought up the mike. "Turn on the external."

Andrews hit the switch.

"This is Sergeant Evans of the Pennsylvania State Police. I want to see both hands, LeFavor. Start walking toward the marked car. Slowly."

LeFavor shot a fast look over his shoulder and edged closer to Lanie.

"Damn it," T.J. muttered. "He's trying to get to her."

"LeFavor. Do it. Now!" Evans shouted into the loudspeaker. He lowered the mike and muttered under his breath, "Come on, you bastard. Give it up."

T.J. scanned the area. To his right was a brick wall with names etched on each individual brick. He looked behind them.

"Back there." he pointed twisting around. "Between the wall and that building. We can cut through there and cross the playground."

Evans swung around and stared out the back window.

"He's on the edge of the dunes, sir," Andrews snapped. "What do you think? Let T.J. and me get closer. We'll scare the livin' shit out of him."

"All right." The sergeant scraped his hand over his face and blew out a quick breath. "I'll stay here, then bring Sullivan's car down. You go make your move."

He opened the door, stopped, and gave each trooper a hard look. "Use your heads, guys. I'll have too much fuckin' paper work if either of you get shot. And for God's sake, don't trash this unit." Then he was gone.

As soon as the sergeant slipped out, Andrews slammed the car into reverse.

"Hang on, T.J." He stomped the gas and they shot backwards, the engine whining. Then he hit the brakes and nosed the front end of the cruiser onto the cement pad between the wall and the restrooms.

"Go, go!" T.J. urged, hanging on to the seat as they shot through the opening.

Les jerked the wheel. "Oops."

A trash can flew straight up and bounced off the front bumper. The front end of the car dipped, and they skidded sideways down a sharp grade. Seconds later, the back end whipped around, and Les punched the gas.

"Hang on," he repeated over the engine's loud roar.

Luckily the playground was almost clear of snow due to wind blowing in off the lake. The strong breeze swept through a grove of trees that acted like a giant wind tunnel and kept snow from accumulating. The cruiser's lights bounced off the trees, creating ghostly patterns in the falling snow. They skidded around a few empty picnic tables, flew past deserted slides, and dodged two sets of swings. Up ahead, boulders blocked access to the beach.

T.J. braced himself and said a short prayer as they rocked to a stop and Les slammed the car in park.

"Piece of cake," T.J. uttered, heaving a loud, gusty sigh. At least now, they were closer.

Close enough to see the weapon clutched in LeFavor's right hand.

A long moment passed. Then the radio crackled, and Sergeant Evans asked, "Both of you still in one piece?"

"No problem, Sarge." Andrews glanced back at T.J., who nodded.

"Thank God," the sergeant muttered. "I'm going to work my way over to your position. What's the situation?"

"LeFavor's armed," Andrews said, "and he's moving closer to the girl. We--"

Unable to wait, T.J. opened the opposite door and climbed out.

"Whoa, T.J. Where in hell are you going?" Andrews demanded, whipping his head around.

The sergeant shouted over the radio, "What's going on, Andrews?"

Crouched low, T.J. ignored them and pulled his weapon. He stood, braced his arms on the roof of the cruiser, and took careful aim at Jack LeFavor.

*****

"I see three of them, Jack." Light-headed from shock, Lanie swayed on her feet. Through chattering teeth, she continued to taunt LeFavor, "Maybe more. You're a dead man unless you do what they tell you."

"Shut the fuck up. Let me think." Jack shifted and paced back and forth, all the while, she noted, making sure he blocked her escape by placing himself between her and them.

Lanie peered through the deepening dusk as the shadows lengthened. Steady snow sifted down like fine sugar, forming a gray curtain in the fading light. She focused on the cruiser. Fixed her eyes on the pulse and sweep of its colored lights. Was T.J. one of the men looking for her?

"Come here," Jack ordered.

She flinched. Her heart skipped a beat, and then lodged in her throat. He waved the gun wildly. Closer now. Almost within reach.

Lanie shook her head. "You're outnumbered. Look. There's more." When he turned his head, she moved several steps along the dune. A solid foot high ledge of ice blocked her escape. She stepped up, tested it, and held her breath. The frozen wave stayed firm.

Another unmarked car arrived and swung around to face them, its headlights streaming over the barren beach like twin spotlights.

Teeth clenched, eyes wild, Jack spun to face her.

"Shut up, I told you." He raised the gun. "Where the hell do think you're going?"

"You can't shoot me now, LeFavor, because I'm your ticket out of here."

Understanding winged over his face, while behind him, a man on foot reached the marked patrol car.

Seconds later, a voice boomed over the loudspeaker, "Put down your weapon, LeFavor. There's no way out. Give it up."

"I'll kill her!" LeFavor shouted. His gun hand wavered, but he kept the pistol trained on her and cast quick glances up the beach. Swiveling his head, squinting against the sudden light. "Come any closer and she's dead. Back off."

"No!" Lanie shouted.

Jack's head snapped around.

"He's a damn coward. He won't come after me. Shoot him!"

With a growl, Jack scurried along the shoreline, keeping pace with her measured steps. He stopped whenever she did, blocking a clear shot from up by the car. She knew they wouldn't shoot if it might endanger her. She had to get out of this herself -- and to do that, she had to make him come after her. She had to get him out on the ice. Time was running out, and this would be her only chance. She was strong, but what if the ice broke? Could she claw her way out?

Didn't matter. This had to end.

The voice boomed over the speaker, "Get down, Elaine! Get down on the ice."

LeFavor lunged at her, stumbled on the sharp ledge, and sprawled face down on the ice. Before she could twist away, he slithered forward and latched on to her leg.

The ice cracked and shifted.

"Let go of me!" she yelled. Her breath came in strangled sobs. She kicked at him wildly, balanced on one leg.

"Bitch," he snarled, just before her foot connected with his jaw and his head jerked violently. He released her leg and bellowed his rage. His gun skittered across the dune and slid into a shallow gully.

Time stood still. The ice shifted and parted at her feet. The gap widened, and she dropped down, scuttling backward as chunks of ice dropped away. Right before her eyes, Jack LeFavor slid clawing and screaming into the black abyss.

Then only the wind screamed. He was gone.

Her legs wouldn't respond. She lay inches from the jagged hole in the ice, paralyzed, and could only stare at the widening gap.

"Lanie, I'm here. Look at me." T.J.'s familiar voice broke through her trance.

She turned her head. He *was* here, and he'd come for her.

*****

T.J. wanted to leap onto the ice and pull Lanie to safety. His legs quivered from his mad dash across the beach. His voice shook as he called to her.

He'd been off and running before LeFavor had lunged onto the ice. She had to be crazy. Taunting a madman, daring him to come after her. He'd raced forward, coming in low, ready to fire. Others streamed in on his left, indistinct shadows pounding up the beach.

He'd stopped at the edge of the dunes. Seconds later, another trooper moved up beside him and swept the scene with his powerful flashlight, illuminating a huge, dark hole in the ice only inches away from Lanie.

A cold, hard knot formed in the pit of T.J.'s stomach, and for a second his vision blurred.

"Here. Throw her this." One of the men shoved a tangle of rope at him. He glanced up, handed Andrews his weapon, and took the rope.

"T.J.?" Her almost soundless whisper nearly cut him in two.

He braced one foot on the craggy dune, scared shitless he'd make a wrong move and she'd slide into the abyss at her feet.

"Look at me," he said.

Very slowly, she turned her head and fixed her gaze on him.

"I'm going to toss you a rope. Grab it and wrap it around you. Do you understand?" He worked blindly, frantically forming a loop on the rope while keeping his gaze locked on her wide green eyes reflected in the flashlight's powerful beam.

She nodded a jerky affirmative as he slid the other end of the rope though the loop. She had to be scared, but she eased around to face him and reached out her arms.

He tossed her the rope. She grabbed it, and after a few fumbles, slid the lasso he'd created over her head and fixed it snug around her waist.

T.J. pulled on the rope until it went taut. Finally, he had her.

Andrews and the sergeant flanked him.

"Just slide forward on your butt," T.J. said. "I won't let go, no matter what. I promise."

She did as he asked, and he slowly pulled her to safety.

When she finally collapsed in his arms, his whole body trembled. Almost unable to believe she was safe and the monster who'd nearly taken her from him was probably dead, he cupped her face and gazed into her tear filled green eyes.

"Oh, God, Lanie. What were you thinking?"

"Who had time to think?" She blinked several times and loosened her grip on him to wipe moisture from her cheek.

Barely holding himself together, he choked out a rough laugh and pulled her against him.

Trooper Andrews approached them. "Here's your weapon, T.J."

He released Lanie long enough to snap the semi-automatic back into his holster, and then he gathered her close again. He almost felt cheated. The satisfaction of blowing away LeFavor and *then* seeing him fall through the ice would have been sweet.

Behind him, Mark Evans barked out orders. The beach was now considered a crime scene, and he was laying the groundwork for what was to come. T.J. scooped up Lanie and headed for the playground and the warm patrol car. In the distance, sirens screamed.

Soon rescue personnel would swarm the beach. This wasn't a rescue, though. This was a recovery. Didn't matter to T.J. one way or another. As far as he was concerned, they could wait until spring to fish Jack LeFavor out of the lake.

Once he got into the car, he pulled Lanie inside and settled her against him. "Are you all right? I'm sorry. I didn't even ask if he hurt you."

"I'm fine," she murmured, her shaky smile lacking its usual spark. She buried her face against his chest.

Chapter Twenty-Five

Bundled beneath layers of blankets in front of the roaring fire, Lanie dozed. She'd been shuttled to Nick and Cassi's place after she'd refused to go to the hospital. She'd just plain dug in, insisting the scrapes and cuts on her hand were nothing, though they'd stung like hell when Cassi had cleaned and dressed her wounds.

She wanted to be left alone, wanted desperately to sleep. Yet every time she closed her eyes, she saw him. Time after time, heart pounding, she jerked awake to the fading echo of Jack LeFavor's screams as he plunged into the lake.

She'd turned down Cassi's soup and her offer to make Lanie's favorite chicken dish. To erase the worry from her friend's eyes, Lanie had choked down a piece of toast and sipped some hot tea. Every move had left her weak and trembling. Not from the cold. No, this was different. Her first encounter with Jack LeFavor on the highway had scared her, then made her angry, and her battle with hypothermia had knocked her flat for a few days. Yet this wasn't the same. Tonight she'd fought for her life, face to face with a monster.

She'd survived, barely, and that reality had left her numb and unable to function. A state so unfamiliar to her it scared her more than all the rest combined. She closed her eyes and burrowed into the soft quilt. If only she could sleep. Push aside the moment he had lunged for her, the thud when her foot had struck him and she'd sent him to his death.

The room spun, and her eyes popped open wide. She wanted to cry, to sob until she had no sorrow left. Until the overpowering hopelessness inside her dissolved.

Until she felt *normal* again.

"I wish you'd eat more, honey." Cassi crouched down and pressed a cool hand to Lanie's forehead.

Lanie grasped Cassi's hand and hung on to blessed reality. "Don't worry. I'll be okay. I just want to sleep." *Stay with me, don't let go.* "And I'm sorry."

"About what?" Cassi shifted, blocking Rufus when he attempted to nose between them. He slid to the floor with a pitiful groan.

Lanie touched his silky coat, another familiar reality. "The pies. I wanted to help you bake the pies for tomorrow."

"We'll have plenty of time in the morning. We aren't expected at Rich and Ada's until afternoon. Everyone's concerned about you," she added when Lanie tightened her grip. "Ada called. She wanted to know if there was anything she could do. T.J.'s mom called, too."

"Is T.J. all right? I hardly remember anything after he helped me off the ice." Lanie's hand stilled, and she brought it up to rub between her eyes. "I-I can't think."

"He brought you here, and then went to his place to rest. He's on third shift tonight. Nick suggested he call off, but I'm not sure he agreed. He looked pretty rough when he left here."

A wave of nausea clawed at Lanie's throat. T.J. could have died tonight, and the thought tore her heart in two. She wasn't aware she was crying until Cassi handed her a tissue.

"Hey," Nick soothed. He knelt down beside Cassi. "He'll be fine after some shut eye."

"You're right." She shuddered and blotted away her endless tears. "I don't know if I would've trusted anyone else to pull me off that ice. I think he knew that, and it became personal."

"It's always personal. No matter whom we're helping. It's the job."

Nick's words stuck in her mind, and her eyes finally slid shut.

*****

Last night, Lanie hadn't thought sleep would ever come, but now light poured in through the skylights overhead and the aroma of cinnamon filled the air.

The fire simmered, and Cassi hummed under her breath as she moved around the kitchen. Judging from sunlight slanting across the floor, Lanie had slept all night. She should feel rested, recovered, and ready to face the day.

Only, she wasn't. Fatigue still plagued her, along with an unexplained sadness and a pressing desire to *avoid* the day ahead. Even while scents of the upcoming celebration surrounded her, she just wanted to be left alone. To withdraw into mindless oblivion and to heal.

Body, mind, and soul.

Beside her lay a thick, terry cloth robe. Not hers. She couldn't remember what she'd packed the day before, but that robe didn't belong to her. Where *was* her overnight bag? She breathed deeply and rubbed her bleary eyes. After a jaw-cracking yawn, she slipped into Cassi's lovely blue robe.

Like magic, her friend appeared with a steaming cup. "Morning, sleepyhead. I brought you some hot tea."

"Thanks." Lanie wrapped her stiff fingers around the welcome warmth. "Your place smells heavenly. Guess I slept through the baking marathon."

Cassi laughed and wiped her hands on the towel tucked into her waistband. "I hope you were comfortable. We have plenty of spare beds, but you were sleeping so soundly I didn't have the heart to disturb you."

Lanie didn't say anything. Instead, she swallowed some tea, and it burned a welcome path down to her empty belly. Nausea didn't rear its ugly head, but she sensed a hollow emptiness inside herself. She took another long, deep sip.

Then she asked, "How bad do I look?"

"You'll look fine after you eat breakfast and take a shower. I've got some eggs ready for those omelets you love. Do you want to eat first?"

"Oh, God, Cassi. I don't know if I have the energy to face today." She set the tea aside and flexed her injured hand. She adjusted the gauze. The tiny slices in her tender skin burned like a million paper cuts. She pulled aside the collar of the robe. "Look at me. I'm not only using your robe, I'm also wearing sweats that don't belong to me, either. Where are my clothes, and how can I show up for Thanksgiving dinner looking like this?"

"Hey." Cassi knelt and gave Cassi's knee a brisk rub. "You need to eat something. Nick went to get your car, and I think your clothes are in it."

"My car. The rental. I'd forgotten." She couldn't concentrate. Everything ran together, and tears threatened to erupt again. "Is it still at the beach?"

"No, no. Relax, honey. Someone drove it to the state police barracks last night. Nick's Uncle Tom picked him up about an hour ago. They're going to bring your car back here for you."

"I'm nothing but trouble." A single tear spilled down her cheek. "It's a holiday, for God's sake, and T.J.'s dad has to take time to run after me. I need to go home. I don't want to ruin the day for everyone."

She pushed herself to her feet. The room tipped, and Cassi grabbed her arm. Lanie's throat ached. If she let go now, she'd drown in a flood of tears.

"Lanie, let me--"

"Sorry." She held up her hand, palm out. "I don't know what's wrong with me. I'll go take a shower while you fix breakfast. I have to pull it together, Cass. Just give me some time, okay?"

Cassie nodded.

Lanie retreated to the bathroom, and once she was alone under the pounding hot spray, she finally let the tears come.

*****

T.J. took Nick's advice and called in, then felt stupid as hell when the officer on duty reminded him about the eight hours required between regular shifts. He'd awakened at first light, dragged his butt out of bed, and driven to his parent's house.

The cold air cut like a knife, but the sun beat down from a cloudless sky. Hershey went wild. The crazy dog leapt through drifts and scooted along on her belly. She popped up, snow piled on her quivering nose, shook, and did it all over again. T.J. laughed until his sides ached.

After last night, he needed to laugh.

Exhausted and covered with snow, he finished playing with the dog and entered his mom's kitchen. He stomped snow from his boots and took time to dry Hershey's paws. The dog made a beeline for his water bowl.

"Hey, Mom. It smells good in here. There's nothing like your homemade rolls. Bet you've been up since dawn." He leaned in and pressed a kiss to the cheek she offered. "Gonna be different this year, having the big day at Rich and Ada's."

She paused from rinsing her mixing bowls and smiled. "I love the sound of that. Rich and Ada's," she clarified. "Ada gets to show off her new kitchen, and I get to relax and let someone else do the turkey. Getting up early to bake my rolls is nothing."

"Yeah, right. As if you'll just sit back and let Ada do all the cooking." He frowned. "You're still doing our Christmas Eve thing, aren't you?"

Ever since he could remember, his parents had hosted a Christmas Eve open house. A much loved tradition. One T.J. looked forward to year after year.

"Wouldn't have it any other way." She loaded the bowls into the dishwasher. "How's Lanie this morning?"

"I drove past Nick's earlier." He helped himself to hot coffee. "He and dad were just leaving, and they told me she was still sleeping. I figured, why stop? Better for me to come here and spend time with my neglected dog."

Mary topped off her coffee and joined him at the kitchen table. He leaned back and stretched out his legs beneath the spacious table, his family's time worn gathering spot. A familiar scenario that had played out countless times throughout his life.

As a young boy, he'd drink milk instead of coffee. His mother would pour him a glass and dig into the big jar on top of the fridge for cookies. Then she'd sit down at the table with him and listen. Just *listen*.

He looked up, and his eyes met hers.

She set a plate of cookies on the table between them. "What's on your mind, T.J.?"

He selected a cookie, took a healthy bite, then chewed and swallowed. "My sergeant asked me something last night. He caught me off guard, because it was right before all hell broke loose on that beach."

"And what was that?"

"He asked if I'm in love with Lanie.

She nodded, and her eyes softened. "Not if you loved her."

T.J. studied her calm, clear eyes. How did she do that? How did she always know what was in his head?

"I'm sure it's no secret that I'm involved with her," he admitted, then he shook his head. "Nick can't keep his mouth shut. How in hell did he do detective work all those years in Philly?"

Mary chuckled and helped herself to a cookie. "I didn't need Nick to tell me what was right in front of my eyes."

"Loving someone or being in love. Is there a difference? Maybe I'm the one in the dark."

Hershey padded over and laid her head on T.J.'s lap. He absently stroked the dog's broad head. "I don't have a clue how Lanie feels about me. Last night she hung on to me for dear life after I got my hands on her. But by the time we got to Nick's, she'd withdrawn and put up some kind of invisible wall. I couldn't do anything about it, because I was near exhaustion myself. So when Cassi took over, I left."

"Have you talked with Lanie this morning?"

"No. I came straight here after Nick said she was still out of it. Figured the rest would do her more good than anything I had to offer."

"What are you offering, T.J.?" She slid her hand across the table and closed it over his.

Warm, bright sunlight streamed in through the window. So different from the day before, when the gray and the cold had brought death to Jack LeFavor.

"Mom, I don't know if Lanie will accept anything I have to offer," T.J. finally said. "She's a puzzle sometimes. Most of the time," he corrected. Except in bed, something he'd keep to himself.

She gave his hand a pat, stood, and went to rinse her cup. The oven timer buzzed, and she slipped on a pair of oven mitts to remove the last batch of rolls. "Here's my advice, for what it's worth. I've only know Lanie for a short while. She's got a big heart. A lot of pent up love. I doubt there's anything she wouldn't do for a friend or lover."

Heat poured out when she removed the sheet of golden brown rolls from the oven. One by one, she placed them onto a cooling rack, and then she set the pan into the sink. She pulled off the mitts and leaned back against the counter.

"How Lanie behaved last night is not unusual for someone who's had a tremendous shock. I think an attempt on her life qualifies. She pulled away, disconnected emotionally. Am I right?"

"So far."

"I think today will be very difficult for her. She'll feel vulnerable, not to mention exhausted. From what I know, her background is different from what she's going to encounter at Rich and Ada's house. And that might upset her even more."

"She's been to our gatherings before, though." Using a napkin, T.J. scooped up his cookie crumbs. "Last year, when Rich and Ada announced their upcoming marriage, she was there all afternoon. She celebrated with the rest of us and looked as if she were having the time of her life."

"Ah, but she wasn't invested then. She had no real involvement with the family, no expectations. All she did was have a good time, then walk away to her own private world."

"No expectations," he repeated, mulling over exactly what the meant. He blew out a long, slow breath. If he loved her, she'd equate that to *him* having expectations. Finally, he concluded, "She doesn't want to fail. Does she?"

"You'll figure it out." His mom just smiled. "Now, go. I have work to do."

"Thanks, Mom."

"You're welcome." She kissed his cheek. "Don't push her, honey. Just be there."

T.J. drove to his carriage house. Working third shift over a holiday weekend wasn't the best time for clear thinking. So he'd give Lanie some space. He'd back off and give her a chance to get on her feet. At some point, though, they'd have to face the future.

To decide if they had one... together.

Chapter Twenty-Six

The shower helped Lanie, but nagging fatigue and a haunting sense of apprehension lingered. Nick returned with her car and her overnight bag. At least now she wouldn't look like a refugee in Cassi's borrowed sweats.

They arrived at Ada's, and she managed to help Cassi unload the pies. She hadn't been to Ada and Rich McConnell's since they'd completed their renovations. Marriage agreed with Cassi's aunt, and for a brief time Lanie's mood lifted as she enjoyed the couple's interactions. Rich would touch Ada's arm, rest his hand at the small of her back, and exchange secret smiles with her whenever she pointed out something they'd shared.

How lucky they were to have found one another.

They'd positioned an oversized table in front of a large, unadorned window overlooking Ada's gardens. A centerpiece of dried fall flowers, colorful gourds, and miniature pumpkins ran the entire length of the polished wood table. Bright yellow placemats enhanced the centerpiece.

Keeping to herself, Lanie strolled closer to the fireplace.

Platters loaded with specialty cheeses, crusty bread, and plump green grapes sat on the counter. Both rich red and crisp white wines were plentiful as well, set off in long stemmed glasses. Family and long time friends talked and laughed together, creating a picture suitable to frame. Lanie kept her distance and admired the portrait from afar.

Nursing a glass of crisp Pinot, she nibbled on crackers and smiled when Rich bragged about his new workshop.She laughed when Rufus and Hershey plowed through the room, and Nick snatched up a toppling vase of flowers, narrowly averting disaster; but she barely held it together when Mary McGraw surprised her with a warm hug and asked how she felt. Thankfully, Mary didn't seem to notice her struggle.

Will this day never end?

Then just as the setting sun turned Ada's snow covered gardens crimson, T.J.'s SUV swung into the driveway. Lanie's pulse quickened, and nerves jittered in her stomach.

A messy mixture of wanting him, yet needing to back away.

He entered the house, handed Rich a bottle of wine, and gave Ada a hello peck on the cheek. After removing his coat, he looked around the room. His gaze slid past Lanie, and then snapped back to her.

In that instant, the memory of the first time they'd met flashed through her mind. She recalled the jolt of awareness she had experienced when he'd first walked through the door. And then seconds ago, he'd done the same thing. Walked in, scanned the room, and zeroed right in on her.

The first time had been a million years ago.

Now, with his gaze locked on hers, he made his way across the room.

"Hi." He touched her shoulder and then gently took her hand.

"Hi, back."

"I see you got your things. I like the red scarf," he added, touching the soft flow of the garment she'd wound around her neck. He lifted their joined hands and studied the thin layer of gauze covering her knuckles. "How's the hand?"

"It's nothing. Just a few cuts and scrapes. I only left the bandage on to keep it clean. It's really not that bad," she repeated.

He pulled her around to face him. "Lanie, we need to talk. I--"

"Come on, everyone. Time to eat." Rich motioned for all of them to gather around the table. "We'll say a blessing, and then I'll carve the bird."

The meal passed in a blur. Food, laughter, and more food. Conversations ranged from sports, to snow, to ice fishing on Pine Shadow Lake. How well retirement agreed with T.J.'s father. They enjoyed laughing over their shared memories. Wine flowed, water glasses clinked, and freshly brewed coffee accompanied slabs of pumpkin pie topped with real whipped cream.

At times, T.J.'s gaze swung to her, but they had no time alone.

While everyone lingered over desert and after dinner drinks, Lanie excused herself and slipped away to the powder room. She moistened a guest towel and pressed it to her face. The cool cloth soothed her and allowed her to catch her breath.

When she returned to the living area, the table had been cleared and darkness had fallen. Lamps scattered about the room cast a welcome glow, and she thought of her cabin.

Her sanctuary.

She needed time to decide where she would go from here.

T.J. spotted her and threaded his way across the room to her.

"I'm afraid I have to leave," he told her. "I'm sorry we never got to talk, but I have to catch a few hours sleep before going in to work."

The tension that had knotted between her shoulders loosened. She'd survived the day, and T.J.'s leaving early presented her with the perfect opportunity to slip away.

"Would they mind if I left with you? It's been a long day."

"I'm sure they'll understand." He scrutinized her face. "I'll drop you at Cassi's. You can get some rest, and Cassi and Nick can stay here as long as they like."

"Let me say goodbye to everyone and tell Cassi I'm leaving."

"Midnighters take a toll," he explained. He lifted his hand and then dropped it. "I may not see you for a few days."

"Maybe that's better for now, T.J.," she said.

His tired gray eyes told her nothing, and he didn't say anything as he drove her to Cassi's and walked her to the door.

To her surprise, however, he drew her into his arms and kissed her.

His kiss was gentle, just a soft, lingering brush of lips.

Once T.J. pulled away, he murmured, "We're far from done, Lanie."

"Goodnight, T.J.," she said softly, her throat slamming shut and refusing to allow her to say anything else. She eased from his arms and slipped into the cabin.

Before she could think about it, she packed her overnight bag and scribbled Cassi a hasty note. After a quick call to Jen, she was on her way.

A short time later, she climbed Hilltop Road. Smoke curled from the chimney, and the porch light cast a welcome glow. She parked and slipped out of her car.

Stars dotted the black velvet sky. Wind whispered through the evergreens, and snow crunched beneath her feet. She walked to the door, unlocked it, and stepped inside. Then she scooped up Sam Cat and buried her face in his warm fur.

Drawn to the warmth of the fire, thanks to Jen, she sank onto the sofa.

One by one, the knots inside her finally dissolved.

*****

Lanie fell into a deep, dreamless sleep. A blessing after the turmoil, the nightmares, and the raw fear that had assailed her from the moment she had faced Jack LeFavor alone on that deserted beach.

A full twenty-four hours passed. She napped often, ate leftover turkey courtesy of Jen's family, snuggled up to Sam Cat so often he protested, and eventually convinced Cassi she was going to survive.

Cassi's outrage over how Lanie had run off unannounced had diminished after she had apologized, begging her friend's forgiveness and understanding. They'd been friends too long, and Cassi knew her too well to *not* understand. They would talk soon.

Lanie grew stronger. In body, in mind, in heart.

Thanksgiving with T.J.'s friends and family had opened her eyes and shined a spotlight on the glaring difference between them. He'd called her several times, and at her insistence, had updated her on the ongoing recovery efforts at Freeport Beach.

He had offered to drop by, but she'd said no. She needed more time.

Since every police officer working that day had witnessed LeFavor's attempt on her life, they themselves were considered witnesses, making it necessary for an independent source to interview each and every one of them. A Corporal Volk from the crime unit had contacted Lanie and made arrangements to interview her as well.

Ice continued to form on Lake Erie, making it difficult to close the case and thwarting the efforts to recover Jack's body. For some reason, that saddened Lanie. From what she had gathered, unless a mid-winter thaw occurred, Lake Erie would hold him in its icy grip until spring.

Jen stopped by every day and even brought Lanie the Sunday edition of the *Erie Times* . Lanie hugged her breathless.

"Wow. I guess you're finally feeling better." Jen huffed out an exaggerated cough. "I brought you the paper. Thought you might like the blow by blow rundown, complete with pictures, on the front page."

No one had taken any photos that night, but the long shots of the ice dunes and the deserted Freeport Beach the paper's photographer had taken the next day were enough to make her skin crawl. The paper had highlighted the spot where Jack had fallen through the ice and had also included stock photos of both him and Lanie.

She studied Jack's face. He'd had a square jaw, a trim haircut, and he was clean shaven. Not your average drug lord. At least, not the kind of man *she* considered to be one. But what did she know?

Jen removed her coat and came to stand behind Lanie while she skimmed the article. "Are you going back to work tomorrow?"

"Yes. I spoke with Kitty yesterday. I have no reason to stay home. And besides," she said, angling herself to look at Jen, "I need to get back to normal. I've had time to rest and think." She shook her head. "I was a mess, Jen. Looking back, I realize shock was partly to blame, and that's something I never want to experience again as long as I live."

"That bad? It must have been difficult to spend Thanksgiving with T.J. and his family."

"I haven't seen T.J. since he dropped me off at Cassi's after dinner that day."

Jen's brow shot up. "Really?"

"He's working third shift until late next week. He calls every day, and has offered to stop by more than once, but I told him no. I wasn't at my best on Thanksgiving Day, and to be honest, the big family thing kind of scared me."

Jen laughed. "Big families can do that. But they're there when you need them."

"I guess you're right," Lanie murmured. "My Uncle Charley was always there when I needed him. I'm not so sure I was there when he needed me, though. Or *if* he ever needed me."

Her friend smiled.

"How about some lunch?" Lanie asked, sliding her chair back and coming to her feet. "I plan on eating, taking a very long walk, and then tackling the boxes I haven't unpacked."

*****

T.J. rolled over and smashed a pillow over his head. He needed more sleep. This set of midnighters was grueling. They were always exhausting, but holidays were the worst.

Tonight would be bad. Travelers heading home after Thanksgiving would jam the roads by nightfall. Worse than Christmas, worse than the Fourth of July.

With a sigh, he tossed the pillow aside. Might as well get up.

He pulled on jeans and a sweatshirt, splashed a little water on his face, and put on a pot of coffee. Decaf, because he really needed to catch some more sleep before tonight. Four more nights to go, then he'd be off for a long weekend. *Thank God.*

Sun filtered through the clouds on this gray, overcast day. Kind of fit his mood. The sleep, wake, work, and then sleep again marathon had wiped him out.

He slapped together a cold turkey sandwich and scraped the last of the leftover coleslaw onto his plate. His mom had dropped off leftovers the day after Thanksgiving, bless her, or he'd be down to eating scrambled eggs. He'd already plowed through the tin of cookies she'd left.

He'd agreed on Monday to come in early. Corporal Matt Volk from crime wanted to wrap up his interviews and arranged to meet T.J. an hour before his shift started.

That was a pain in the ass for Matt, having to interview every frigging one of the guys who'd been at Freeport Beach that night. But that was the way it had to be. T.J. had talked to Raife on the phone over the weekend. The guy had busted his butt for years chasing LeFavor, and his ear splitting whoop had damn near deafened T.J. when he'd relayed how Jack LeFavor had met his maker -- or whoever he'd met. T.J. had his suspicions.

The cocky agent had promised to give Lanie a big, fat, juicy kiss the next time he saw her. T.J. wasn't sure how he felt about that.

After a fast shower and a shave, he felt almost human again. He tried to call Lanie, but got her machine. He left a message, the best he could do for now.

The afternoon before, his dad and Rich had helped him move more stuff from his duplex. He glanced around. His place was shaping up. They'd hauled out the last of Rich's tools and put the finishing touches on the newly installed door. The new addition off the kitchen still needed something, however. Maybe a few chairs, or a couple of end tables. He'd have to take care of that in the spring.

Right now, his much loved recliner by the fire and the new, deep red area rug he'd bought gave the place a homey look. He caught himself wondering if Lanie would like what he'd done with the place.

He grabbed a bottle of water and dropped into the recliner.

No sense trying *not* to think about her. At times on Thanksgiving, she had appeared dazed, overcome. She'd tried to hide it, but more than once he'd caught tears glistening in those gorgeous green eyes. Part exhaustion, part shock, probably. They went hand in hand with each other. Even still, he had admired the way she'd handled the holiday turmoil after what she'd gone through the day before.

He'd almost lost it that night. When he'd first seen her on the ice dunes, his heart had nearly stopped. He'd known LeFavor would stop at nothing, and the only thing that mattered was keeping the sick bastard from hurting Lanie. He still wished he'd gotten the chance to empty his weapon into that son of a bitch.

Lanie had come face to face with death, and she had survived. He admired her courage and her ability to overcome. Her warmth and her compassion. Her complexity, and yeah... even her feistiness.

He couldn't get her out of his head. Had she wormed her way into his heart, too?

The warmth from the fire made him drowsy. He tipped his head back, and was gone.

Chapter Twenty-Seven

Down to the last box. Lanie sat back and rubbed her dusty hands on her thighs. The boxes had been in her Miata the night of the accident and held the final remnants of her life in Fox Chapel. The first three she'd opened had contained a mix of odd papers and a few old pictures.

She'd lingered over a framed shot of her and Uncle Charley taken the day she'd graduated from college. She looked ecstatic; he looked tired.

Her heart ached. He must have known then that he was dying. Yet he'd kept it to himself because he wouldn't have wanted to mar her perfect day. She'd hugged him so hard. That was the only time she'd ever seen tears in Charley's eyes.

She set the picture aside. It needed a new frame, and once she'd bought one, she'd put it somewhere special. A reminder of what she'd had... and what she'd lost.

With a deep sigh, she pulled the last box closer. This one was different. Much neater than the ones she'd sealed with duct tape after scrawling a hasty list of contents on top. This box was sealed with clear packing tape, with her name printed in one corner in neat block letters.

Elaine.

She closed her eyes and pressed her hand to her trembling lips. Uncle Charley had packed this one. She vaguely remembered when he'd given her the neat little box, because shortly after he had, he'd been rushed to the hospital and she'd forgotten. She must have packed it with her other boxes when she'd moved.

She lifted it and tilted it from side to side. Not a sound came from within it.

With a smile, she wiped a stray tear from her cheek. Whatever Charley had put in there, he'd made sure it was secure in his usual, thorough way. Very carefully, she slit the tape and peeled back the top flaps.

Folded newspaper lay on top. That was another of her dear uncle's quirks: recycling.

She lifted the top layer, and an envelope dropped into her lap. Her name was written on the outside in the same handwriting as the one on the box. She ran her hand carefully over the outside of it. In all probability, this was one of the last things he'd done, and knowing it had taken her this long to read it broke her heart in two.

The envelope contained a single sheet of paper neatly folded in half. Lanie slid it free, leaned back on the sofa, and read her uncle's cramped scrawl.

My dearest Elaine,

Of all the things I had to leave you, what lies within this simple box may be the most precious. We never created memories or traditions of much account in the few years we had together. I focused on keeping you fed and clothed, and on giving you the best opportunities I could to help you deal with the hand life has dealt you.

I never got a chance to tell you the history of the simple treasures within, but they come to you with love and a rich sense of tradition. They were left to me when the last of my dear family passed away, long before you entered my life.

Now I leave them to you. Find happiness, my dear. When you do, don't hesitate or wait to share the love you have inside you. Believe in your heart and know you will always be in mine.

With all my love,
Uncle Charley

One by one, Lanie unpacked Charley's last gift to her. Tears blinded her as she carefully unwrapped the fragile ornaments and the delicate strings of colored beads, each wrapped with care and nestled together.

She remembered the red edged star that had adorned the top of their tree that last year. Charley had been forced to fix the plug and replace the tattered wire. How beautiful the tiny tree had looked. In previous years, they'd had a strange parade of trees. Some purchased already trimmed, complete with lights.

He'd insisted that last year be different, stating that her upcoming graduation was reason enough for them to dig out some *old stuff* and start a new tradition to celebrate her future.

If only she'd known what his future held.

Sam Cat nosed the box and touched a tentative paw to the rolled up papers she'd set aside. She gathered him into her arms and sobbed until she had no tears left.

*****

Insistent ringing dragged T.J. from a bottomless pit of dreamless sleep. He opened one eye and squinted at the luminous dial on his watch. Who the hell had the balls to call him at two in the afternoon after his last night on duty?

He'd planned to sleep until the next day, if possible, or at least until the damn sun set.

"All right, all right," he mumbled. The ringing stopped, and his machine clicked on. Seconds later, the ringing started all over again.

Something was wrong.

He tossed the covers aside.

"Aw, shit," he said when his bare feet hit the cold floor. He was wide awake now, and a strange foreboding edged out his initial anger. He'd disconnected the extension in his bedroom, always keeping his cell beside

165

the bed. The ringing came from near the kitchen. A small alcove there housed his desk, a filing cabinet, and his answering machine.

Shivering in shorts and a tee-shirt, he just made it before the machine kicked in again.

He grabbed the receiver and croaked gruffly, "McGraw."

"About time you hauled that lovely ass of yours out of bed."

"What the... Lanie?" It couldn't be. But the tone and the *ass* remark said otherwise.

"Hi, T.J. I have a question."

"Can you hold on a minute? I'm freezing my lovely ass, and I need to get a drink so I can talk normally." Gripping the portable phone, he swung past the fridge and grabbed a bottle of water, then veered into his bedroom.

"I'm getting a nice visual, McGraw. Sleep in your skivvies?"

"Have you been drinking?" he asked, chuckling now as he tucked the phone beneath his chin, hopped on one foot to pull on sweat pants, and balanced his water all at once.

"Nope. Just need to ask you a question."

He pulled up his pants and took a deep drink of water. "Okay, I'm decent and lubricated." This whole conversation was a bit surreal. "What is it?"

"I know it's early," she said. "And because you've been working third shift, you probably haven't had time."

"For what?" He plopped down onto the bed, feeling around for the socks he'd peeled off just before crashing a couple of hours ago.

"For your Christmas tree."

"My what?"

"Your Christmas tree, T.J. Like I said, it's early yet." She paused.

Fully awake now, he sat up straighter. Something was happening here, and he didn't know whether to be excited or scared shitless.

"Elaine, are you all right?"

"Yeah, T.J. I'm all right." Her voice grew softer. "Or rather, I will be very soon. Please don't ask questions. Not right now. I'm sorry I woke you, but I've been watching the clock and hoped you'd be up by now."

"Well, you were wrong. But it's no big deal," he added hastily. "I don't have to go in tonight. So I'll live." He took another deep swig of water. "What's the deal with the tree?"

"I'm still at work." She took a huge breath. "I have to run some errands after I get off, and like you, I need a good night's sleep. Here's what I want you to do." She paused, and then rephrased what she'd just said, "Here's what I'm *asking* you to do. For me."

"I'm listening."

The next morning he made a call, relieved when Gifford's Nursery in Wattsburg assured him they were open and had cut trees ready for the holidays. He'd never paid attention to when his parents got their tree each year. Only that by the week before Christmas, it was up, decorated, and the house smelled like a pine forest.

What was it Lanie had said? Don't get one that's too big, but don't get a little shrub, either. Okay, he'd go with a six foot Scotch pine.

They put it through a neat machine that wrapped the entire tree in netting. Made it damn easy to toss on his SUV and tie down. The drive from Wattsburg to Pine Bluffs wasn't far, so no big deal. Of course, he'd had to stop at McConnell's Ace Hardware and pick up a stand. Lanie had said to get lights, too, so he'd bought a couple of strings of white and some multicolored.

"Getting ready for the holidays early?" Rich asked, eyeing what T.J. had balanced in his arms while waiting to check out.

"Can't be too early," T.J. remarked. He held out one of the boxes. "Do people usually get all colored or all white? I've covered all the bases. What do you think?"

Usually his questions for Rich were about tools. He'd been coming to Rich's hardware store all his life and couldn't remember *ever* buying colored lights in the past.

"Hmm. Lanie didn't give you instructions? White's fine," he added, laughing when T.J. gave him a pokerfaced stare. "How big is your tree?"

Rich plucked up the stand T.J.'d chosen and studied the box.

"About six feet tall. It's out front."

Rich stepped over and looked out the front door. "You're right on top of things, aren't you? Be right back," he added, and disappeared down an aisle.

He returned a few minutes later with a different stand and placed it on the counter with the lights. "This one's better for a tree that size. Gives you the option to go larger if you want to in the future."

"Thanks, Rich. I don't think I'll go much larger and--"

"Trust me, T.J. If a woman's involved, they'll want larger."

He thought about Rich's comment on the way back to the carriage house. Rich hadn't asked any questions, and T.J. hadn't offered any information. Because so far, he had nothing to tell.

He wrestled the tree inside, cut a few inches off the trunk like the guy at Gifford's had suggested, and whacked on the new stand. After a few adjustments, the tree stood upright.

With a little extra effort, he hauled it upstairs. Before leaving, he'd chosen a spot in front of the window and put down an old sheet. Surprising how much he remembered about setting things up, and what to do. He'd never given Christmas trees much thought before, but guessed now he knew the basics.

He'd planned on getting Hershey this morning, but after Lanie's call had decided to wait one more day. He turned in a slow circle to make sure the place looked descent.

With a fire in the fireplace and his furniture filling up what had been empty space up until a couple days ago, the place looked pretty good. Damn good, in fact. Once they got those lights on the tree... well, it would feel just like home.

Along with tree shopping today, he'd fit in time to restock his fridge. Lanie hadn't mentioned anything about dinner. She'd just told him she'd be here before dark, nothing more. So he'd gotten stuff for a salad and some chicken. He had all the bases covered.

He glanced at the time and frowned a little as he turned on a few lamps scattered around the room.

He walked to the window just as headlights appeared through the deepening twilight.

*****

Lanie gnawed on her bottom lip. Her stomach did flip flops as she gathered the resealed box and started up the winding walkway to T.J.'s door. The light outside the carriage house cast a warm glow on the path, but before she had a chance to ring the bell, the door swung open and T.J. filled the opening. Light came from behind him, casting his face in shadow.

Her heart bounded into her throat. She stopped and shifted the box.

Then she took a deep breath and looked into his eyes. "Hi."

"Hi. Can I help you with that?" He reached out, and she handed him the box. He skimmed his gaze over her face. "Come on in."

She slid past him into the foyer. He closed the door and waited patiently as she removed her gloves. The last time she'd been here, packing boxes, a couple of odd pieces of furniture, and lots of tools had filled the foyer. Now the floor gleamed, coats hung neatly from brass hooks, and the oak bench along the wall looked newly refinished.

"You've been busy," she commented, sitting on the bench to remove her boots. She dug into her oversized canvas bag and pulled out a pair of shoes. As she slipped them on, she could make out soft music drifting down the stairs.

"Did you get a tree?" she finally asked, his patient silence and half smile unnerving her.

"You wanted a tree. I got a tree."

She let the breath out she'd been holding.

He raised one brow and lifted the box. "This for the tree?"

"Yes." One look at his face, and she knew she'd made the right decision. He hadn't questioned her or demanded to know why she'd kept her distance for so long. He'd literally saved her life, and he had every right to resent the way she'd pushed him away. Without question, though, he'd done as she'd asked. The rest was up to her.

At the top of the stairs, she stopped dead when she saw the tree. "Oh, T.J. It's perfect."

He slid his arms around her from behind and she leaned back, resting her hands on his arms when he wrapped them snugly around her waist. She tilted her head back to look at him. Being here felt good. It felt *right.*

He turned her around and pulled her against him. "I need to kiss you now."

Words clogged her throat, and all she could do was nod.

She sank into the kiss and drowned in the sensation of T.J. holding her. She'd missed him so much. Until he'd opened the door a few minutes ago, she hadn't realized how much. He kissed her breathless, yet so tenderly her heart all but melted. The air around them simmered with emotion, and the wild scent of pine permeated the room.

He eased back. His eyes made it impossible for her to look away, and in her heart she knew they'd come full circle. Starting with their first kiss, followed by the first time they'd made love, and ending the night on the dunes when her life had hung by a thread.

A meandering path wrought with stumbles and uncertainty.

And fear.

The blinding fear for her life, and the fear she'd never find happiness. One so different from the other, yet both connected to the man in her arms.

"I don't know where to begin." She searched his face and touched her hand to his cheek.

"How about we start by trimming the tree?"

She rose up and brushed her lips over his. "It's a good way to start."

Lanie discovered the boxes of lights by the tree. Without a word, she opened them. He joined her, and together they strung them onto the feathery branches.

"I've missed you," she said, pausing and turning to face him. "I don't think I've ever said that to anyone before."

"There's a lot I've never said before, too, Lanie." He laid the lights aside and studied her. "At least where you're concerned. Give me a minute."

He blew out a long breath and tucked his hands into his pockets.

"I remember the first time I saw you," he said. "Or at least, your picture. Then I met you in person." He shook his head and scooped one hand through his hair. "I believe I told Nick you looked like nothing but trouble."

She started to speak, then bit back her words. Other then checking out his body, she'd felt pretty much the same and had deliberately avoided him most of the time.

"The night of the accident, fate stepped in and dropped you right into my lap. Literally. Then there was no turning back. I felt as if I'd started to read a book, one that wasn't my usual taste. I liked the cover, though." His lips curved, and his gaze drifted over her.

She arched a brow.

"Then I got a taste of what lay between the pages. Humor, intelligence, and a touch of mystery."

"How about passion?" Lanie rose and opened another box of lights.

"You said you liked the cover, and to me that's a physical attraction, not what's on the inside."

"That came later." He grinned. Then his eyes turned dark and serious. "What got me was your heart. Brave, yet soft. An entangled combination so strong it took my breath away."

The string of lights slipped through her fingers and pooled at her feet.

He came to her, took her hands, and drew her down onto the rug beside him.

Behind the glass doors, the fire burned steady, flickering and dancing. The first strand of tiny white lights twinkled amidst the tree's green branches, and Lanie gazed into the eyes of a man she'd come to treasure.

She pressed her hand to T.J.'s lips when he started to speak. "Wait, there's something I have to share with you."

She went and got the box he'd carried upstairs. Lifting the top, she pulled out the note from Uncle Charley and turned to T.J. "I knew the first time I kissed you it would be hard to walk away. You were different. You grew up surrounded by love and family, ingrained with traditions to enrich your future. You had so much to share. I was terrified I'd fall in love with you and have nothing to bring to our life together. I was ready to walk away, T.J., until I found Uncle Charley's note."

She took his hand and pressed the note into his palm.

T.J. opened it and read her uncle's words. When he'd finished, he carefully refolded it, laid it aside, and pulled her into his arms. "Just let me hold you."

"I've finally found happiness." She wound her arms around him and rested her head on his chest. His heart beat strong and steady beneath in her ear. "I want to share the love inside me, too. I love you, T.J."

"Oh, Lanie." His arms tightened around her. "In the beginning, I looked into your eyes, and my heart stumbled. You're a complicated woman, but I can't imagine my life without you... because I not only love you. I've also fallen *in* love with you."

*****

They undressed in silence and came together on his cool, smooth sheets. Lanie's subtle scent filled T.J.'s senses. This time, they would savor each other.

He glided his hands over her. She moaned as he touched her, arching into his caress, and giving a contented sigh when he brushed her tender flesh with his lips. They had no need to rush. She was his now. If possible, his desire for her had grown stronger and more urgent.

So much more.

They didn't just share the slide of their bodies, but taste, touch, tenderness and the same wild, breathless craving. Her body moved with his, and he reveled in her soft whimper of pleasure as his mouth covered her breast.

Her breath caught as he entered her, a quick hard tremble, and she shuddered beneath him as his body released.

In the aftermath amidst his rumpled sheets, she rolled against him and stroked her fingers through his hair. "I know I said this earlier, but it bears repeating."

"Hmm. I'm listening, just don't ask me to move. Not yet." He tucked her closer to him and lazily trailed a gentle finger over the swell of her breast. "You want us to get up and finish decorating the tree now, right?"

She stiffened and angled to look at his face. "I was going to tell you that I love you."

"I'm sorry." He kissed her, and the stubborn set of her mouth softened. "I love you, too, with all my heart. But damn it, I just can't be all serious and somber about it. I want to celebrate. Open some wine, call our friends. And I want to decorate *our* tree," he concluded with a smacking kiss.

She grinned up at him. "Let's do it naked."

"I thought we just did."

"No, silly. Let's decorate the tree naked."

"Well… okay." He rubbed his chin. "It could be our first tradition."

Chapter Twenty-Eight

"It's snowing!" Lanie rushed into the bedroom.

T.J. fussed with his tie in front of the mirror. "Uh huh. Where's your cat?"

Lanie had arrived at T.J.'s early. They intended to spend Christmas Eve together, and to her way of thinking, that included Sam Cat. He'd protested the whole way from Harborcreek, and then sulked in his carrier, refusing to come out until they'd secured a curious Hershey.

"He finally came out, ate a bit, and prowled around. I think he likes the place." She grinned and took over straightening T.J.'s tie. "There, that's better," she said, and turned him around. "You look very handsome tonight McGraw," she remarked, peering over his shoulder.

His eyes met hers in the mirror, dipped to the low scooped neck of her red knit dress. "You look gorgeous. Maybe we should stay home. Skip the madness at Mom and Dad's and finish trimming the tree."

"The tree's all trimmed." She laughed and dodged his hands when he swung around and grabbed for her. "I'll go check on Sam Cat, and then we can get going."

"I'll be there in a minute," T.J. said. "Why don't you get the wine we picked out and put it in that fancy bag you bought?"

She hummed along with Jim Brickman's flowing rendition of *Jingle Bells* while tucking red tissue around the wine they'd chosen as a hostess gift for his mom. The tree looked perfect. She'd wound fluffy cotton around the base of the tree. Charley's ornaments sparkled, and the fragile colored beads draped elegantly over the branches.

T.J. strolled into the room. She frowned at the box he carried. "What's that?"

"Come here," he instructed, and knelt by the tree.

When she joined him, he opened the lid.

"Mom called while you were out shopping the other day," he said. "She asked me to stop over. I'd forgotten about this." He glanced up. Her eyes filled as he placed the small wooden manger beneath the tree. "This was mine. Mom said they got it for me my very first Christmas. Until recently, they put it out every year."

He handed her a tissue wrapped figure, and she unwrapped a leggy camel.

"It's been packed away." He unpacked more figures. "She said I had a place of my own now, and a future," he added, leaning in to gently wipe a tear from her cheek. "She thought this would be the perfect compliment to your traditional ornaments."

"Give me a minute," Lanie said, shaking her head. "Or I'll have to redo my makeup and we'll be late."

They worked together in silence, arranging the tiny manger beneath the tree.

*****

As dusk fell, snow drifted down like confetti, blanketing the ground and coating the trees and buildings.

"Christmas Eve snow." Lanie touched T.J.'s thigh and gave it a little rub as he turned up the drive to his parents' home.

Grinning, he covered her hand with his. "Keep that up, and we'll have to turn around and miss the party."

Lanie laughed. Happiness bubbled inside her, along with a few nerves. She'd been to the McGraws one other Christmas Eve, the year Cassi and Nick had announced they were getting married, and Rich McConnell had fallen for Cassi's Aunt Ada.

Looked like this year might be the catalyst for another new beginning.

Because Lanie had fallen in love with T.J. A big splat in love, and she had yet to wrap her head around it all. Other than declaring their love for one another, they had yet to discuss their future together. It remained a mystery.

T.J. parked beside Nick's Ridgeline.

"Dad outdid himself again." Tiny white lights adorned the thick evergreens flanking the front porch. Graceful swags of ground pine intertwined with more white lights draped the porch railing. He opened his door and then came around to open hers.

Once she climbed out, he took her hand and led her past the house to a spot overlooking Pine Shadow Lake. Christmas lights shined through windows, creating colorful patterns on untouched snow.

"Before we go in, I have to ask you something." He drew her in and laid his lips on hers.

She wrapped her arms around him.

"Lanie?"

"Hmm?"

"Do we have a future together?" His words hung in the cold frosty air.

She brushed away the snow clinging to his hair and cupped his face in her hands. "I had to make sure, T.J. I had to step back, push *you* back, and make sure."

"I didn't like your stepping back or pushing me back."

"I know, and I'm sorry for that. You gave me the time, though. You did what I asked, what I needed." She stretched up and touched her lips to his. "Aside from my uncle, you're the only man I've ever loved. I want you in my future."

He drew something out of his pocket. Standing in the glow of

Christmas lights with snow drifting down, he slid off her glove and slipped a ring onto her finger.

"Oh... oh, T.J. It's beautiful." Tears clogged her throat. She hadn't expected this level of commitment and trust. The square cut emerald flanked by a swirl of three tiny diamonds on each side glistened in the night. "I don't know what to say."

"Emeralds are a symbol of beauty, of health and happiness." T.J. brushed his knuckles over her cheek. Then he kissed her and traced a finger over her trembling lips. "You have beautiful green eyes. Your life revolves around health, and I see nothing but happiness in our future together."

*****

The holiday surrounded them the minute they stepped inside Tom and Mary McGraw's home. Scents of Christmas -- pine, vanilla, and ginger -- filled the wonderful space.

A flurry of hugs, handshakes, and kisses followed.

Lanie was speechless, with tears welling in her throat. T.J. clamped his arm around her and kept her knees from folding. Otherwise, she would surely have sunk into a delirious, happy puddle at his feet.

Somehow amidst it all, T.J.'s father pulled out a bottle of champagne and passed around tall, frosted flutes filled with the bubbling liquid.

Tom McGraw handed one to T.J., one to her, and then he stepped between them. "I'd like to propose a toast."

The room grew silent. Tom took a deep breath.

"I have a few things to say," he said. "And tonight seems like the right time to say them. If this sounds like a speech, so be it."

His warm gray eyes, so like T.J.'s, filled with emotion. "This tradition of family and friends gathering in our home is a long standing one. A good one. Many years ago, Mary and I announced the upcoming birth of our son this night, one of many happy beginnings. More recently, Nick and Cassi started their life's journey with one another on Christmas Eve."

Lanie's heart filled as Nick gently kissed his wife, and she noted that Cassi touched the shiny penny on a gold chain encircling her neck. The symbol of commitment Nick had given Cassi that Christmas.

Tom turned to Rich and Ada. "It took a while, but my best friend finally opened his eyes and fell like a rock for Pine Bluffs' lovely lady gardener."

Ada stretched up and placed a chaste kiss on Rich's cheek. "He's made up for lost time."

"Now I'd like to propose a toast. Each year, Mary and I open our home on this special night. As I've mentioned, the tradition has been blessed. Tonight, I raise my glass to my son and his new fiancé. May they carry on the McGraw tradition."

He raised his glass. "To Lanie and T.J."

Swamped with emotion, Lanie struggled not to cry. One after another, everyone embraced her, admired her beautiful emerald, and wished them well. When T.J.'s mother finally served the food, platters of everything imaginable, T.J. drew Lanie to a quiet spot by the tree.

He lifted her hand. The stunning green stone sparkled in the lights from the Christmas tree. He raised his gaze to meet hers. "Your uncle was right, Lanie. You've made me a happy man by sharing your love."

"I remember Charley always told me to look ahead to what I could be." She shook her head. "I made the mistake of looking back. Each and every person here tonight brings something to one another. I see that now. I can't change the past, but together we can make a future."

"All right, cousin, can you stop pawing the woman and mingle a little?" Nick handed each of them a steaming cup of hot cider. He bent and kissed Lanie's cheek. "I knew from day one he was hooked, even though he didn't want to admit it."

He grinned at T.J., then took Lanie's hand and admired the flash of green. "One of the first things he asked after meeting you was if I'd noticed your eyes."

"Really?" Lanie arched her brow at T.J.

"Oh, yeah. Then he said you weren't his type. What a bunch of bullshit," he said, walking away chuckling.

"You know what I think?" she murmured, leaning in and smoothing T.J.'s lapel.

He looped his hands around her waist and pulled her against him. "What do you think?"

"I think when we get back to your place, I'd like to add some lovely old ornaments your mom gave me to our tree." Her eyes twinkled with mischief.

He had to think a minute before he got her meaning, and then he curved his mouth in a slow smile. "Can't forget tradition."

The End

About Nancy Kay

Nancy Kay resides near Lake Erie in Western Pennsylvania with her husband, a former member of the Marines and the Pennsylvania State Police Department, thus providing valuable insight for her stories. At various times in her life she has worked in banking, as a veterinary assistant, and as an aerobics instructor. She pursues a healthy lifestyle and enjoys her part time job in an exclusive lingerie boutique. As a member of Romance Writers of America and three affiliated chapters, she keeps involved and informed while pursuing her writing career. Her stories are set in small towns and inland communities scattered along the shores of the Great Lakes amongst rolling grape vineyards and glorious sunsets. They focus on romance, intertwined with the love of hearth, home and family, yet are sprinkled with suspense, danger and intrigue.

Learn more about Nancy at **www.nancykayauthor.com**

Made in the USA
Middletown, DE
08 July 2015